THE ME

This edition first published 2020 by Fahrenheit Press.

ISBN: 978-1-912526-91-8

10 9 8 7 6 5 4 3 2 1

www.Fahrenheit-Press.com

F 4 E

The Mermaid's Pool

By

David Nolan

Fahrenheit Press

For Benny Rothwell

Useful Mancunian Expressions

And all - as well
Any road - anyway
Conk - nose
Dob you in - tell on you
Ginnel - alleyway/passage between houses or shops
Gob - mouth
Keks - trousers
Kinnell - shortened version of ‘fucking hell’
Owt - anything
Mam - mother
Mard - a person who is easily upset
Mard arse - a person who is very easily upset
Mither - to bother or cause trouble for someone
Nora - woman’s name often attached to swear words. EG:‘Bloody Nora’
Nowt - nothing
Soft Mick - a mysterious Mancunian character who has a great deal of everything. So, to have ‘more shoes than Soft Mick’ means you possess a huge number of shoes

PROLOGUE

9.30 pm Thursday 31 March 1988

When they came for her, she fought.

Hard.

She kicked, scratched, screamed and spat at the men, grabbing at their balaclava masks… trying to find a way out.

But there were five of them. And there was no way out.

She shouted too, of course. And tried to scream. But the hand that covered her mouth and the forearm that cradled her neck were both strong and practised.

The leader - she instinctively knew he was in charge - put his covered face next to hers. He put a finger up against the wool of his mask, where she imagined his mouth was.

'Shhhh now,' was his advice.

She nodded. A moment of silence.

'It's time,' he stated.

The grip on her mouth loosened.

Slightly.

She said something in a language the men didn't understand. 'English!' another man screamed. He poked her hard in the face once with the flat, handle end of the baseball bat he was carrying. Then he hit her again after every subsequent word: 'This. Is. England. Speak. Fucking. English.'

As they took her, bare toes dragging on the carpet, she dared speak one more time: 'Where are we going?'

The leader replied: 'Swimming.'

PART ONE

'Manchester Radio News at six - this is Beth Hall. Police are investigating a series of apparent race hate attacks in Oldham last night. White paint was splashed on houses, restaurants and a mosque in the town centre as Robert Crane reports…'

'Police were initially called in the early hours after the owner of a restaurant in the Glodwick area said his premises had been targeted during the night.

White gloss paint had been thrown at the restaurant's windows. The front door, walls and even the pavement outside had been daubed with swastikas and what appeared to be paintings of a wolf's head.

Several homes in the area were also targeted, and white paint was also thrown at a mosque in Coldhurst. One local man whose home was vandalised - but who didn't want to be named - says the police aren't interested in attacks on the South Asian community:'

> *"We are on our own. They don't care about our homes, our businesses or our kids. If it happens around here, the police don't want to know. It's scary right now, I mean it. These are frightening times and the authorities don't seem to be on our side."*

'Police believe the incidents are linked but say they're keeping an open mind as to whether they were racially motivated. They're urging anyone who saw anything suspicious in the area at the time to come forward. Robert Crane, Manchester Radio News in Oldham.'

CHAPTER ONE

9.45 pm Thursday 31 March 1988

Looking closely at the little girl's swollen and bloodied lip, Detective Inspector John Smithdown sighed, rubbed a hand across his unshaven chin and shook his head. 'It's nasty,' he conceded. 'I'm not saying it isn't, because it is. It's definitely nasty. But it's not nasty enough, that's the problem.'

He looked again, his tired, grey face just inches from hers. Nearly everything about Smithdown seemed tinged with grey - grey hair, grey bog-brush moustache, grey suit, even blue/grey eyes. There were some tonal differences in his appearance - light grey to dark grey - but it was all pretty much grey.

As he continued to look at her lip, she stopped crying - largely because she was so puzzled as to what the policeman was up to. She lay still on the examination table.

The girl's lip was slightly split, just to the right of the bow. Again, Smithdown looked hard at the cut. 'Fuck,' he muttered, after much deliberation. Then he remembered the girl was just ten years old. 'Sorry, love,' he said by way of an apology. 'But, honestly. It's just not fucking nasty enough.'

'I don't follow, Mr Smithdown,' the young photographer said, looking at the girl's face and then at the detective. 'Sorry. Am I being thick? I was just told to take some snaps of her injuries. That's all I know. I have to say, it looks pretty nasty from where I'm standing.'

Smithdown motioned for the photographer to come with him to the rear of the examination room, one of several at Oldham's brown, pebble-dashed police station. The detective looked at him. *Twenty-two. Twenty-three, tops. Straight out of*

Manchester Polytechnic. Streaked-blonde hair and wearing jeans and his dad's old suit jacket. Fucking Nora.

The detective placed a hand on the young man's shoulder, then subtly moved it so he cupped the nape of his slim neck. Smithdown then pulled the photographer ever-so-slightly towards him. 'So, you're the new staff snapper… What's your name, lad?'

'Paul, Mr Smithdown. Paul Rees. I'm new. Yes. I only started this week.'

'Look, Paul,' the DI said in a whisper, turning his head away from the girl. 'It's like this. The doctor will be here any minute. He'll take one look at that kid's lip, see straight away it doesn't need stitches, wipe her face, give her a lolly and send her home. Straight back into the hands of the twat that did that to her in the first place. The same twat that probably did it to her last month. And the month before that. And that is unacceptable in my view. Un-acc-ept-able, Paul. Let me give you an alternative scenario. Instead of that happening, we could get her into the Royal Oldham Hospital for the night. Then - are you following all this, Paul? Then, social services can work a bit of their hippy bollocks magic, get her made a ward of court and then get her out of that shit pile she calls her home - and away from that shithead she calls her mum's boyfriend. Me and you. We could do that, Paul. We could make that happen. So - are you with me, or against me?'

'I'm very much with you, Mr Smithdown,' the photographer replied after a few moments. 'I think.'

DI Smithdown gave the young man a hearty double slap on the back of the neck. 'Absolutely top notch. Now, put your camera down, Paul, face the wall and shut the fuck up.'

'The wall?' the photographer asked.

'The wall,' DI Smithdown confirmed. 'It's the big pile of bricks over there.'

Paul lifted the strap of his Hasselblad camera over his head and carefully laid it onto the table in the corner of the room. Then he turned to face the examination room's yellowy-white wall.

'Cracking,' said the detective. He checked the paperwork connected to the case then walked over to the young girl. He popped a mint into his mouth, aware that the two pints he'd had earlier in The Old Bill bar next to the police station were probably still wafting about on his breath - it was the favoured drinking spot for Oldham detectives and hard to resist of an evening shift. Smithdown bent down so that his eyes were at the same level as hers and spoke quietly to her, his hands deep into the pockets of his grey suit trousers. 'Hi, Rebecca.'

'It's Becky,' she said in the quietest of voices.

'Sorry… Becky. Hello there. Can I ask you something?'

She nodded. Her hair was greasily dark. There was dirt underneath her fingernails and her eyes were underscored by dark semicircles. She was wearing a Mel and Kim t-shirt, jeans that were too small for her and scuffed, pink plastic sandals. Smithdown recognised them. He saw a lot of kids wearing them in his line of work. *Woolworths' sandals. Bless her. She's wearing plastic sandals from Woolies. Never a good sign. The cheapest shoes in town and probably second-hand. Poor, poor little Becky.*

'Right then,' the detective said. 'Do you want to go back home tonight? Back to your mam's?'

A pause.

'And back to her boyfriend? Or would you rather stay the night somewhere else? Maybe with some nice nurses at the hospital? They could look after you while we get this all sorted out.'

The girl looked at him – her dark brown eyes were locked onto Smithdown's - but she said nothing.

'Home? Or somewhere else?' he reiterated.

There was silence as Becky continued to think. She seemed slightly embarrassed to give the DI a reply and looked away for a minute. But eventually she answered: 'Somewhere else,' she said. Then she looked directly at the policeman and added: 'Please.'

Detective Inspector John Smithdown nodded. He turned to check that Paul the photographer was still looking at the wall. He was. 'Right then,' the DI sighed. 'Sorry, love.'

With one quick move he slid a finger into the girl's mouth, yanked his hand back and split the child's lip a third of the way up to her nose. A thin squirt of blood jetted onto his overcoat. *Shitting hell, it'll have to get its annual clean a little earlier this year.*

'You can take your photo now,' Smithdown said to the photographer. But the girl was screaming so loudly, the young man couldn't quite make out what the detective had said. Paul made as if to turn around several times but was clearly nervous about seeing anything that he wasn't supposed to see.

'I said you can take your photos now lad!' Smithdown said loudly as he crossed the room and leant against the far wall. He folded his arms and watched as the photographer took a reading with his light meter and bent over, looking into the camera's reverse image viewfinder. He held the electronic flash over his head - his hand was still shaking - and took four pictures of the girl's face. He turned to look at DI Smithdown. 'Okay?'

'Perfect, Paul,' the detective replied, just as the on-duty doctor came into the room. He was a slight man in his late fifties, his hair scraped across his head in an inelegant combover. He looked at the blood on Smithdown's coat. 'Christ Almighty, John. I can remember the days when you at least tried to be a bit subtle about these things.'

'I can remember the days when I didn't have to do such things at all, Clive. I'll ring the hippies and get her booked in. Then I can start rattling a few bins to find the twat that did it to her. Pint later?'

'Absolutely, John. I'll just clean up your fucking mess and I'll see you for last orders.'

CHAPTER TWO

11.45 am Friday 1 April 1988

Smithdown stood on the steps of the children's care home and thought for a moment. *What's the best way to play it? Doesn't really matter, Brenda will give me a gob full either way.*

The large, red brick house on the semi-rural estate of Alt on the south eastern outskirts of Oldham would have looked out of place and lopsided to anyone looking at it from the road. It was actually two, semi-detached houses that had been knocked into one large property. Three separate strains of dance music could be heard coming from the open windows of the upstairs rooms. The detective recognised at least one of the songs as something his daughter listened to, but they all sounded the same to Smithdown. *Car alarm music. Wah-Wah-WahWah. I bloody hate it.*

He popped open the glove compartment and rummaged through the cassettes that filled it: Kilburn and the High Roads... Brinsley Schwarz... Dr Feelgood. Meat and two veg pub rock - that was Smithdown's kind of music. He'd lost interest after the mid-70s. *You'll never improve on 'Surrender to the Rhythm' by the Brinsley's, so what's the point?*

He opted for Dr Feelgood's *Down By The Jetty* and shoved the tape into the car's player in readiness for his return. *I'll need a bit of Lee Brilleaux after the bollocking I'm about to get.*

Smithdown locked his dusty, dark blue Ford Escort then checked it was secure by pulling up the door handle. *Can't be too careful around here.* The detective liked to use his own car; he hated the pool vehicles that were provided for detectives at Greater Manchester Police – beige Morris Marinas, mainly. There was never enough of them to go around and on one occasion Smithdown had to resort to catching the bus to get to an incident. Never again.

Using his own car also meant he wasn't at the beck and call of the 'GK' radio fitted as standard in the police pool cars. And that suited him just fine. Especially when he accidentally forgot to take a portable PF1 Pocketphone unit with him too. He was always doing that.

Smithdown walked towards the front door of the care home; it opened before he could ring the bell and a woman in her 40s wearing a baggy, brightly coloured jumper put her finger close to the detective's face, held it there and began shouting. 'You absolute fucking lunatic, John Smithdown!' Brenda Graham shouted, a twist of south west Ireland in her accent. 'The state of that girl's face when she arrived this morning. Like she'd been mauled by an animal. Which she fucking had been, by the way… You! I said give her lip a squeeze, not tear it in half, you useless fucker. Anyway, how are you? Come in.'

Head down, Smithdown walked through the hallway into the large, open-plan kitchen which acted as the central hub of the care home. Although it was nearly lunchtime, the kitchen was humming with chatter as a dozen youngsters ate cereal, made toast, chatted, laughed, bickered and smoked. Smithdown noticed how the older kids – aged about 15 – helped the younger ones without any fuss or complaint. 'Too noisy in here,' Brenda shouted to the detective. 'Outside.'

The detective nodded, followed Brenda through the house and stepped outside into the warm, late-Spring breeze that eased across the large, overgrown garden. There were so many bikes, scooters and outdoor toys scattered about the lawn that they seemed to be growing out of the long grass. Brenda sat on the back step as Smithdown offered her a John Player Special cigarette from a battered, black pack pulled from the inside pocket of his grey suit jacket. He'd dropped off his overcoat at the cleaners on the way.

She took the cigarette, tucked it behind her ear and then rolled one of her own from a pouch attached to the belt of her red, corduroy trousers. She lit it with a Micky Mouse Zippo lighter - offered the flame to Smithdown - then flicked it shut with a loud clack. 'Anyway,' she sighed; her voice was much quieter now. 'Thank God you got that girl out of that house. I don't care for the way you did it, mind, but you got it done. Fair play. You're still a fucking animal, though.'

'I had to make sure that Dr Clive would definitely sign her away,' Smithdown explained. 'He's half-pissed most of the time. It had to be a dead cert. Black and white.'

'Black and blue, more like,' Brenda pointed, her voice going up a few notches again. 'The state of her this morning after she'd come back from the Royal.' She shook her head slowly from side to side to make sure that the detective was in no doubt about how annoyed she was.

'It could have been a lot worse if she'd gone back to her mum's bastard boyfriend,' Smithdown offered quietly. 'Dread to think what he would have done to the poor little mite.'

'Becky,' Brenda stated. 'Her name is Becky.'

'Right. Becky. Yes. Is she okay? Apart from the whole lip thing, obviously.'

'She's okay. Just about. It's her mam I'm more worried about.'

'I see. So, there's more to you asking me here than just the mere pleasure of bollocking me, then?'

'The bollocking is just a bonus, to be honest, John. Her mam's not been seen for at least 24 hours.'

'Right,' said Smithdown, searching for his notebook. 'That's… what day is it today?'

'Friday, John. It's Friday. Good Friday, to be precise.'

'Okay. Of course.'

'Little Becky says there was trouble at the house yesterday teatime - and that's all she'll say. The neighbours rang social services because they were worried about her, but your lads ended up getting there first because of all the screaming and shouting.'

'Her mum's Naomi Wells, right?' the detective asked rubbing the side of his nose with the end of a betting shop pen. 'I know her. Christ. She's not had the greatest life so far, but she's more sinned against than a sinner, I'd say.'

'She's a good person, John. And a good mam to Becky.'

'Have you seen her boyfriend about?' the detective asked, the ash from the cigarette dangling from his lips landed on his notepad as he wrote. 'Jimmy Todd isn't it?'

'That's him. Thankfully, I haven't seen him, no. He's a piece of dirt. Describes himself as a DJ but he's basically a drug dealer with a big record collection. He's only been with Naomi for about a year. She's been known to do a bit of sex work on the side, as you know, and I think he encourages it. Probably got his eye on little Becky too, the shit bag.'

'Don't suppose you have a photo of mum, do you?' Smithdown asked.

'I don't,' said Brenda, squeezing off the end of her roll-up and popping the tiny dimp down the backyard drain. 'But little Becky has one. It's in her room by her bed. Perhaps you could pop upstairs and ask her for a lend of it? Seeing you is sure to bring a smile to her face. Oh no. She can't smile just now, can she? I forgot.'

'Kinnell,' sighed Smithdown, jabbing his JPS out against the back wall, causing a small tumble of sparks to fall into the grid. 'Okay. Lead on.'

The detective felt the angry stares of at least a dozen pairs of young eyes as he followed Brenda and walked back through the kitchen and then up the stairs. They passed several doors – all with customised variations of KEEP OUT signs on them - before stopping outside the last door on the first-floor landing. Brenda knocked. Nothing. She tried again, louder this time. 'Becky. It's Brenda. I've got a policeman with me. I'm afraid it's the same one you met last night. He wants to talk with you. You don't have to talk to him if you don't want to. But he wants to try to find your mum. That picture of yours will definitely help.'

Silence.

'It's up to you Becky,' Brenda continued. 'I'd completely understand if you don't want to see him.' She looked at

Smithdown and shook her head in disapproval. 'I wouldn't blame you in the slightest, I really wouldn't.'

Silence again. Brenda was about to try one more time when the door opened. A little. Becky Wells' bruised face could be seen through the small gap. There were stitches in her lip. Her hair looked clean and shiny. She was wearing what looked like a new, plain white t-shirt and clean but clearly second-hand jeans. Smithdown looked at her feet through the opening. *Woolies' sandals.*

Becky passed a photo to Brenda through the gap, caught John Smithdown's eye for the briefest of moments, then closed the door. Music started from the room: Mel and Kim's '*Respectable*'. Brenda motioned for the detective to follow her back down the stairs. When they got to the hallway Brenda stopped, took a look at the photo and handed it to the DI. It showed a woman in her late 20s punching the air and laughing in what looked like a nightclub. She was wearing a black vest top and army-style grey and white camouflage trousers. The red date stamp on the bottom right-hand corner of the photo showed that it had been taken just two months previously: 11.2.88.

'Yep, that's Naomi. Quite the party girl,' offered Smithdown.

'You can be a good parent and have a good time as well, John. I'm sure your mates down at the Old Bill will agree with that. How's your daughter doing, by the way?'

'Point taken, Brenda. Point taken. She's doing great, thanks. Still at uni. She's quite the party girl too.'

The pager on Smithdown's belt buzzed an interruption. It was his one concession to being contactable as he could very easily just ignore it. The display's message wasn't the usual instruction to ring a phone number.

<ALEX PARK NOW>

The detective looked at it with a frown. He didn't like carrying a pager at the best of times, but he liked it even less when the messages sounded like he was being shouted at. He re-attached the pager to his belt and placed a hand on Brenda's upper arm, giving it what he hoped was a reassuring squeeze. 'Right, I'll get this circulated and do some digging. My presence is required at Alexandra Park, apparently.'

'Thank you, John,' she said, placing her hand on his and returning the squeeze. 'You're still a massive fucking arsehole, but I'm glad you're on our side.'

'Beautifully put, Brenda. I'll be in touch.'

Smithdown walked back to his car then paused. He took another look at the photo - it still had a yellowed curl of Sellotape stuck to the back. He looked at Naomi's happy face then tucked the photo into his jacket pocket. He got in the car and pushed the Dr Feelgood cassette he'd found earlier into the slot. As he switched on the engine the tape mechanism kicked in and '*She Does It Right*' wowed into life.

~

It took him just a few minutes' drive to get to Alexandra Park; it ran along the south western edge of the town. As he drove past uniform roads tightly packed with corner shops, takeaways and terraces he wondered exactly where in the park his presence might be required. He quickly got an answer; half of Oldham's police force seemed to be swarming around the park's boating lake. Smithdown pulled into the car park, nodded to the uniformed constables herding afternoon school kids out of the main gates and headed down the sloping path, past the tennis courts towards the main lake. In between the main boat house and a separate launch building was a slipway that led into the shallow, brown water. There were two police officers already there, talking to a very distressed looking man with a red setter dog. The dog was also extremely agitated, yanking and straining in the direction of a plastic bag by the water's edge. *A man out walking his dog. It's always a man out walking his dog.*

He caught the eye of Detective Constable Bob Donaldson

as he approached the lake's shoreline. Donaldson, in an old blue suit, light blue shirt and a dark blue tie had an unusually cheery face for a police officer. He looked more like a friendly butcher than a detective. But his face was currently set to 'very stern indeed.' By pursing his lips, exhaling and shaking his head, Donaldson managed to tell Smithdown a great deal about what was going on as he approached the scene. Essentially, it was along the lines of: 'This is grim and you're not going to like it one little bit'.

The red setter was barking loudly now. Smithdown spoke to one of the PCs who was trying to calm down both the man and his dog.

'Could you get this pair away from here for the time being, please?' he told one of them. 'Tell him to take the dog up behind the boathouse, to wait there and to say nowt to anyone. Wait with him until we're done here. And tell him to shut that fucking dog up - I can't hear myself piss here with all that racket.'

He turned to Detective Constable Donaldson. 'Bob. On a scale of one to ten, how badly are the contents of that placcy bag going to put me off my tea?'

'What are you planning on having for your tea,' the DC said. 'If you don't mind me asking, boss?'

DC Donaldson was in the habit of being overly curious about things that most people wouldn't ordinarily bother with. A good trait for a policeman to have, some might say – but an annoying one, nonetheless. Smithdown knew it was quicker to indulge him. 'Chippy tea, Bob', he replied. 'Steak pudding, chips, peas and gravy. And a can of dandelion and burdock.'

'No fish? Not like you. It's Friday…'

Smithdown took a look across the lake and back down to the bag. There was a puddle around it where the lake water had seeped from the bag's holes. The water was speckled with what looked like soot. 'I'm off fish today, Bob, if I'm honest.'

'In that case,' Donaldson offered, 'I'd say a good strong nine.'

'Cracking...' Smithdown said. 'Absolutely cracking.'

Smithdown pulled a pen from the inside pocket of his jacket, squatted down and eased apart the handles of the bag with the pen's tip. Inside, somewhat puffy and wrinkled from the lake water it appeared to have absorbed, was a human hand. The detective did what he always did in these circumstances and followed the advice he'd been given by a senior detective he'd worked with in the late 70s: think with your eyes open and your gob shut.

DI John Smithdown looked long and hard at the contents of the bag. And kept his gob shut.

It was a left hand. The cut at the wrist was neat. The fingers were slender. The nails had chipped traces of dayglo nail varnish on - the colours alternated between orange and lime green on each fingernail. Smithdown didn't feel that he was jumping to a conclusion by considering it to be a young woman's hand. But he was, as ever, prepared to be convinced otherwise. While the main, fleshy part of the hand was blanched white - not unlike tripe from Oldham market - the tips of the fingers were blackened. Smithdown, again not unreasonably, felt they could well have been badly scorched, as if a harsh flame had been held to them. Three of the fingertips had been burned so badly the skin and flesh had flaked away. The thumb and forefinger got his attention - they seemed to have had less time in the flames.

'Fucking Nora,' Smithdown sighed, sensing that his chippy tea was now looking increasingly unlikely.

'I know,' offered DC Donaldson. 'Not nice. Not nice at all. Any missing-from-homes that might fit the bill? Or indeed, fit the wrist.'

'Brilliant Bob. You've been waiting half the afternoon to use that line, haven't you?' said Smithdown. 'Let's see if we can get some dabs off those fingers that haven't been totally barbecued and take it from there, shall we? We're not in the business of jumping to conclusions.'

'I reckon you know whose mitt that might be, don't you, boss?'

'Potentially. Get them to do a check against a Naomi Wells.

Age 26. One of our regular clients. I hope I'm wrong, but it might save time. In the meantime, go and take a statement from the bloke that found it and tell that twat if he breathes a word of this to anyone, I'll drown him and that noisy fucking dog of his in the lake myself. Okay?'

'I'll tell him that word for word, boss.'

CHAPTER THREE

3pm Friday 1 April 1988

Smithdown was at his desk listening to the radio, when DC Donaldson approached with a file under his arm. The DI held up his hand for a moment as he monitored what Manchester Radio was saying about the find.

'…Murder squad detectives in Greater Manchester are investigating after a human hand was found at a park in Oldham.

The grim discovery was made by a man out walking his dog in Alexandra Park yesterday afternoon. Robert Crane has more.'

'It's always a GRIM DISCOVERY, boss,' Donaldson said. 'Ever noticed that? Always.'

'Shush.'

'The hand, thought to be that of a woman, was found wrapped in a plastic bag in the boating lake at the park yesterday. Brian Sharples was out walking his dog at the time and became suspicious when his red setter spotted something in the lake.'

> *"Me dog… it were going mad. Barking and that. Barking at this bag in the water. So, I let him off the leash and he dragged it out. Wish I hadn't now, when I saw what were inside. Horrible. Never seen anything like it in all my days. You just don't expect it, like, do yuh?"*

'Forensic tests are now being carried out to try to identify the victim. In the meantime, police are trying to reassure local residents who say they're fearful that more remains will be found. Robert Crane, Manchester Radio

News, in Oldham.'

'Fucking Nora, Bob,' Smithdown said, turning the radio off. 'Didn't you tell that bloke not to speak to the press?'

'I absolutely did,' Donaldson replied.

'I was hoping to keep some of those details back. We don't actually know it's a woman's hand. It could belong to a bloke with a sensitive disposition for all I know.'

'That's what I wanted to talk to you about,' Donaldson said, standing in the doorway. Smithdown's office was so tiny it was more comfortable to stand outside it than to try to squeeze into it. 'We've got a preliminary ID on the hand. It'd been torched alright, but not quite torched enough. They manged to get a fingerprint match from the thumb and the pointing finger.'

'Forefinger, Bob,' Smithdown said with a sigh. 'That's what we tend to call it. Not pointing finger.'

'Aye, that as well. Looks like you weren't wrong boss. Prints seem to match those of a Naomi Laila Wells, D.O.B 12th of the second 1962. Half-caste girl…'

'Mixed-race is my preferred option here Bob, we have spoken about this.'

'With respect, boss,' Donaldson replied, 'Half-caste is still the term used by the GMP press office in their descriptions.'

'I think we can aim higher than the GMP press office, don't you Bob?'

'We can but dream, boss. Any road, she was known to the Manchester Criminal Records Office, so her dabs were in the system: theft, soliciting…'

'… I know she had a MANCRO number, Bob. It was me that did her for most of the crimes in question.'

'Can't say I'm surprised. The boyfriend is top priority now, I'm guessing.'

'Your guessing right, Bob. Cancel your plans for tonight, because we need to get that dickhead into custody, sharpish. We can get him in on suspicion of murder, but without the rest of her, technically speaking she's still just a missing person. That's what we say to the outside world and that's what I'll be saying to her daughter - for the time being, at least. I've upset that little girl quite enough so far this week, without having to tell her that her mum's probably in bits across half of Oldham.'

'Can't blame you there, boss.'

'We need a press statement for now, saying that we're growing increasingly concerned for Naomi's safety - the usual holding line - that'll see us through the weekend. Then we'll need to get a press conference on the go for first thing Tuesday morning…'

'Why wait 'til Tuesday?' asked Donaldson.

'Monday's a Bank Holiday, Bob. Glance at a calendar from time to time, will you?'

'Will do. In fact, I'll make a note in my diary to do it…'

'I'll tell DS Pym about the presser. We need to have a total blackout on any mention of her previous convictions. Public sympathy goes right out the fucking window as soon as you mention it, especially soliciting.'

'Aren't you supposed to check with the DS before you organise a press conference?' asked Donaldson. He was smiling. He knew the score between Smithdown and James Pym, their Detective Superintendent.

'Of course, Bob,' Smithdown said, his tone of voice bone dry. 'How remiss of me. I'll get right on it.'

'He'll be wanting to buy himself a new suit if he's going to be on the telly at Tuesday teatime.'

'I'll call ahead to *Stolen From Ivor* and let them know he'll be round for a fitting.'

'Very decent of you.'

'Right,' said Smithdown, waving the DC away. 'I've already rung the landlord of Naomi's flat. He's dropping the keys off any time now. Let's give it an hour to get everything else on the go, then meet me out front.'

DC Donaldson's eyes darted to his left by way of a signal - Smithdown immediately understood. 'Good stuff DC Donaldson. Well done. First things first - let me appraise the

DS of the situation and I'll be with you shortly.'

'Looks like I've arrived at just the right time then, doesn't it?' said DS James Pym, approaching from Donaldson's left. The DS, five years younger than Smithdown but looking at least ten, was smartly dressed and looked like he'd just come from the barbers. He smelled strongly of Aramis. 'Always good to be kept abreast of the latest developments,' he said. 'Especially where it comes to body parts being left in the grounds of our local leisure spaces.'

'Vital, I'd say,' agreed DC Donaldson. 'I'll see you downstairs Mr Smithdown.'

'Looking forward to it, DC Donaldson,' Smithdown responded, switching from dry to sarcastic. 'Take a seat, Jim,' the detective offered with a smile, knowing full well that there wasn't a seat in his office other than the one he was already sitting on. Pym didn't move.

'Hand. Lake. Bag,' stated DS Pym. 'Appraise me. Now.'

'Of course. The hand belongs to Naomi Wells - known to us but nothing earth-shattering.'

'Prossie, wasn't she?'

'Soliciting is how I tend to refer to it. Occasional sex worker at a push. Bit of theft, handling stolen goods, low-level dealing. A bad life rather than a bad person. I think we should have a presser on Tuesday if nothing else has turned up. Her daughter's currently in care up at Alt. She's only little. Nice kid. She's had a time of it too. We were called out to a domestic yesterday. The daughter had certainly taken a knock. We think that Naomi's boyfriend banged the kid against a few walls at their flat over in Glodwick. Jimmy Todd is his name. He's a dealer. And a DJ. And a dickhead. So, we are looking for the boyfriend for assault on the girl and he's clearly a person of interest in terms of the hand and Naomi being missing. We're off to their flat, now.'

'So, we've a DJ who likes chopping up bodies and beating up little girls? Lovely little town this, isn't it? Well, you'd better find him, John. Sharpish. We like our murdering dickheads in custody, not running around Oldham on an Easter weekend.

Never mind a presser on Tuesday - I want to be on the telly saying we've caught the bugger before I have my Bank Holiday lunch on Monday. Clear?'

'Of course, Jim. You've never been clearer.'

'And please remember to take a fucking radio out with you.' Pym said as he walked away. 'If I didn't know better, I'd say you were doing it on purpose.'

CHAPTER FOUR

4.25 pm Friday 1 April 1988

The address the detectives had been given for the house that Naomi and Becky Wells shared with Jimmy Todd was a flat above a South Asian sweet shop, barely a mile from Alexandra Park. Smithdown knew the owner, who'd dropped off a small set of keys to the flat at the police station reception half an hour earlier. He'd also left the DI a small, neatly wrapped box of mixed barfi, his favourite. Nice touch, Smithdown thought, as he popped the key into his pocket and slipped his thumbnail through the round sticker that sealed the box. The sticker featured a drawing of a friendly-looking man with a huge moustache winking, with "Mr Aleem's" written underneath it. The cardboard lid popped open and a sweet waft of condensed milk and cardamom was released. A pretty reasonable consolation prize for missing my chippy tea, he thought, taking an oblong of cake and popping it into his mouth. Making inroads with the local South Asian community was one of Smithdown's ongoing projects, but the DI was under no illusions about how long this was likely to take. He knew the kind of language some of his colleagues used about the ever-growing Pakistani and Bangladeshi presence on the east side of town; was it any wonder that many of the local South Asian youths mistrusted the police to the point of hatred?

'You drive, Bob,' Smithdown said. 'Get us there in one piece and I'll save you a bit of barfi.'

'I don't like it, boss, as you well know,' the DC said as they pulled out of the car park and cut across the town centre to the sound of Ian Dury's '*What a Waste*' on the cassette player. 'I like a nice Eccles Cake. Or an Iced Finger. Or a Manchester Tart. Not up my street that Asian gear.'

'Bob, you're in The Raj for a lamb biriyani at least once a week. You talk shite.'

'That's different, boss. Savoury is fine. It's when they do sweet that I don't approve of. A cake that smells like pilau rice? It's not right.'

'You're not right, Bob. Just drive.'

It took a matter of minutes for them to get to Naomi Well's flat. It was on the corner of a terraced cul-de-sac off the main road between Oldham and neighbouring Ashton. Identical streets stretched out in every direction, featuring identical houses: same red stone front doorsteps, same two-up, two-down design. Many had windows that were boarded up with metal sheeting. Smithdown could see one street where only one or two houses remained occupied.

Naomi's flat was above Mr Aleem's sweet shop which, unlike many of the surrounding houses, was very much occupied. There was a queue out of the door as people waited to be served. Through the shop window Smithdown caught the eye of the owner, who was chatting to people as they made their purchases. The staff serving wore green and white hats and tabards with "Mr Aleem's Sweet Centre" written on them in an extravagant, signature-style script. Aleem himself wore a three-piece suit; his tie pushed out by a gold pin. His moustache wasn't quite as huge and lustrous as the cartoon suggested, but it wasn't far off. He was in his early 50s like Smithdown, but his hair and his moustache were matching jet black. The detective gave him a thumbs-up, waived the two keys he had been given, pointed to the flat upstairs and held five fingers up to indicate how long he would like the shop owner to wait until he joined them. Mr Aleem smiled and returned the thumbs-up.

'Business is booming for Mr Aleem, I see,' Donaldson commented as Smithdown opened the door next to the front entrance of the shop that led to Naomi Wells' flat with the larger of the two keys.

'Big noise in the local Tory party, isn't he?' Donaldson added. 'Running to be a councillor soon, I believe.'

'So I hear,' Smithdown acknowledged, struggling with the lock.

'Everyone calls him Mister Aleem, don't they? Even you. Mister Aleem this and Mister Aleem that. Don't get me wrong – smashing bloke and all that. But, he always gets the Mister treatment. What's his full name?'

'Mr Aleem,' Smithdown replied.

'No, but what's his actual first name?'

'Mister,' confirmed the DI, pushing open the door and shifting a small pile of free newspapers, takeaway menus and general post in the process.

The two detectives climbed the steep stairs which led to a small landing and another door. Smithdown opened it with the smaller of the two keys he'd been given, and they walked straight into the flat's main living room. It was a plain affair - largely clean but not particularly tidy. There was woodchip wallpaper throughout; some of it darkened with scuff marks and crayon. Several ashtrays - the metal kind often found in pubs - were full of dog ends on the low slung, smoked glass coffee table. Some of their contents appeared to be legal. Some weren't. The rest of the furniture seemed to date from several different decades - mainly the 1970s. It looked as if the items in the flat had been cobbled together from junk shops and relatives having a clear out; they even included a coffin-sized radiogram with records piled up in matching towers either side of it. A dark brown settee dominated the room - it sagged in the middle and one of the seat cushions had been stitched in several places. The TV and accompanying video recorder were both huge by 1988 standards - dating from the start of the decade. There was a mantlepiece framing a log-effect gas fire with at least a dozen photos on the top of it. Some pictures were in frames, some were loose, propped up against the wall. Most were of Becky Wells. Several were of

Naomi, Becky and Jimmy Todd. Smithdown looked at Todd's face. Late 20s, slim face. Nice white teeth. Hair cut short at the sides, streaky blonde on top. *Half the lads in Manchester have that haircut.*

Smithdown zeroed in on one photo: little Becky was in the middle of the shot - her eyes were closed - and she was laughing. The faces of her mum and of Jimmy Todd were pressed against her cheeks, one either side. They were laughing too. Smithdown looked. He said nothing.

Eyes open, gob shut.

Smithdown took the picture and eased it into the inside pocket of his jacket. He felt the corner of the other photo - the one of Naomi nightclubbing that Becky had given him - with the edge of his fingers.

He walked into the kitchen. There was a similar feeling here as there had been in the living room - a hodgepodge of items that looked like they'd been begged and borrowed from friends and relatives. Smithdown opened one of the drawers. It held a mix of knives, forks and utensils. He looked at them then rummaged for a moment. He found a tin opener, looked at it then tossed it back in. Smithdown turned when he heard a knock on the kitchen door. Mr Aleem was trying to get the detective's attention rather than asking for permission to enter. It was his property after all. 'I'm not disturbing you am I, John?' Aleem said. His voice was clear, his diction crisp; only the elongated vowel sound in *disturrrbing* gave him away as being Oldham through and through.

'No, no. Just looking, Mr Aleem.'

'And thinking, John,' Mister Aleem added. 'That's you to a tee. Always thinking.' Aleem walked across the room and shook Smithdown's hand. It was a perfect handshake, just the kind that the detective approved of. *Not too firm - a bullshitter's handshake, no thanks. Not too weak – like a wet lettuce, a vicar's handshake, no thanks either.*

'Well, I think that I'll definitely have to get some more of that barfi before I leave,' Smithdown said. 'Paid for this time, obviously.'

'Obviously, obviously,' Aleem said, with a wink.

'Tell me about Naomi Wells, Mister Aleem.'

The landlord sighed and put out his hands in a gesture that suggested disappointment, resignation and slight regret all in one. 'So nice. A nice, nice girl. Dotes on her daughter - little Becky. She's okay? Please tell me she's being well looked after.'

'She's being very well looked after,' confirmed Smithdown.

'Naomi didn't have much,' Mr Aleem continued. 'But Becky was her top priority. Number one. Always. Sometimes she was late with her rent, but I knew she'd pay at some point, so I let it pass. She always paid eventually. Always. Then that boy moved in and things went downhill, seriously downhill.'

'In what way?' chipped in DC Donaldson, who'd been quietly taking notes.

'Noise. Parties. Complaints. Big trouble the other night,' Aleem said. 'Rent not paid… at all. He treated her badly, I believe. Very badly. And now there's this terrible business over in the park. Please tell me they're not connected John. Please.'

'We're anxious to trace the boyfriend Mr Aleem, put it like that. That's our priority. The boyfriend.'

'I'm told he sells drugs. He goes from nightclub to nightclub on a bike. Demand is so high, he uses a racing bike, John. Can you imagine? A racing bike like you see on the Olympics so he can get around at double speed. Imagine.'

'What's his favourite spot?' Smithdown asked.

'The new place in the town centre. It used to be a regular club, now it's changed. Kingdom it's called. Different music, different drugs. Changes, John. Big, changes.'

Smithdown had seen the changes first-hand. The old-style white shirt, slacks and loafers crowd were morphing into a new type of clubber. There was less need for the police outside the clubs at the moment because there was much less drunken fighting. Former hard cases were coming out of nightclubs hugging people they'd been punching in the face a few months earlier. Beer sales were down, water sales were up. Ecstasy had come to town and Oldham's's nightclub bosses were having to adapt accordingly. A bottle of water now cost nearly as much as a pint of bitter. A bottle of Lucozade cost even more. There were rumours that cold-water supplies to the toilets at Kingdom had been cut so people couldn't slake their E-fuelled thirsts for free. Smithdown had heard that the owner of Kingdom - one Richard T. King - was raking in cash by selling ice pops worth pennies for the price of a cocktail.

Smithdown didn't like Richard T. King - he insisted on being called that - one little bit. Most of the town's troubles seem to inevitably snake back to him. The local press liked to call King a 'flamboyant businessman'. That was just a euphemism for 'crook who likes to show-off' as far as Smithdown was concerned. When asked what the T stood for, King was in the habit of answering: 'The'.

'Yes, Mr Aleem,' Smithdown said. 'You're not wrong. Big changes.'

CHAPTER FIVE

9.45 pm Friday 1 April 1988

'These balaclavas are itchy as fuck,' the masked man said as he waited in the orangey glow of the street near an unkempt set of deck-access flats. He wasn't alone. There were six of them - at least five seemed to be having a competition as to who could look the most suspicious. Mr Itchy Face was currently the clear winner. Tapping out a beat on his thighs, accompanying it with a tsk-tsk-tsk noise of exhaled air through his teeth, he stared up the road, then down, then back again. Unable to bear it anymore, he pulled up the balaclava exposing the lower half of his face, removed one glove and scratched both cheeks.

'I swear there's nits or something in them,' he carried on. 'Were they second hand? They're itchy as fuuuuck, I tell ya. These gloves are just as bad.'

'Shhhh now,' the tallest of the group said. 'We'll be done soon. Until then keep it shut.' The tall man alone seemed in control of his movements. Like Itchy Face, the others jogged on the spot or stepped from one foot to the other - not to keep warm, but to drain off the excess energy that seemed to ripple around them. As they waited, they scanned the area. One spotted a youth crossing the street about 150 feet from where they were standing. He was wearing headphones and had his head down. 'Him there,' Itchy Face said. 'The lad in the white hoodie. He's a Paki. He'll do.'

'He's supposed to be from Bangladesh,' the leader said. 'That's the point. Bangladesh. Not Pakistan. That's the whole point. That's why we're here. I think his family run a business on Coldhurst Street. A restaurant, yeah? You know him don't you, Tariq?'

There was silence. Tariq Shamsi - also wearing a balaclava - was staring at the pavement. 'Tariq?' the leader shouted, 'Do you, or do you not know that lad?'

Tariq glanced in the youth's direction for the briefest of moments. Then his eyes returned to the pavement. 'I think so, yes,' he confirmed.

'And does his family run the restaurant on Coldhurst Street, or do they not?'

'Yes. I think his name is Musta.'

'And where are they from? The family, where are they from?'

A pause. 'They're Bengalis.'

'So, he's a Bengali Paki then?' asked Itchy Face.

'His family are from Bangladesh, yes,' Tariq confirmed.

'Right then. If that's the kind of Paki we're after, let's get cracking.' He pulled the balaclava back over his chin. 'Itchy as fuck,' he reiterated. The leader gave a nod. A red and white Adidas holdall was produced, and weapons were handed out. One each. Tariq shook his head when he was given his.

'Take it,' he was told. He did. The group headed down the street - the leader and one other member of the gang hung back a little. Itchy Face raced ahead.

Sixteen-year-old Mustafizur Rahman hadn't been paying much attention to what was going on ahead of him. But a blur of peripheral movement made him look up slightly. He saw the gang framed under the curved upper edge of his hoodie. A group of lads walking towards him was a fairly serious worry at the best of times. The fact that they appeared to have baseball bats meant that it was time for him to make the swiftest exit possible.

Go.

Go, go, go.

Go now.

Go!

Still moving at walking pace, he turned sharply into a passageway between two blocks of flats. The moment he was out of sight, he ran. Hard. The sound of several pairs of feet immediately followed him. He heard a shout too: 'Yeees! Here we go. The thrill of the chase - fookin' brilliant.'

The boy ran harder. Across the square, through the passage, up the stairs. Flat 24. He'd be home in a minute. If he ran really, really hard. Halfway across the square he risked a glance back. He was pulling away from the group.

Yes.

But keep going. The greater the distance, the safer you'll be. Nearly home.

He faced forward again, entered the final alley and ran straight into the balaclava-clad leader. He'd pulled away from the main group and gone another way into the square. 'Hi,' the big man said. He pointed the end of his baseball bat directly into Mustafizur's face. The bat was tilted down slightly - the man was nearly a foot taller. The others were there now, buzzing around them. The teenager could hear their laughter, smell their beery sweat, see their breath hissing from the mouth holes of their balaclavas.

A moment of stillness. The bat's tip inched forwards and touched the young man's forehead. The big man winked. The teenager grabbed the end of the bat and shoved it away from him, hitting the big man in the eye.

Mustafizur turned to run but one of the gang swung his bat hard into the boy's stomach. A second bat then smacked across his shoulders and he hit the pavement. He was surrounded now. In turn, each took two swings with their bat. The boy instinctively put his hands over his head, but the blows all connected with his arms, legs and torso.

All but one of the gang took a swing. Tariq was at the back, several feet away, until the leader pushed him forward. As he did so, his balaclava was pulled off by one of the group exposing his face. 'No! Why would you do that?' Tariq shouted.

'So you can see better,' said Itchy Face, handing him a weapon.

Tariq tried and failed to avoid the boy's frightened eyes as he took it, his fingers flexing around the handle. The leader leaned in. 'Say it,' he whispered.

A pause. 'Say. It.'

'Fuck Bangladesh.'

'Again. And put some life into it.'

'Fuck Bangladesh!'

'Now do it. Do it! Fuckin' do it!' Itchy Face screamed.

Tariq pulled his balaclava back over his face, as if it somehow made the situation better and afforded him some protection from Mustafizur's hurt and hateful stare. He swung once at the top of the teenager's arm. Despite the slightly half-hearted way it was done, the boy screamed.

'Proper! Do it proper!' Itchy Face screamed.

He swung again. This time the machete - because that was the weapon he'd been given - cut right to the bone.

CHAPTER SIX

11.15 pm Friday 1 April 1988

Smithdown and Donaldson made absolutely no effort to blend into their surroundings as they walked slowly - very slowly - around the dancefloor of the Kingdom nightclub that evening. It was as if they had gone out of their way to stand out even more from the club's Friday night clientele. Most were young, late teens, early twenties, and were far too busy earnestly concentrating on their repetitive dance moves to pay the two detectives much notice. The heat inside the club was intense. Overwhelming. Kingdom was in an old, art deco-style bingo hall and despite the post-modern, industrial stylings that had been added to the interior, it had retained many of its original fixtures and fittings. The DI placed a hand on an ornate iron radiator that had been painted grey and gold; it was hot. To Smithdown's eyes, the clubbers clothes looked strangely uniform yet practical: baggy tops mixed with cycle shorts; vests and combat trousers; bandanas and sweatbands. *They're not here to fight and pull like normal. They're here to dance and try to stay cool while they're doing it. And Richard T. King is making it as difficult - and probably expensive - for them to do that as possible. The sly twat.*

As Bang The Party's '*Release Your Body*' segued into '*Voodoo Ray*' by A Guy Called Gerald, the two detectives approached the bar. Smithdown leant in to speak to the barman; he was in his late 20s with a black polo shirt, shaven head and a beard. Ornate, animal-themed tattoos could be seen across his arms, neck and head. Nearly all the staff seemed to sport a similar look. The staff at Kingdom seemed to be exclusively male; the only females Smithdown had seen were on the dancefloor.

It took Smithdown three attempts to make himself understood. The barman nodded, held up a finger indicating he'd be one minute, flipped up the counter and walked briskly down a corridor to the left of the bar. Smithdown looked at the pained expression on his colleague's face. DC Donaldson was more of an ELO man and the music and its eardrum-rattling volume was visibly distressing him. Donaldson mouthed two words to Smithdown, 'fookin' shite'.

The barman reappeared and indicated that they should follow him. Smithdown and Donaldson made their way down a grey and gold corridor. It was lined with exhausted clubbers, sheened with sweat, taking a break from the dancefloor. Some were still performing tiny dance steps as they chugged on bottles of water. Others were in small groups of two or three, with their arms around each other, glassy-eyed and smiling.

They reached a door marked PRIVATE - STAFF ONLY. The barman punched a four-digit code into a keypad on the wall, pulled the door open and invited the officers to take the stairs. As the heavy-duty door closed behind them the noise level dropped by 75 per cent: 'Absolute bliss,' sighed DC Donaldson as the two detectives climbed the stairs. Each step they took reduced the decibels from the dancefloor. As they reached the top of the stairs, another door was opened by a tall, well-built man in a smart, well-cut black suit, shirt and tie. He seemed different to the other members with their shaved heads, polo shirts and tattoos. His hair was short and neat with a side parting. 'Evening officers,' he said in a soft Oldham accent. 'Please, come in.'

Smithdown recognised him. The detective knew a lot of people in Oldham and he had been at school with Tom Lennon's mum. 'Evening Tom,' he replied.

The room opened out into a huge office. The walls were bare brick and the wooden floors had been stripped and oiled to an expensive-looking finish. Framed posters and prints lined the walls, each hung with exacting precision at exactly the same distance from its neighbour. They highlighted pop culture moments that reflected the tastes of the man at the end of the office: films (*Battleship Potemkin*), music (*Solid Air* album cover, signed by John Martyn) and gigs (Slaughter and the Dogs + Sex Pistols, Lesser Free Trade Hall, Manchester, 1976). The centrepiece of the room was an oblong granite table that seemed to be floating in mid-air. As Smithdown got closer he saw that it was suspended from the exposed beams in the ceiling by thin black wires. Behind the desk sat Richard T. King. He was eating. Mixed tandoori grill with salad and a nan, Smithdown noted. *Christ, I'm fucking starving.*

King stood up, motioned to the bouncer that everything was fine and wiped his hands and mouth with a baby wipe from a pack on his desk. He bounded across the room and offered both the detectives an overly firm handshake. His dark blonde shoulder-length hair bounced slightly as he greeted them. He was wearing a dark blazer with white piping that appeared to be modelled on the style favoured by Patrick McGoohan in the TV show *The Prisoner.* Underneath the jacket he wore a Mickey Mouse t-shirt, knee-length multi-coloured Bermuda shorts and light blue flip-flops. His toenails were painted black. 'DI Smithdown!' he cried. 'Welcome, welcome. So very pleased you've decided to spend your Bank Holiday weekend with us. Soy contento. Please, please… won't you and your colleague take a seat.'

In the space of four sentences King's accent had pinballed between Manchester, London and New York with a little touch of Spain for good measure. Smithdown had read that the nightclub owner was in fact from Tintwhistle, to the east of Manchester just over the Derbyshire border. King liked to boast that he was the second most famous person to come from the village, after clothes designer Vivienne Westwood.

The detectives both ignored King's offer of a seat and Smithdown produced the two photographs that were in his jacket pocket. He placed them one after the other on King's floating desk as if he was playing pontoon. The desk wobbled slightly. 'Naomi Wells. Missing person. Known to frequent this club. Jimmy Todd. Person of interest in said missing person case. Also known to frequent this club. Any information gratefully received, Mr King.'

One of the wires holding up King's desk was close to Smithdown's face. The detective reached out and gave it a twang. It made a satisfying noise, not unlike a harp. King didn't look at the photos. 'I know them both. They've set up home together across town, I believe. Naomi is a regular; she sometimes dances on the podiums. Really lovely girl with an equally lovely daughter. Jimmy pretends he's a DJ but he's not. He's a scumbag and a dealer and I won't have him in the club. He's barred. I don't allow drugs in my club therefore I won't allow drug dealers in my club. I told Naomi to have nothing to do with him too. She ignored me, of course. Quel dommage.'

'What a shame indeed, Mr King,' said Smithdown, quietly pleased that he'd managed to dredge up a little O Level French to understand what King was talking about. 'Because if I find out that you know where either of them are, I'll have the licensing authority close this sweaty shithole down so fast it'll make your flip-flops spin. Capisci?'

'Naturalment', replied a smiling King, his hands apart in a wide, peaceful gesture. He leant back in his chair and put his hands behind his head.

The detective picked up the two photos and returned them to his pocket. He turned to leave. DC Donaldson glared at the nightclub owner for a few seconds, then followed. 'And turn the fucking heat down on that dancefloor you money-grabbing bastard. Some kid's going to die of exhaustion while you're selling ice pops at 20 times the usual price.'

As the two detectives left, Smithdown nodded to the tall man at the door. 'Give my regards to your mum, Tom.'

'Will do Mr Smithdown. Have a good evening.'

With jackets over their arms to ease the effects of the heat, the detectives made their way down the stairs and around the edge of the dancefloor in silence. They nodded to the bouncers on the door and were relieved to feel the night air cooling their faces. They both took out a cigarette each - John Player Special for Smithdown, Benson and Hedges for

Donaldson - and lit up. 'What do you think?' asked DC Donaldson.

'I think he's full of shite,' replied Smithdown. 'The flip-flops, nail polish and cod French don't fool me. You don't get your hands on as much money and property as Richard T. King has without being a hard-faced fucker. He knows more about this than he's letting on, but he's saying nowt. What I want to know is why he's saying nowt.'

'Good to know that he won't allow drugs in his club though,' Donaldson observed, as he passed a small group of young men walking arm in arm down the street.

'It's a weight off my mind, it really is,' Smithdown replied.

The two detectives walked through the town centre as they smoked and watched as the local pubs emptied. The further they got from the Kingdom club the more a grumbling sense of trouble increased in the air. Their night shift police colleagues were maintaining a quiet presence at the periphery of the precinct, waiting for the older, pub crowd - mullet haircuts and moustaches for the men, mini-skirts and heavy makeup for the women - to start the inevitable Friday night fighting sessions. Having been a night-time PC himself, Smithdown knew that there'd be just as many fights among the women as the men. He compared the atmosphere outside the town square pubs to that around King's nightclub. Outside Kingdom there were smiles and hugs, laughter and dancing. 'Maybe if the pubs served ecstasy on draught there wouldn't be all this mither at the weekend,' offered DC Donaldson, pulling on his cigarette from a cupped hand.

'An interesting suggestion Robert,' replied Smithdown. 'I'll raise it with the Chief Constable next time he's buying me a pint in The Old Bill. Now, shall we have a crack at a few of these delightful pub-goers and ask them if they've seen our missing Romeo and Juliet?'

Donaldson looked directly at his senior officer: 'Look. you get yourself off. I think I can handle chatting to a few drunks. Go home.' A pause. 'How's Jean doing?'

Smithdown looked at the pavement. It was studded with a

grey carpet of dried chewing gum. He didn't look up. 'Okay, I suppose. But she's tired, mate. Dog tired. This chemo… it's worse than the cancer, I swear it is.'

'Get home then,' Donaldson said quietly. 'Look after her. It'll be right; you know what they say…'

'If you're going to get cancer, get it in Manchester,' Smithdown cut in, saying the words in a sing-song voice. He'd heard this particular pep talk so many times, but still found it strangely comforting. The Christie Hospital in South Manchester was world-renowned as a cancer treatment centre and it was just a 40-minute drive from their house. *We're lucky really. Really lucky.* Smithdown dropped his cigarette, put his shoe to it and popped a mint into his mouth. *She'll kill me if she knows I'm still smoking. I wish cancer was transferable, like money in a bank account. I'd ring the hospital and say, take it from her and transfer it to me. All of it.*

'Spot on, boss,' Donaldson confirmed. 'Yet another reason why we live in the greatest place on earth. Now, give me those snaps and get on your way.

Within half an hour Smithdown had returned home. Jean was half asleep and squeezed his hand when he got into bed beside her. He carefully placed his arm around her surgery-damaged chest. He looked at the knot on the brightly coloured paisley-patterned bandana she wore to cover her hair loss. She had quite a collection now.

He stared at the bandana and thought about what the cancer - and the treatment for it – was doing to his wife. Smithdown had lost count of the number of times he'd sat with her at the Christie as the red chemotherapy liquid was fed into her. He'd smile thinly at the other couples that shared the treatment room, but inside he was furious at the reasons for their enforced confinement. He hated the proximity of the other couples and families and the self-consciously comfortable chairs they were provided with - not like the hard, plastic ones in a normal hospital. As the chemo liquid went in, he would read a book and chew half-heartedly on one of the pre-packed sandwiches the staff had handed out. He remembered that there was a choice of three sandwiches that first day they'd attended. The choice had remained unchanged: cheese, ham, or cheese, and ham. He'd never eaten a cheese, ham, or cheese and ham sandwich outside of the hospital since.

He remembered how sick she'd been after that first cycle - and the reasons why. The doctors wanted to know how she'd react to the chemo so they had withheld any anti-sickness medication, which coincidentally was very expensive. Unsurprisingly, she had reacted very badly.

There'd been hours and hours of tears and vomiting. Then more tears.

Jean Smithdown's hair had gone after the first cycle. She had bought a bandana in time for the second and third sessions. The start of her collection.

She was probably fully awake now - the steroids kept her from sleeping. But she stayed still and silent.

Please. I'm begging. Give it to me. Not to her. Anyone but her. I'll do anything. Give it to me.

CHAPTER SEVEN

11.55pm Friday 1 April 1988

'Fuck! Paki! Stan! Fuck! Paki! Stan!'

The gang kicked the door of the house with each syllable. The chant continued as petrol from a small plastic bottle was squirted through the letterbox of the impressive, three story townhouse overlooking Alexandra Park.

The liquid was followed by a burning, rolled up copy of the *Oldham Messenger* newspaper. Voices - screaming and shouting, male and female, young and old - came from inside the house. The door opened and the burning paper was kicked outside. The homeowner shouted to people inside the house as he stamped on the paper at the doorstep, pulling his dressing gown around himself as he tried to put out the flames. The gang stood either side of the door on the wide porchway. As the man came out, one slammed the door behind him. Another two hit him with their bats. But he didn't go down. It took a third hit to do that. Once he was on the floor, the machete came down: once to the upper leg, then another to the arm just above the wrist. Instinctively, he put his other hand in front of his face to protect himself. The third blow hit his hand between the second and third fingers and split it in two. He was screaming now. They didn't understand what he was saying but they could tell that he wasn't begging – he was cursing them, furiously defying them. A baseball bat swung in from the right and connected with his head, the second swipe knocked him unconscious.

'Go. Go. Go,' commanded the leader and the gang ran

down the driveway, crossed the road and shot into the park.

'Fuckin' 'ell, did you see his paw?' Itchy Face shouted. 'Did you see it? Fuckin' 'ell, it split like a kipper! Like a big, brown stinkin' kipper. Fuckin' ell!'

The leader ignored him. 'There are bins near the lake,' he said as they ran. 'Head there. Go!'

They ran past the tennis courts, down the winding path past the boathouse and arrived at the lake. There was a concrete bin sunk into the ground near the lakeside toilets. The gang stripped off their masks, jumpers and trousers and shoved them into the bin, pressing down the chip wrappers and aluminium cans that half-filled it. Underneath they were wearing jeans and t-shirts. It was a warm evening and they wouldn't look out of place. The leader produced a tin of lighter fuel, doused the pile and then set it on fire.

They stood for a moment around the bin as the flames caught hold. Their breathing was rapid - partly from the run, partly from the adrenaline hit of the second attack. All were tall and well-muscled with hairstyles that ranged from short to shaven. All were white. Apart from one. Tariq Shamsi was staring at his feet rather than the burning bin. 'Give me your gear, then fuck off, Tariq,' the leader said. 'Do nowt. Say nowt. A word about tonight - a single word - and we'll dob you in to the cops.'

'It was you what did the nasty stuff, anyhow,' added Itchy Face. 'Not us. That swing is really coming along, by the way. What a swipe that last one was!'

'You do understand, don't you, Tariq?' the leader said. 'Tell me that you understand this simple instruction and that you won't say anything.'

'Course I won't say anything,' the young man said. 'How can I?'

'Exactly,' Itchy Face said. 'We'll have done your mum and your sister in before you're halfway to Oldham nick anyway.'

'I know.' Tariq said. He pulled off the balaclava and gave it to the leader.

'After the lads have all had a crack at them, obviously,' Itchy

Face added. 'One at a time. Maybe two at a time. We'll see.'

Tariq pulled off his trousers - he had a tracksuit on underneath. He started to take off the jumper, but it got stuck as he tried to pull it over his head. The gang laughed at him as he struggled. Itchy Face pulled it off him, sending the young man staggering around the burning bin. He was crying now.

There was a growing swell of noise and light around the park. The sound of sirens came from the police station to the north of them; ambulances came from the west. A set of fire engines appeared from the east - the gang could see the crews stop at the edges of the park, so close they could hear the firemen's voices.

'You'd better get off home Tariq. Make sure your mum's alright,' the leader said.

'And your sister,' added Itchy Face. 'She's sweet. For a Paki.'

Tariq headed east though the park. The leader nodded to one of the gang, who quietly peeled off from the group and followed the teenager down the path on the south side of the lake. Tariq was crossing a small bridge that separated two sections of the pool when he was hit across the back of the head with a baseball bat. He fell to the floor. The bat came down again and again.

Such was the force of the blows that the deadly assault mercifully lasted only a few moments. When it was over, his attackerused the baseball bat to push Tariq's now lifeless body towards the edge of the bridge where it slipped silently over the side and into the water below.

It would lie there undiscovered for almost a week.

~

The gang dumped the last of their clothes into the flames but left Tariq's by the side of the bin. They went north, keeping their distance from the commotion outside the house, but remaining close enough to see and hear snatches of what was happening. Pockets of noise were springing up around the park. The voices of young men could be heard, shouting. Swearing. Making threats. Some of the voices spoke in English, some didn't. Windows were being smashed. Security alarms began ringing out. A wave of violent energy was sweeping across the town centre. The gang seemed pleased with their work.

There were streetlamps in this section of the park. Itchy Face caught sight of the leader's face, his eye in particular. 'You'll have a shiner there tomorrow, Tommy lad,' he noted.

CHAPTER EIGHT

2.15 am Saturday 2 April 1988

When the trimphone chirruped a double ring next to his bed, Smithdown wasn't sure whether he'd actually slept at all. He still seemed to be staring at the knot on his wife's bandana. He turned and his hand shot out to grab the receiver, to stop it ringing again. 'Smithdown…' he whispered.

'So sorry to disturb,' said Bob Donaldson, 'but I've two bits of news that I thought you ought to know about.'

'Go on,' Smithdown said, as quietly as possible. His wife stirred next to him.

'We've got Jimmy Todd in custody. He's saying nowt at the moment but I'm sure we can soon change that.'

Smithdown sat up in bed. 'I'll be right there.'

'No. Your services are required elsewhere. We've got a body, out at Kinder Scout near Hayfield. Not my decision, it's down to you - but I reckon you'll want to go there.'

Jean Smithdown was looking at her husband through the half-light now. He mouthed the word 'Bob' to her. She switched on the bedside light, put on a pair of reading glasses and took out a paperback book. It gave Smithdown the go-ahead to speak in a normal voice: 'I'm assuming,' he said, 'that you're going to give me a compelling reason why I should give a shit about a body that is not only outside our division, but outside our county? Hayfield is in Derbyshire, Bob, as you well know.'

'I do indeed, boss. The thing is, the body has got a hand missing.'

‘I see,’ said Smithdown, getting out of bed and looking for his trousers. ‘To be fair, that is a fairly compelling reason.’

CHAPTER NINE

2.40 am Saturday 2 April 1988

Smithdown knew how to get to the village of Hayfield without looking at the crumpled A-Z map he always kept in the glove compartment of his car; at this time of night it was barely a half-hour drive south east of Oldham. Marooned in the green folds of the Derbyshire countryside between Glossop and Chapel-en-Le-Frith, he remembered coming to the village on days out as a kid. Indeed, he'd taken his own daughter here when she was young.

She was at university now, studying journalism of all things. *Bloody journalism.* In London, of all places. *Bloody London! God, I miss her.*

Hayfield was easy enough to locate, but Smithdown wasn't quite so sure about finding his way to the Hayfield Mountain Rescue Centre. The directions that he'd been given seemed simple enough though: turn right into the village. Big pub on left. HMRC is in the pub car park.

Smithdown had heard that the rescue teams liked a pint - particularly after a hard night pulling idiots off Kinder Scout - so positioning their HQ behind the Old Ship Inn was clearly good planning on their part. *I like these lads already.*

The village seemed largely unchanged from the mental image his childhood provided: two pubs, a fish and chip shop, a boutiquey antiques place and an all-purpose corner shop. Kinder Scout was the big attraction that drew people to Hayfield. The moorland plateau looked, from a distance, like someone had taken a giant tenet saw to a normal mountain and cut it in half, creating a bizarre table-top oddity that could be seen by half of Manchester. And, as every student of North West England history knew, it had a way of drawing people to it, like a truncated beacon.

In 1932, disaffected young ramblers and communists from Manchester and Sheffield had taken it upon themselves to organise a mass invasion of the moors around Kinder Scout, a place that they were forbidden to walk on by moneyed landowners. Their act of youthful class warfare had ultimately opened up the British countryside - thanks to those brave souls woefully ill-prepared townspeople could now come freely to places like Kinder Scout and be rescued by the volunteers of the Hayfield Mountain Rescue Centre.

~

The HMRC was set in a strip of stables at the rear of the Old Ship Inn.

Volunteers of all ages and shapes were to-ing and fro-ing from the stables with vital-looking pieces of outdoor equipment like a team of industrious, bearded bees. Their headtorches sent wobbly beams of light across the early morning darkness of the car park as they loaded gear, checked kit and quietly chatted. Smithdown checked his watch as he parked up. *2.45am. Fuckin' Nora.*

He had to dip his head to get through the main door of the centre. 'Detective Inspector John Smithdown, Oldham Police,' he announced as volunteers squeezed past him to get out into the night. 'Which one of you extremely energetic gents are in charge, please?'

A man who looked to be in his early 40s - slim as a stick of liquorice and wearing tight-fitting dark blue running gear - leant back slightly from the huddle of people he was involved with so he could see who was asking. 'For tonight's purposes, that would be me,' he said with the flat hint of a Derbyshire accent. He put out a hand to Smithdown: 'Brian McIntyre,' he said, giving Smithdown's brown shoes and suit the once over and smiling slightly.

'I believe there's been a spot of mither up on your moors,' the detective said.

'You could say that,' McIntyre replied. 'One of your lot?'

'Potentially,' Smithdown nodded. 'I believe there's a Detective Constable from the local Con-stab-u-lary about too?' the detective added, pronouncing every syllable of the archaic sounding word for the local Derbyshire force. It tickled him to think they still held onto the title of Constabulary.

'DC Seddon is unavailable,' McIntyre said, the smile subtly easing itself from his face.

'Well,' Smithdown sighed. 'While I'm waiting for the DC to find a moment in their busy schedule, maybe you could fill me in?'

'With pleasure,' McIntyre offered, gesturing for the detective to come over to a map of Kinder Scout and the surrounding Dark Peak area that covered most of the far wall of the rescue centre. 'The body was spotted from up here at Red Brook,' he said, jabbing his forefinger at an area of the map three quarters of the way along the v-shaped rim of the plateau. Smithdown struggled to see so McIntyre shone a torch onto the map and wiggled the beam over Red Brook. On the map it looked like a stream, but the contour lines showed it was almost vertical.

'A guy walking the edge of Kinder saw it lying right next to the Mermaid's Pool,' McIntyre continued. 'It's a small lake tucked away under the Kinder plateau below the edge. I've got four volunteers up there already. They've staked out the area, taped the scene off and they're making sure no one gets near. They'll stop there with the body for as long as it takes.'

He knows his stuff this guy.

'Are you in radio contact with them?' he asked.

'After a fashion, yes,' McIntyre said. 'There's no point-to-point comms from here to the pool, so we've sent two of the team up to an adjoining area to set up what we call a repeater. We talk to them; the repeater relays the message to the team at the pool and vice versa.'

'And where exactly are they?' the detective asked.

'Here,' McIntyre said, punctuating his words with another jab on the map. 'On Mount Famine.'

'Of course,' said the detective, peering at the map. 'The Mermaid's Pool. Mount Famine. Does everywhere around here have a weird name?'

'Pretty much, yes. They don't call it the Dark Peak for nothing.'

'I'm beginning to realise that. And the body… it's definitely deceased?'

'Oh yes,' McIntyre nodded. 'Most definitely deceased.'

'What makes your lads so sure?'

'A couple of reasons. One, because they all have a reasonable degree of medical training. Two, because the body was on fire when they got the call out - it took them nearly an hour to get to it and it was still smouldering when they got there...'

'Fair enough...'

'...and three, because DC Seddon from the local Con-stab-u-lary based at Glossop is already at the scene. DC Seddon also happens to be one of our rescue volunteers and is currently at the pool, keeping the site secure.'

'And I'm sure he's doing a grand job,' Smithdown offered with a weak smile.

'Yes. She is. Jenny's doing a proper grand job.'

Smithdown felt that a change of tack was called for: 'And the body has got a hand missing, I believe?'

'Yes, that too; gets better all the time, doesn't it?'

'Do you know which one?'

'Does it matter?'

'Yes. It does.'

'Let's ask the team up at the pool then, shall we?'

McIntyre reached across the detective and pulled a handset from its cradle on a sturdy-looking radio set. It looked old and took up a considerable amount of space on the cluttered desk tucked into the corner of the rescue centre. 'Kinder Link,

Kinder Link this is Kinder Base. Over,' said McIntyre.

A pause. Then a crackly click; a voice came from the set's speaker: 'Kinder Base, this is Kinder Link. Over.'

'Kinder Link, please ask Kinder Jenny at Kinder 2 the following. Which hand is missing from the deceased – left or right? Over.'

The voice came again through the speaker: 'You want to know which hand is missing from the deceased – left or right? Over.'

'Affirm. Out.'

McIntyre waited. 'They'll relay the message up to the Kinder 2 team at the pool. Everything is double-checked to make sure nothing gets lost in translation. Simple, but effective.'

After about ten seconds, the radio crackled back a reply: 'Kinder Base, Kinder Base. This is Kinder Link. Kinder 2 confirms that the deceased's left hand is missing.'

McIntyre double-checked the message: 'I understand - Kinder 2 confirms that it's the left hand on the deceased that is missing? Over.'

'Affirm. Over.'

McIntyre looked directly at Smithdown; his expression suggested he was checking that the detective was satisfied with the answer. Smithdown nodded his approval. Without breaking eye contact with the detective, McIntyre spoke again: 'Kinder Link. This is Kinder Base. Please tell Kinder Jenny at Kinder 2 to take care. And that me and the kids love her very much. Base Out.'

He returned the handset to its cradle and smiled at Smithdown. 'Right then, looks like we need to get you up to the pool, doesn't it?'

'And get that body down,' added the detective, feeling the heat of embarrassment around his collar.

'Well, that's where the fun will really start,' McIntyre stated. 'It'll take 18 volunteers to bring that body down to Hayfield. Minimum.'

'Eighteen volunteers to carry one person?' queried

Smithdown. 'Who's up there, the fucking Pope?'

'No, Mr Smithdown,' McIntyre pointed out. 'Not the fucking Pope... at least, as far as I'm aware. It's only the early stages of the enquiry though, isn't it? So, no - probably not His Holiness. Just a poor soul that deserves care and respect to get them back off those moors. That's fair, isn't it?'

'Yes, it is - perfectly fair,' Smithdown said, quietly.

'It's a bit wet out,' McIntyre continued. 'And we have a saying around here: the wetter it is, the harder it is. Every time you put a foot down, there's no telling where it could end up. There are peat hags, dykes, rocky gritstone cliffs, steep piles of scree, boulders the size of Mini Cooper's, hidden streams and gaps in the rocks to trap and snap your ankle - all the fun of the fair around Kinder Scout. It takes an eight-man team to operate a stretcher safely - plus short and long navigators to look out for hazards and plot a safe course through the terrain. The first team will need relieving at some point. They'll be exhausted. So, another eight will take over the stretcher. So, 18 souls in all. It's not a Sunday stroll through Oldham up there, you know. That corpse has decided to set up camp in one of the trickiest spots in the Dark Peak to get to.'

'And the weirdest,' said another rescue volunteer, taking a metal Bell Tangent stretcher from a rack on the wall and smiling at the detective.

'What do you mean,' asked Smithdown. 'The weirdest?'

'I'll tell you on the way up,' McIntyre smiled. He glanced at Smithdown's scuffed brogues with a small shake of his head. 'Like I say, this won't be a stroll through Oldham, Mr Smithdown. What size boots do you take?'

CHAPTER TEN

3.45 am Saturday 2 April 1988

After leaving the rescue centre, Smithdown had taken a ride in the mountain rescue team's Land Rover along a service track near to Kinder Reservoir, in the shadow of the plateau. The vehicle had then begun the much bumpier job of tackling the uphill lower slopes of the moors. The detective was jammed into the vehicle with Brian McIntyre and three other rescue team members. He held onto an internal strap to stop his head banging onto the ceiling of the vehicle. There was silence as they made the journey. 'Go on then,' Smithdown said. 'I know you're dying to tell me. What local cross-eyed country crap are you going to give me about this Mermaid's Pool, then?'

McIntyre was driving. He looked into the rear-view mirror at one of the men squeezed up against the detective. 'Go on, Barry,' McIntyre said. 'You tell him.'

'Well,' Barry said, rubbing his beard and smiling. 'It's believed that the ancient Celts would carry out water worship rituals in this area…'

'Here we go…' muttered Smithdown.

'… and that this pool we're heading for was a particular favourite with the Celts because the water is salted. Like the sea. And no-one's quite sure why. They also liked it because of the mermaid that's said to swim in it.'

'Jesus Christ,' muttered Smithdown, folding his arms.

'It's said that once a year, if you visit the pool on the right day and the mermaid appears - and if she takes a shine to you - she'll grant you eternal life.'

There were smiles and quiet laughter from the other

members of the rescue team. 'Is this the bit where I ask what happens if she doesn't like you?' Smithdown said.

'Yes, it is,' Barry confirmed.

'Okay. What happens if the mermaid doesn't like you?'

'She'll rise up out of the water and kill you,' Barry stated.

There was silence. 'Ooooooooooh,' howled another of the team. The rest laughed.

'Brilliant,' Smithdown said. 'I'm so glad I came. Just for fun, which day of the year are you supposed to visit the mermaid to test this story this out?'

McIntyre spoke this time. 'Joking aside, this bit is actually rather weird. Easter Eve. The day before Easter Sunday. Which given the time right now, is technically, today.'

Smithdown looked across the moors. The ridge of Kinder was getting closer now, a huge black wall of moorland rock blocking out the stars. The yellowy light of the dawn was just starting to pick out its shape against the Dark Peak sky. 'Fuck off,' Smithdown said, closing his eyes. 'Wake me up when we get there.'

'No need,' McIntyre said. 'This is as far as we can go. The rest will be on foot.'

'Fantastic,' grumbled the detective.

The Land Rover had stopped next to an identical mountain rescue vehicle. They got out and Smithdown felt his boots - which were a size too small - sink slightly into the wet, mossy peat. The detective found himself in a large group of mountain rescue volunteers. They flicked on their head torches; four of them began walking up a barely visible path that led up the moor in the direction of Kinder Scout. 'Follow them,' said McIntyre. 'Do exactly as they say. Nothing more, nothing less.'

Smithdown did as he was told. The mountain rescue team members walked just ahead and just behind him. McIntyre and Barry were by his side. Occasionally the volunteers in front would offer advice about hazards that were approaching. *They're protecting me from the moors.*

The path initially followed the left-hand line of a stream,

then crossed the water back and forth several times. The detective tried to keep his boots dry as he went, but soon gave up and just splashed his way across the water as the mountain rescuers did.

Then the path peeled away from the stream and cut though a walled plantation of pine trees. It became darker, the light of the stars extinguished by the density of the small forest. They picked their way carefully through, stepping over logs and negotiating their way around fallen branches; the floor of the plantation was thick with a soft carpet of fallen pine needles. Then the stars reappeared as they cleared the plantation - the landscape opened up again to wide, rolling moorland. To Smithdown's eyes, the path had disappeared, but the rescuers seemed to follow a route only they could see.

McIntyre pointed up to his left. There was a deep scar in the vertical landscape that disappeared into the night. 'That's the Downfall. It has a waterfall that sometimes goes up instead of down, depending on the wind.'

'Course it does, muttered the detective, tripping over a small hole in the moor and finding himself briefly in the arms of a burly, bearded volunteer.

'It's true,' McIntyre offered. 'I'll take you there sometime, if you fancy coming back.'

'I think that's unlikely, but I'll bear it in mind.'

After a further fifteen-minute walk across the upper moors they crested a small hill. 'There it is,' McIntyre said.

In front of them was the Mermaid's Pool. It was strangely unimpressive to Smithdown's eyes - brown and shallow-looking, with a few rocks and reed banks scattered around the perimeter. It was about 40 feet long and less than 20 feet wide in the middle. It was uneven, shaped not unlike a map of Ireland. Behind it, the ground rose up sharply to meet the edge of the plateau above. Blue dragonflies flitted and swooped around the water's edge and Smithdown could hear a light chakka-chakka-chakka sound. A series of metal stakes had been pushed into the soft ground around the pool, connected by tape. The sound was the tape fluttering in the moorland breeze. There were four mountain rescuers stood in a line at the far end of the pool, guarding the area marked out by the tape.

The dawn air smelled foul, like a rotting butcher's bin that had been set on fire. At the far end of the water, steam rose from what appeared to be a tangle of blackened sticks, laid out as if someone wanted it to look like a body. *There were some recognisable shapes: legs, torso, arms, the notion of a head - but too burnt, too wrecked, too alien to have ever been a human being. Surely?*

Any chatter among the newly arrived rescue team members petered out and then stopped entirely. At first, they stared. Then they looked elsewhere, the lights on their head torches slowly dipped and pointed away from the Mermaid's Pool as they turned their eyes to look somewhere - anywhere - rather than at the remains in front of them.

There was pity in their faces; pity for the poor soul at the edge of the pool. But pity also for their friends and fellow rescuers who had been standing guard at this terrible scene for the best part of five hours. Smithdown looked at their faces. Some were holding hands. Several were in tears. He caught the eye of one member of the team. She wasn't crying - from the look on her face, she seemed to be in a fury. *DC Jenny Seddon, Derbyshire Con-stab-u-lary. Fucking Nora.*

Smithdown nodded at her and dipped under the tape. As he did so Brian McIntyre leant in and spoke quietly to her, their conversation was silent yet clearly heated. As they spoke, Smithdown approached the body. The ground around it was scorched, like a small bomb had gone off. One hand was stretched out, as if the victim had been reaching to grab a fistful of the peaty brown water of the Mermaid's Pool. The fingers looked like black twigs. *Jesus. She was trying to save herself… trying to get to the water to douse the flames.*

The other hand was missing. The body was wreathed in mist now, as the sun began to heat the ground around it.

Smithdown wasn't sure how long he'd been silently staring at the body when he was joined by one of the mountain rescue team. 'DI Smithdown?' she stated, in a clear, no-nonsense tone. Smithdown knew what was coming. 'Detective Constable Jenny Seddon. Glossop CID.' A pause. 'Derbyshire Con-stab-u-lary.'

Smithdown turned and looked at her. 'Morning DC Seddon. You must be starved.'

'Not heard that expression for a while.' the Derbyshire detective said. 'Starved instead of cold. My dad used to say it. He was a Manc. Wonderful man my dad. But very, very old-fashioned. Know what I mean?' Seddon's Derbyshire accent slid the words into each other: norwharramean?

'I do,' Smithdown said, trying to sound apologetic. 'Message received. Let's start again, shall we?' He put out a hand. DC Seddon removed a glove and gave Smithdown a firm handshake. Her hand was red with cold. Smithdown's fingers left white marks where the grip of his hand had been. She was about 30 with round gold-rimmed glasses; her dark blonde hair was cut into a smart, short style. She was small but looked extremely fit. She also looked completely at home there in the hills. 'How are you doing, DC Seddon?'

'I am tired, hungry, wet, cold and a bit pissed off,' she replied. 'But things could be worse. I could be her…'

'Her?' Smithdown queried.

'Well, you've been fishing female hands out of your local boating lake - a left hand, I believe. And you've got a female missing-from-home. And we've got a body with no left hand. And you're here. Plus, there are female belongings scattered over there on the other side of the pool. So yes. Her.'

'Belongings? Okay. Can I see?'

'Sure.' DC Seddon leant sideways to see around Smithdown. 'Brian. I'm taking the DI to see the personal effects. Get one of the lads to cover my spot, please.'

A shout of 'will do' came from a huddle of rescue volunteers. 'Brian's your bloke, is he?' Smithdown said, trying to make conversation.

'He is,' confirmed DC Seddon.

'Kept your maiden name, though.'

'I said he's my bloke, not my husband, DI Smithdown.

Christ, you really are like my dad.'

'I'm fucking glad I'm not your dad,' he muttered with a smile, just loud enough for her to hear. 'Let's take a gander at this gear then, shall we?' he added. The two detectives gave the steaming body a wide berth and walked towards a spot behind a clump of reeds at the far end of the Mermaid's Pool. Several items were there: an inside out canvas shoulder bag was first. Close to it was a Williams & Glyn bank card with "Miss Naomi Wells" embossed on it. Next to it was a photo of Becky Wells – she looked a few years younger than when Smithdown had seen her at the children's home and her front teeth were missing. She was smiling for the camera, showing off the gap with pride. Sundry items of makeup were also scattered about, along with a lip balm and some green Rizla papers. Next to the papers was a small plastic pouch with several bright pink pills inside.

Smithdown looked long and hard at the items. Then he looked at DC Seddon. She said nothing; she just looked, taking in the scene.

Thinking with her eyes open and her gob shut.

A voice came from behind them - it was young and scared-sounding. 'Mr Smithdown?' said Paul Rees. 'I suppose I need to photograph those items, don't I?'

The photographer was wrapped in a snorkel parka. His face was peering out through a ring of synthetic fur around the hood. The DI saw the young man had tears in his eyes. 'Yes lad,' Smithdown confirmed. 'You do.'

'I've already done the... is that technically still a body?' he asked. 'Yes. Course it is. A body. A very, very burnt body. Is it burnt with a T or burned with ED on the end? I can never remember. Either way, I've snapped it. Didn't like it one bit, but I did it.'

'It's never easy, Paul. Yes, these items by the water too, please. Just do your best.'

Paul wiped his nose with the sleeve of his parka. 'Christ Almighty, what a way to die, Mr Smithdown. What kind of fucking wrong 'uns would do something like that?'

'I don't know, Paul. I really don't. Just take the pictures and get yourself off home.'

'Right, yes,' Paul said with a sniff. 'I'll do these last pictures. The items. Then I can go. Go back down. Away from here. Yes. Okay. Right. Snaps.'

'Yes please, Paul. Snaps. Then you can go. Then we can all go. Including that poor soul by the side of this… Mermaid's Pool. Fucking stupid name.'

Paul nodded, took his camera from his shoulder bag and began by taking wide shots of the scene, before picking out the individual items for more specific shots. The two detectives watched him. Eventually, DI Smithdown spoke. 'What do you make of it then, DC Seddon?' he asked, quietly.

'Christ Almighty,' she sighed. 'To do that to another human being, all the way out here. Fucking animals. I've never known anything like it.'

'Neither have I,' Smithdown agreed. *What had the victim done to generate that kind of hate?*

CHAPTER ELEVEN

7.05 am Saturday 2 April 1988

Sitting in the snug bar of the Old Ship Inn, eating a second bacon roll and contemplating a third, DI Smithdown thought about what he'd witnessed coming down from the Mermaid's Pool.

He'd watched as the mountain rescue team had eased what was left of the victim into a body bag. At least two charred limbs had snapped in the process; the rescuers had carried on despite the distress several of them were clearly in. He'd seen the care they'd taken in keeping the metal stretcher straight and level, despite the up and down unpredictability of the Kinder terrain. He'd waited as a second team took over as the first became exhausted. And he'd seen them slowly push the body into the waiting Land Rover, then wait until the vehicle had been driven away and crested the hill on its journey down to Hayfield, before allowing the emotion to take over. There were hugs and quiet tears. Now he saw them sitting quietly in the Old Ship Inn, clearly unable to process what they'd just been party to. Some had curled up into any available seating and gone to sleep. Others stared at the walls. *These are volunteers, Plumbers and teachers and shopkeepers. They shouldn't have to deal with this.*

'Can I join you?' asked DC Seddon. She smiled at Smithdown and offered him a plate. She'd bought him another bacon roll.

'Please do,' he said, shifting his jacket to make a space next to him. *She looks younger in the daylight, tough as anything though this one. Took her turn on the stretcher for as long as any of those big, bearded bastards on the rescue team. Good on you, our kid. We could do with a few more like you back at Oldham.*

Despite his approving internal monologue, what actually came out of Smithdown's mouth was: 'Good butties these. This'll be my third.'

'So I see,' she noted. 'We'll need a stretcher for you too at this rate - straight to coronary care.'

Brian McIntyre brought over two mugs of tea - he smiled at DC Seddon then left the two detectives to it. 'They're good people, this mountain rescue lot,' Smithdown said. 'Your lot, I should say. Really good people. How do you find the time to volunteer for this as well as being a detective?'

'Well,' she replied. 'Working for the Con-stab-u-lary largely consists of sheep rustling incidents, mint cake theft and the odd bit of rambler disorder, so I have bags of time on my hands to do other things - like drag smouldering bodies down the side of Kinder Scout.'

Smithdown winced at her response. 'Fair enough, I deserved that. I'm sorry. I really am. What you and these people did tonight was amazing. It really was.'

'I should think so, you cheeky old bastard. Apology accepted.'

There was silence now between the two police officers. The small shoots of respect that were growing between them were still tempered by caution. DC Seddon spoke first. 'They must have watched her burn. Chucked petrol on her, set her on fire and watched as she tried to drag herself towards the pool to try to put out the flames.'

'Did you notice how the head was more badly damaged than any other part of the body?' Smithdown asked.

'I did,' she replied. 'That's where the fire burned the hardest - where the accelerant was most concentrated. It was probably petrol - they made her swallow it, didn't they?'

'Yes,' said Smithdown. 'I think they did.'

'So - no teeth.'

'Definitely no teeth.'

'Christ Almighty,' sighed DC Seddon, finishing the last of her bacon roll.

'Did you read about that case the other month?' Smithdown asked. 'The double rape and murder in the Midlands solved by DN whatsit genetic evidence?'

'DNA - yes I did,' DC Seddon replied. 'Colin Pitchfork - he was sentenced in January. Good job that by the Leicestershire Con-stab-u-lary.'

'Okay, okay. No more,' Smithdown said. 'They're talking about setting up a national DNA database, you know. That'd make life easier, wouldn't it?

'Don't hold your breath for it to arrive in Oldham. Let alone Glossop.'

Both detectives sipped at their tea. 'What happens now?' DC Seddon asked.

'We've got the boyfriend of our missing person in custody,' Smithdown stated. 'I'm going home to freshen up and then I'll go and have a chat with him. Can't see him taking long to cave in and that'll be that, I suppose.'

'Really? That's that?'

'That's that. Why? What's on your mind, DC Seddon?'

'I can't stop thinking about what we saw up there,' she said.

'That's understandable. It was a distressing thing for anyone to see.'

'I didn't mean that,' she cut in. 'I meant the whole scene; the body, yes but the belongings, the bag, the bank card. The whole bit.'

'What about it?' Smithdown asked.

Detective Constable Jenny Seddon of the Derbyshire Con-stab-u-lary pulled at the sleeve of her fleece, took off her glasses and cleaned the lenses by pinching them through the material between her thumb and forefinger. Then she put her glasses back on. 'I thought it was the biggest load of stage-managed bollocks I've seen for quite some time.'

'Manchester Radio News at seven - this is Beth Hall. Murder squad detectives are investigating the discovery of a badly burnt body close to a Derbyshire beauty spot. Officers from Greater Manchester Police and the Derbyshire Constabulary are thought to be linking the find to an incident in Oldham where a woman's hand was found in a local lake. Henry Matthews is at the scene and sends this report.'

'The body was found next to the Mermaid's Pool in the early hours of this morning. The remote spot lies underneath the edge of Kinder Scout close to the village of Hayfield.

Local officers and mountain rescue volunteers have been at the scene since the alarm was raised by a walker late last night. Now, detectives from Oldham police have also become involved in the case - it's thought they're investigating a connection between the body and the discovery of a hand at Alexandra Park. It's understood the body at the Mermaid's Pool had a hand missing but is so badly burnt that a positive identification is thought unlikely.

Mountain rescuers spent the night carefully removing the charred remains from the scene. This morning the area around the Mermaid's Pool is still sealed off.

The pool is a notorious part of local legend. It's said that anyone who goes there the day before Easter Sunday risks the wrath of the mermaid that lives in the water. By a grim coincidence, today is Easter Eve. Henry Matthews, Manchester Radio News, Hayfield.'

CHAPTER TWELVE

7.45 am Saturday 2 April 1988

Smithdown's head nodded slowly downward as the need to sleep tugged at him. He snapped back awake. It happened again. Sleep was pleading with him now. Then a third time and just for a moment his eyes shut fully. *Just a little kip. That's all I want. Twenty winks will do me. Ten, maybe.* Then his head jerked, the steering wheel of his car jarred to the right and he was suddenly very awake and aware of the steep drop to the left of the moorland road that twisted its way to his house on the outskirts of Oldham. *Just another mile. That's all. Then home. And sleep.*

He wound down the driver's window and the car flushed with cold, clear air. He switched on the fan and set it to cool. He turned on the car stereo and put the volume up as high as he could bear: '*What a Waste*' by Ian Dury drifted across the moors. He slowed the car right down, crawling the last half mile at less than 30 miles an hour. Finally, he turned into the short gravelly drive of the detached cottage that had been the Smithdown's home for 20 years.

He killed the engine and rested his head on the steering wheel. Sleep was coming again. The detective banged his head twice on the steering wheel, widened his eyes and made a "baaah" sound. He shook his head until his lips flapped and stepped out of the car.

The front door was unlocked. Jean liked to leave it open. Friends from the nearby village and the wives of other officers were in the habit of calling in, often with homecooked food in Pyrex bowls - food she rarely ate but that Smithdown was very grateful for.

He saw that his daughter Kate's rucksack was lying in the hallway.

The house was quiet. He went into the living room. His wife was sitting on the sofa with her legs tucked up to one side. Smithdown's daughter Kate had her head in her mother's lap. Jean Smithdown was stroking her daughter's hair. It was shorter and spikier than when Smithdown had last seen Kate at Christmas. She also seemed to have more piercings in her ears, though he couldn't be sure. One thing the detective did know - both his wife and his daughter had clearly been crying.

'Where have you been, Dad?' Kate Smithdown said, in a quietly furious voice. 'I mean literally, where the fuck have you been? Mum shouldn't be on her own. Not now. Not ever. But definitely not now. In case you hadn't noticed, she's sick.'

Jean Smithdown looked at her husband and shook her head. *Don't. Not today.*

The detective toyed with the idea of telling his daughter about the hand in the lake; about the trek to the Mermaid's Pool; about the steam coming off the body; about the haunted faces of the mountain rescue workers. But he decided against it. 'Bit of trouble down at Alex Park. And then I had to go out Hayfield way. Couldn't be helped. You're here now, Kate. All three of us are here. That's the main thing.'

'You should sleep, John,' Jean said, continuing to stroke her daughter's hair. 'You look absolutely awful. Your trousers are filthy too, what have you been up to?'

'Classic mum,' Kate said, raising her head from her mother's lap and wiping her nose on the sleeve of her baggy red top. 'Looking after everyone else. Looking after you while you're out being The Great Detective.'

'Not fair, Kate,' Smithdown said, quietly. 'You're not here. You've got university. That's just not fair.'

'Well I'm here now and I'm staying,' Kate said, running her hand through her black hair and making it stick up even more. 'I'm packing in uni. I want to be with mum. Someone needs to be.'

'I don't want that, Kate,' Jean stated, taking her daughter's hand. 'Really. I don't. If you want to help, then finish your course. It's important. The first person in our family to go to university! Please. Make me proud. That's the kind of support that'll keep me going.'

'Christ,' Kate said, tears appearing in her eyes. 'Hear that, Dad? You're so fucking brave, mum.'

Smithdown was about to speak when his wife cut in: 'It's not fucking brave, Kate. Trust me. It really fucking isn't.'

The detective and his daughter were surprised into silence. *She never swears. She's really upset now. Shit.*

'Brave is choosing to do something that's really hard,' Jean Smithdown said, adjusting her bandana as she stood up from the sofa. 'I've got no other bloody option. I'm not sick from the cancer - they've cut that bit of me out. I'm sick from the chemo - it's the price I've got to pay to stop it coming back. I'm going to be fine. Just fine. It was a decent cancer to get. I can recover from it. But I need your help. Both of you. Together. Will you do that? Will you help me? Both help me?'

Smithdown and his daughter looked at each other for the briefest of moments, then nodded. They both independently decided that the best option right now was to just stare at the carpet. So that's exactly what they did.

'The best thing for me would be a house with no angry voices in it,' Jean Smithdown said, quietly. 'If they could bottle a bit of niceness and inject that into me, I'd be right as rain.'

Silence again. And carpet staring. 'Kate, make me some toast. John. Go to bed.'

Kate did a mildly stroppy walk to the kitchen. Smithdown headed for the stairs. He kissed his wife on the way. He was aiming for the side of her face but connected with the edge of her bandana. 'Just let me sleep for an hour,' he said quietly. 'An hour and a half, tops. No more. Okay?'

'Okay.'

Four hours later, the phone rang. It was DC Bob Donaldson. 'Boss. I know you've earned that kip, but I think you need to get down here to the station quicksticks. The place is going mad.'

'The news from Granada Television this Saturday lunchtime, I'm Hazel Barrett, good afternoon. Community leaders in Oldham have hit out at the local police force, saying not enough is being done to stop violent attacks in the area. They claim people from both the Pakistani and Bangladeshi communities have been subjected to a growing number of violent incidents, culminating in two separate machete attacks late last night. They've accused the police of turning a blind eye as Andy Gill reports.'

'At around 10 o'clock last night a 16-year-old boy was attacked by a gang wielding baseball bats and a machete. He sustained serious injuries to his arm and a concussion.

A man, described as wearing dark clothing and of Asian appearance, was seen running from the scene. Burnt clothing - including a balaclava mask - was later found in Alexandra Park.

In the second incident, a 52-year-old man was also set upon by a machete gang at his home on Queen's Road, which overlooks the park. The attackers had started a fire at the man's home before the attack took place. Detective Superintendent James Pym of Oldham Police says the two incidents may be connected:'

> *"We're keeping an open mind but in both attacks, inflammatory anti-Pakistani and anti-Bangladeshi statements were thought to have been made. In both incidents the attackers are thought to be Asian, so we'd ask that anyone with information from either community contact us immediately."*

'The attacks follow the death of Naomi Wells earlier this week. The 26-year-old year mixed race woman had been dismembered - part of her remains were found in the boating lake at Alexandra Park. Meanwhile, a body found near Kinder Scout in Derbyshire that had been set on fire is believed to be that of Miss Wells.

Community leaders are this morning calling for calm but are accusing Oldham Police of losing control of law and order in the area. Andy Gill, Granada Newss, Oldham.'

CHAPTER THIRTEEN

1.05 pm Saturday 2 April 1988

Smithdown wasn't in the habit of entering Oldham police station through the public entrance but given the amount of noise that was coming from the front desk area he decided to make an exception.

He lit a cigarette and took in the scene. 'Fucking Nora,' he muttered as two men in their late 50s tumbled through the swing doors and aimed wild punches at each other outside the main entrance. They were being egged on by a group of about a dozen noisy bystanders, making threats towards each other in a language – or maybe two languages – that Smithdown didn't understand. The feelings they conveyed were very much universal ones, though. Anger. Mistrust. Fear.

The detective could have intervened. But he chose not to. Instead, he eased his way around them and walked into the main reception area. The scene outside the station was relatively calm in comparison. Six more arguing men, plus two middle-aged women in tears; a white woman in her late 40s who looked like she'd been out all night, was being restrained by what appeared to be her husband and her son; a reporter from the *Oldham Messenger* was going amongst the various factions with a pad and pen, asking questions and being shouted at.

Sitting quietly in a scooped plastic chair in the corner was Richard T. King. He was, rather ostentatiously in Smithdown's opinion, reading a paperback copy of *The Consolation of Philosophy* by Boethius. King gave the detective a smile, saluted him and carried on reading. Next to him was Tom Lennon. He had a round, red mark over his right eye.

‘Morning, Mr Smithdown,’ King said. ‘Have you been having a lie in? Don’t blame you - but look what happens when you’re not around. Pandemonium ensues!’

‘So it appears,’ the detective agreed. ‘What’s happened to you, Tom? You been messing with your catapult again?’

‘He was assaulted last night in an unprovoked attack, weren’t you, Tom?’ King offered.

‘I was asking him,’ Smithdown pointed out.

‘I was assaulted last night in an unprovoked attack,’ Lennon stated.

‘That’s unfortunate,’ Smithdown noted.

‘All fortune is good fortune,’ King said, gently shaking his paperback in the detective’s direction to make sure Smithdown was aware that he was quoting Boethius. ‘We’ve come to report the matter,’ added King. ‘These people can’t be allowed to rule our streets. Tom’s bravery in coming forward will benefit the wider community when the aggressors are apprehended.’

‘You can count on it,’ the detective added, muttering another quick, ‘fucking Nora,’ under his breath.

The Duty Sergeant buzzed him through and Smithdown took the stairs to the first floor CID department. As he pushed open the double doors from the stairwell the noise of the area was released: typewriters, telex machines, ringing phones, shouting, laughing, swearing, distant furious banging from the cells. *All human life. God, I love it.*

He spotted DC Donaldson walking towards him: ‘An appraisal of the current situation, if you’d be so kind, Bob,’ said Smithdown.

‘Right. Kinnell. I’ll do me best. Here we go: the Asians are up in arms because a Bengali lad got battered and macheted up round Coldhurst way last night. They reckon a Pakistani gang done it. The lad’s family are currently going spare out front.’

‘I’ve just seen them. How badly hurt is the lad?’

‘Broken tibs and fibs, concussion and a couple of machete wounds you can get your fist into, but he’ll live.’

'Next?'

'Report of a similar incident in reverse. Looks like a gang of Bengali lads have macheted a Pakistani bloke on his doorstep at one of those big houses near the park in the early hours.'

'Revenge attack?'

'Sounds like it - classic tit for tat. Neighbours heard anti-Pakistan chanting. Fuck Pakistan - all that. They did a spot of arson with intent for good measure.'

'Not helpful that, is it? What are his injuries like?'

'Similar. Less broken bones, but his machete wounds are worse - absolute shocker apparently, might lose his hand. Waiting to hear.'

'That's going to play badly on both sides of the fence.'

'Yes indeed. Multiple reports of Pakistani and Bengali lads tooling up ready to do more of the same tonight. Bengali community leaders are going barmy about it. Pakistani community leaders are going barmy about them going barmy about it. And vice versa.'

'Inevitably. Next?'

'Got a missing-from-home - also an Asian lad, as it happens. Seventeen-year old Tariq Shamsi. Mum's distraught. She's also in reception. Totally out of character for him to stop out all night, apparently. Last seen yesterday evening in the Coldhurst area.'

'I've a feeling there's more,' sighed Smithdown.

'You would be correct. Richard T. King is also out front. Says one of his lads was attacked by a big gang of Asian lads last night. Hardly on the same scale, clearly, but a crime number is being generated as we speak. It's Tom Lennon, Maureen's lad. Big fucker. Tom, that is, not Maureen.'

'I assumed that,' Smithdown said.

'Anyway, looks like he's poked himself in the eye with a teaspoon quite frankly. Flimsiest Section 47 wounding I've seen for some time, but the "King of Clubs" is demanding action.'

'He was quoting Greek philosophy to me at the front desk.

King, that is, not Tom.'

'I assumed that,' replied DC Donaldson.

'That it?'

'That's just your starters. Main course?'

'Jesus wept. Go on.'

'Jimmy Todd, noted disc jockey and drug entrepreneur is currently in a cell, right here, right now. While you were taking a well-deserved rest, he confessed to the murder of Naomi Wells. He has refused the offer of legal counsel on multiple occasions. All other enquiries - beyond "yes, DC Donaldson, I did it" - are getting a firm "no comment" from Mr Todd. DS Pym wants him charged as soon as possible, probably so His Lordship can get his gob on the telly at teatime and deliver at least one piece of good news to the good people of Oldham. Apart from that, fairly quiet.'

'Where did they find Todd?' Smithdown asked.

'He strolled in while you were hibernating. Looked a right mess, by all accounts. Waited his turn at the front desk like a nice, polite lad, coughed to the murder, then sat back down again. Never seen anything like it. You don't get people queuing politely like that round here, do you?'

'No, Bob. You don't. I need to see Jimmy, sharpish.'

'DS Pym says no one is to see him. We tried to get Todd to see the Custody Sergeant, but he refused to come out of his cell, so we charged him through the hatch. He seemed frightened to death. His 330 paperwork's all boxed off ready for court. Done and dusted, essentially.'

'I might just pop in to pay Jimmy my regards. The DS doesn't need to know, does he?'

'Know what?'

'Precisely. I'm just gathering intelligence, DC Donaldson. No more than that. Perfectly legit.'

Smithdown knew Jimmy Todd by reputation rather than via a great deal of first-hand knowledge. He was aware of him around town and he'd seen him in the photos he'd seen at Naomi's flat: good-looking with a big smile and that shock of blonde hair. *Got the look of a German holiday rep. Eager to please.*

Charming. A bullshitter but relatively harmless. A wannabe, yes - but a murderer? That's a surprise. The person he saw in the cell looked very different to the man in Smithdown's photo. Todd's handsome head of hair was plastered onto his forehead with dirt and sweat. His left eye was swollen shut. His hands were filthy. He was digging dirt from under his fingernails when Smithdown came in. He didn't look up. 'Jimmy, my name's DI John Smithdown. I believe you've confessed to the murder of Naomi Wells, is that right?'

'Yes,' he said, still looking at his fingernails. 'I've made a statement. Nothing more to say.'

'Mind telling me what happened?'

'We had a row,' Todd said, he gently touched the desk with the edge of his hand as he spoke. 'I strangled her in the flat. I started to cut her up, but it was too hard. So, I dumped part of her in the lake and the rest up in Derbyshire.'

'At the Mermaid's Pool...' the detective said, leaving an opening for Jimmy to speak further.

'No further comment to make, Mr Smithdown.'

'This isn't an official interview, Jimmy,' the DI said. 'There's no tape going. We have to tape all interviews now, it's a new thing. Did you know that?'

'I didn't,' Todd said.

'Not required here, though. This isn't going to be used in evidence. It's just you and me. Go through what happened for me, if you don't mind.'

'No further comment to make, Mr Smithdown.'

'I'm trying to help you, Jimmy. Honestly, I am. What were you rowing about?'

'No comment to make, Mr Smithdown.'

'I knew Naomi. I liked her. She had it hard, but she was making a life for herself. And for Becky. I don't get it, Jimmy. It just doesn't fit. Why did you do it?'

'No comment.'

'We've plenty of lakes and reservoirs of our own round here - why drag the rest of her all the way up to Hayfield and beyond?'

'No comment.'

'You burned her beyond recognition yet left her personal effects scattered about for all to see - makes no sense, does it? Why would you do that?'

'No comment.'

'I don't think she died in the flat. She was still alive when she got there, wasn't she, Jimmy? At the pool, I mean. Still alive. She must have been begging and screaming all the way up the hill. I've been up there; it took me ages and I was in a Land Rover for half the journey. She must have been bleeding all over the shop too, but still fighting, I'll bet. Right to the end. But why burn her like that? Domestics that get out of hand don't end like that. She suffered. Really suffered. If it was a moment of madness, why prolong it like that? It. Makes. No. Sense.'

'No comment, Mr Smithdown. No comment. No fucking comment.'

'And you'd been knocking her daughter about too, hadn't you Jimmy? Little Becky. She was here with her face all bashed in. The neighbours heard you smacking her about and found her all alone in the flat above Mr Aleem's. You were obviously busy setting fire to her mum up at Kinder…'

'Please, Mr Smithdown. Please, please, please. No fucking comment.'

Smithdown looked at Todd. He'd closed his eyes, dropped his chin to his chest and folded his arms. *Shutdown. I'll get no more from this lying twat.*

As he left the cell, the first person Smithdown saw was DC Donaldson, who was pulling his 'warning' face. Again. Detective Superintendent James Pym was a few steps behind him. 'John. Morning. I could have sworn I'd told DC Donaldson that Todd wasn't to be disturbed. I must be going mad. Any road - Todd is all sorted and ready for shipping to court - special weekend sitting first, then off to the Stangeways Hotel on remand, I expect. We've got too much on our plates to be wasting time on a domestic. Albeit a fucking nasty one. One less drugged-up DJ to worry about I suppose. And one less prossie girlfriend.'

Smithdown sidestepped DC Donaldson and stepped directly in front of his senior officer. His face was just a little closer to Pym's than normal work etiquette allows for. 'These are people Jim,' he said in a quiet voice. 'They might have fucked up in the course of their lives but they're real people. Naomi was a good person. A good mum. Now what's left of her is in the morgue over at Stepping Hill. And that lad in there isn't telling us the truth about it. Call me an old fusspot, but I'd quite like to find out why he isn't telling us the truth - what with me being a police detective and all.'

'He's confessed, John,' Pym pointed out. 'End of. She's dead and he's coughed to it. We've got too much shit to deal with right now to be dwelling on the whys and wherefores. Plus, we'll never get an ID from that pile of burnt sticks you recovered from Kinder. So, you need to get down from your high horse, get your sleeves rolled up and do some policing. We've got two Section 18 Assaults in the Royal and two sets of community leaders going spare about it. One will probably end up as attempted murder. Our priority right now is to bring a bit of calm to the streets before things really kick off. Oldham was on the verge of serious disorder last night while you were admiring the view up at Kinder Scout. So, let's have you down the hospital sharpish and find out what the victims are saying. Okay?'

The two stared at each other, their noses just a few inches apart. 'The daughter,' Smithdown said after a few moments. 'Someone needs to tell the daughter. Don't send some faceless constable. She knows me. I'll do it, then I'll go to the hospital. Have you got names for the two machete victims?'

'I've written them down for you,' Pym said, offering Smithdown a piece of paper. 'Wouldn't want you to get them tricky Asian names wrong now, would we?'

Smithdown looked at the piece of paper. He could have sworn that he saw the briefest of smiles on DS Pym's face.

CHAPTER FOURTEEN

2.15 pm Saturday 2 April 1988

'That,' Smithdown said, sitting on the back step outside the care home smoking with Brenda Graham, 'Went as well as could be expected.'

'That poor little girl,' Brenda agreed. 'That's no start in life, is it? Bless her. She didn't even cry. Saving it up until we've gone, I'll bet.'

'Maybe, deep down, she knows she'll be better off without her mum,' the detective offered. He regretted it almost as soon as the words had left his mouth, but it was too late.

'John Smithdown, you heartless shite!' Brenda shouted. She immediately realised that with the back door open, her voice could be heard across the house. So, this time, she whispered it: 'You heartless shite! Naomi adored that girl, doted on her. They had it tough and maybe weren't everyone's idea of the ideal family unit, but that little girl was happy. People who live in nice houses like you don't have the monopoly on happiness, you know?'

It was Brenda's turn to regret saying something now. 'Sorry, sorry, sorry. You've got me at it now, talking shite. Sorry. How is Jean?'

'Again, as well as can be expected,' the detective replied in a quiet voice.

'Will you hug her from me. I mean it. A proper hug.'

'Yes, I will.'

'Promise?'

'Promise.'

She squeezed his arm, jabbed out her roll-up on the wall and stood up. 'Time to be changing Becky's status on the system, I suppose. She'll be needing a more permanent temporary home, if you know what I mean. It would be good to get her away from around here, that's for sure.'

'Her mum's inquest will be all over the paper's before you know it,' Smithdown pointed out. 'Every grisly detail of the whole business there for the whole of Oldham to see.'

'I know. This town right now, John. Jesus wept, it's gone mad. Lads with machetes wandering the streets. A mini-riot last night. Communities that have lived peacefully alongside each other for years at each other's throats. The old guard, the 1970s racist fuckers saying: "I told you so." Absolute madness. How are the people that were attacked - a Pakistani and a Bengali, I hear.'

'You hear correctly. I'm on my way to the hospital now. I thought I'd come here first. Just one long cavalcade of fun today, isn't it?'

CHAPTER FIFTEEN

2.45 pm Saturday 2 April 1988

'Mr Aleem. How are you doing?' asked Smithdown. He'd bought some flowers and a small box of After Eights. He'd managed to work himself into a mild state of worry as he entered the Royal Oldham Hospital, concerned as to whether there were any issues with the ingredients in After Eights that might make it an inappropriate gift for Aleem. Maybe for religious reasons?

Then he realised that he had no idea what Aleem's religion actually was. And even if he did, he had no detailed knowledge as to how that affected his chocolate choices either. Then he saw the state his friend was in and he forgot all about the After Eights.

Mr Aleem 's face was so swollen he looked like he'd had air injected under the skin around his cheeks, forehead and eyes. The redness of the bloated skin was in the early stages of turning purple. His left hand and arm were criss-crossed with cuts, scratches and sutures. His right was bandaged so heavily it looked like a white boxing glove. There were two pillows under his upper arm - three under his lower arm and wrist. Aleem's arm was pointed upwards, like a power salute. His eyes followed Smithdown as he entered the open ward and pulled up a seat next to Aleem's bed. The detective placed the After Eights on the small, brown bedside cabinet next to the bed. Aleem looked at them. 'You know, John,' he said, speaking while moving his jaw as little as possible and glancing at his hand. 'I might struggle to open a wafer-thin mint just now. I'll save them for later if that's okay. But the thought is very much appreciated. Very much indeed.'

'Yes, you might find it little tricky just now, but they're something to look forward to, I suppose,' Smithdown said, trying to sound as encouraging as possible. 'Bloody Nora, what a mess, mate. I don't know what's happening to this town - the place is going insane.'

'Something stinks in Oldham right now, John. Something bad has arrived. The hand in the lake; then Naomi goes missing; I hear you've found something terrible over Derbyshire way, too? Now this.'

Smithdown was reluctant to ask Mr Aleem questions but he knew that he had to: 'Look, I know this isn't a great time, but I want to find who did this. The neighbours heard anti-Pakistani chanting outside your door. Were they Bangladeshi lads? Is that who did this?'

'I don't know,' Aleem sighed. 'I heard something. Shouting. Banging. It's what made me go to the door. Then there was the fire too. I don't know. It's hard to remember. My family were in the house. They could have died. Why would these people target us?'

'Revenge?' Smithdown offered. 'A Bangladeshi lad was done over earlier in the evening. There's been multiple reports through the night of attacks from both communities. We've got teenage lads from either side in custody. The attack on the lad in Coldhurst… then you? It kicked off a whole load of trouble right across the town. Fighting, criminal damage. All sorts.'

'I heard. But, baseball bats? Machetes? That's not our town, John. That's not our youth. There's a kind of poison in the air. Poison.'

'It's like someone's put something in the water, alright,' the detective agreed. 'There's too much for us to cope with right now and all of it is off the scale. And it's involving communities that… I don't claim to be an expert in these matters, put it like that. I'm a bit embarrassed about how little I know, to be honest.'

The two men were silent for a moment. 'I came here with my family 15 years ago after the Liberation War,' Mr Aleem said. 'It's not been easy, let me tell you. Abuse? Yes. Violence? Sometimes. Vandalism and graffiti? Sure. Almost constant. You know where that has all come from, John? Of course you do - a tiny minority in the white community. But nothing like this. There's a boy down the corridor with machete wounds too. A boy from a good Bengali family. I know them. They walked past the ward earlier - they turned away when they saw me. Like it was somehow my fault.'

'I know there's always been this undercurrent of animosity between the Pakistanis and Bangladeshis in Oldham. Separate parts of town, worshipping at different mosques. Were they Bengali lads? Did they attack you because you're from Pakistan?' the detective asked.

'Maybe. Maybe not. I don't know. Sorry.'

'It's okay. I'll leave you be. Get well, okay?'

'Sure. I'll be out of here by teatime I reckon.'

'I bloody well doubt it,' Smithdown said.

'John? Can I ask… How's Jean?'

'She's just like you, making life difficult for the good folks of the NHS. But, also like you, on the mend. Take care, mate.'

Smithdown gave Mr Aleem a thumb's up, headed towards the reception and was directed to where he could find Mustafizur Rahman. The 16-year-old was upright in bed talking to another young man, who looked about 20. *A friend? Maybe his big brother. Probably very pissed off.*

'Hey look, it's a man in a grey suit,' the older one said. 'Must be one of Oldham's finest - here to ask some stupid questions instead of being out there trying to find the animals that tried to chop up my brother.'

'And a very good afternoon to you too,' Smithdown replied. The detective turned his attention to the young man in the bed. His arms were bandaged, and his face was bruised. He looked tired too, but overall, he seemed in better shape than Mr Aleem. 'Mustafizur Rahman? I'm Detective Inspector Smithdown from Oldham Police. I'd like to talk to you about what happened. Do you feel up to it?'

'Hey, hey,' interrupted the older of the two. 'He's my

bother and he's only sixteen. Our parents have just left. Mum was too upset. I mean, can you even do that? Can you question a kid of his age without them here? Is that even legal?'

'I'm not questioning him,' Smithdown pointed out. 'I'm trying to find out what happened so we can catch the people responsible. And, for your information, I can talk to him if it's in the presence of a responsible adult. Do you know any?'

'Oh wow. A comedy cop. Nice. Just what we need right now.'

'Look. We're all on the same side here…'

'Are we, though? Are we really?' Smithdown looked at Mustafizur's brother. The young man was sporting a floppy centre-parting and his hair was cut very short up the back and sides. He was wearing a brightly coloured top and baggy jeans. He looked about the same age as his daughter, Kate. *Got a right gob on him too - just like her.*

'Yes, we are. Absolutely,' Smithdown said and put out his hand. 'Sorry, I didn't get your name. I'm John.'

The young man waited a few beats, looked out of the window, then glanced at his brother, before reluctantly shaking the detective's hand.

'Mohiuddin,' he said.

'Sorry?'

'Uddin. Call me Uddin if all those brown syllables are too much for you to handle.'

Fuckin Nora. 'Right you are, Uddin. I just want to get a few details from your brother, that's all.'

'Okay with that, Musta?' Uddin asked his brother.

'Sure,' the teenager replied. 'But I already gave a statement to a uniformed officer,' Mustafizur said. 'I told them what I know. I don't remember much.'

'Did you recognise any of the people who attacked you?' Smithdown asked.

'They were all masked,' the young man replied, occasionally glancing at his brother. 'Gloves too. They hit me with baseball bats. One guy lost his mask at one stage. Not sure how. He was definitely a South Asian kid. He said something anti-

Bangladesh. Then he hit me with the machete.'

'What about the others - were they South Asian?'

'I don't know. The masks, you know? And the gloves.'

'Did the others… well, sound Asian?'

'Oh wow!' exclaimed Uddin, placing both hands on his head with a look of disbelief. 'Mate. Comedy cop. Listen to yourself. You need to go on a course or something. Listen to yourself.'

'I don't know,' Mustafizur replied. 'Sorry.'

'Maybe it was hard to hear because of the sound of the baseball bats and machetes hitting him!' Uddin offered.

Smithdown carried on: 'The lad who spoke. Did you recognise him? Do you know him? Would you know him if you saw him again?'

'I don't know him, but I've seen him about town.

'Is he Pakistani?'

'Whoah, whoah, whoah mate,' interrupted Uddin. 'What's this all about?'

'Not sure yet. We're keeping an open mind.'

'That's a copper way of saying, "we haven't got a clue", I reckon,' Uddin said.

'Well, there was, what appears to have been, a revenge attack on a man from Pakistan shortly afterwards,' Smithdown said. 'He's in a room down the corridor with his hand hanging by a thread. Then there were attacks on shops and businesses from both communities. During the second attack, a gang were heard shouting things that were anti-Pakistan. During your incident… anti-Bangladesh stuff was shouted. That's the line of enquiry because that's where the evidence is leading. That okay? Where were you last night, Uddin when it was all kicking off?

'Brilliant. Try to pin something on me rather than find the people who did this to my brother. Classic.'

'It's not a secret that the Pakistani and Bangladeshi communities don't always exactly see eye to eye around these parts,' the detective offered. 'That's fair isn't it? Different parts of town, separate mosques...'

'Oh, wow listen to the expert - Mr South Asia here - explaining how things work in downtown Oldham.'

It took a lot to agitate Smithdown, but Uddin was doing a pretty good job of it. Mainly because he was right. Smithdown didn't really know what he was talking about: South Asian people accounted for almost a third of the population in the town centre of Oldham, yet he knew next to nothing about the differences between the communities.

'Okay, Uddin. Who do you think was responsible?'

'The Pakistani lad said something against our community. Then hit a kid from our community with a machete. That's all I need to know.'

'It wasn't quite like that, though,' Mustafizur said, pushing himself upright in his bed. 'It was weird.'

'How do you mean?' asked Smithdown, grateful to hear from him rather than his brother.

'There was something about the way he hit me…'

'…with a big machete…' added his brother.

'Like he didn't want to do it. Like he'd rather be doing anything… be anywhere… rather than be there doing what he did.'

'But he did it anyway,' added his brother.

'Why do you think that was, Mustafizur?' Smithdown asked.

'Like… It's weird, really. It was like if he didn't do it, something much worse would happen.'

CHAPTER SIXTEEN

4.50 pm Saturday 2 April 1988

Several weeks earlier, Jean Smithdown had been fitted with a semi-permanent cannula to allow the next cycle of chemo to be pumped in. The treatment was wrecking her veins and it was becoming increasingly difficult - and painful - to put a needle into her.

The fixed cannula meant the discomfort of trying and failing to find a vein was one less thing for her to dread about the process. She'd lost her hair almost straight away; her appetite had followed soon after and her weight had plummeted. Everything tasted like iron filings, she said, and yet she couldn't face anything more flavoursome than vegetable soup. Thanks to the chemo, her urine had gone red too. The steroids she was taking made sleep almost impossible, so she was tired all the time. What's more the pills made her feel spacy and not-quite-there - or 'off her tits' as her daughter liked to put it.

Kate Smithdown was holding her mother's hand - the one that wasn't receiving the chemo cocktail. Both were reading a book with their spare hands: *McNae's Essential Law for Journalists* for Kate, her mum had Stephen King's *Misery*.

John Smithdown watched them from his seat a few feet away. Both had to use a chin, the edge of the chair they were sitting in or even a tongue to help turn a page. It was clearly an awkward and inefficient way to read a book for both of them, but it preferable to the alternative - because that would have meant letting go of each other.

For no apparent reason, Kate turned away from her book. Father and daughter looked at each other for second, maybe two. The detective felt his eyes become warm and itchy and he was worried he was going to cry. Then his daughter jutted her chin at him and gave him the cross eyes - just like she had done since she was tiny. He smiled and the need for tears fell away.

Kate returned to her book. Smithdown shifted his weight in the scooped plastic hospital chair and thought. He should have been thinking about the attacks on Mr Aleem and Mustafizur Rahman. But instead he was thinking about Naomi Wells. He was running through a list in his head:

Alex Park Lake - just a hand? MNFS

Distance from Naomi's flat to the pool? MNFS

Murder scene at the Mermaid's Pool. MNFS.

Destroy body but leave ID? MNFS

Jimmy Todd confession? MNFS

The problem with this whole Naomi Wells business is most of it Makes No Fucking Sense.

'Dad,' hissed Kate. 'Stop muttering and swearing to yourself, you weirdo. You're not at work now.'

'Sorry,' he said with a small smile. 'I was miles away,' Smithdown stared at the chemo drip attached to a stand near his wife. She'd dozed off

Kate gently extricated her hand slowly from her mother's, checking constantly that she was still asleep. She stood up from her chair and carried it over to sit next to her father. They both looked at Jean Smithdown. She looked peaceful; her fine features and naturally pale skin were set off by the sheer white of the hospital pillows tucked behind her head. She'd chosen a pale yellow and white scarf today, as if it had been specially picked to match the light in the room. 'She's the only person who can take the whole no-hair-and-bandana cancer look and carry it off,' said Kate with a sniff. 'She's so beautiful.'

'Yes, she really is,' agreed Smithdown. 'That's one thing we can definitely agree on.'

'Sorry for being a dick the other day,' Kate said. It was time for holding hands again - this time, it was her father's. 'The hospital is looking after mum, mum's looking after me and no one's looking after you. Sorry.'

'It's alright,' John Smithdown said. 'All forgotten about. Though you are a bit of a dick, to be fair.'

'Were you thinking about Naomi Wells?' Kate asked.

'Yes, I was, did you know her?'

'Are you questioning me, Dad?' Kate said, folding her arms across her '*Meat Is Murder*' t-shirt.

'I'm gathering intelligence,' Smithdown pointed out. 'Perfectly legitimate…'

'I did know her,' Kate said. 'Sort of. If you went clubbing in Oldham or Manchester, you knew Naomi. They say she was first through the door on the opening night of The Haçienda in '82. She was one of those people who seemed to be able to be at two different club nights in totally different places at exactly the same time. She was Ms Manchester.'

'And Jimmy Todd?'

'Similar situation. If you go to clubs - and you take drugs - you know Jimmy.'

Smithdown shifted in his chair: 'Well that's comforting for a father to hear, I must say. Probably best not to say anymore. You do know I'm a police officer, don't you?'

'It has cropped up a few times in conversation, Dad, yes. Look, drugs aren't my thing if that helps. Even if they were, I'd be so wary right now. Things are very different right now. It's all too new. No one has any idea what they're swallowing and they're practically giving out ecstasy for free in the clubs - carrier bags full of it.'

'Bob Donaldson reckons that if they served it in pubs, we'd have less people in the cells. Big gangs of lads hugging outside the clubs instead of fighting.'

'Maybe he's right,' Kate said, nodding in agreement. 'Did you know, the original name for it was empathy not ecstasy?'

'I didn't know that. Why did they change it, do you think?' the detective asked, genuinely interested.

'Marketing, I suppose. Why buy empathy when you can buy ecstasy?'

'Good point well made,' Smithdown conceded. 'This is a really weird conversation, by the way.'

'I know. Shall we pretend it never happened?'

'Yes please.'

'Seriously, though,' Kate said. 'The whole thing is bizarre. First the hand in the lake - then taking Naomi all the way up to that weird lake near Kinder. The press is having a field day with that. All the Mermaid stuff. It's a journalist's dream. Then Jimmy coughing to it - just strolling into Oldham nick with his hands up.'

When she was younger, Kate had talked about wanting to join the police force. As she grew older, the idea of being a journalist took over. A good cop and a good journalist are cut from very similar cloth, he'd told her on many occasions.

'So, what do your journalistic instincts tell you about all this, then?' Smithdown asked.

Kate thought for a moment. She glanced over at her mother, then looked at her dad: 'It makes no fucking sense, does it?'

'Language, Kate,' murmured Jean Smithdown, stirring from her nap.

'Sorry, Mum,' Kate said, winking at her father.

'Dad?'

'Yes, Katie.'

'I do love you.' She leant over and kissed his cheek.

'Not as much as I love you,' the detective replied. 'You're still a bit of a dick sometimes though.'

CHAPTER SEVENTEEN

8.35pm Saturday 2 April 1988

After calling her from the hospital, DC Jenny Seddon had agreed to meet Smithdown at the Star Inn, in Glossop. The detective felt that as he'd been so rude to her last time they'd met, the least he could do was to buy her a drink on her patch, and it was him who wanted to see her, not the other way around.

The Star was perched on a corner, tucked between the train and police stations at the top end of the town. It had a rounded front, etched glass windows and as Smithdown noted as he stepped inside, dim lights and reassuringly low ceilings that gave it a warm, orangey atmosphere. A fug of cigarette smoke clung to the room. Plus, they sold Big D peanuts behind the bar - Smithdown's favourite.

Dressed in a tracksuit, DC Jenny Seddon was standing at the bar talking to a group of men - every one of them was at least a foot taller than her. She glanced at Smithdown, nodded and pointed to her glass to ask if he wanted a drink; the detective nodded back and mouthed the word 'bitter' as he squeezed through the crowd to get to the bar. Jenny Seddon gave him a thumbs up, then said something to the group; whatever it was it caused all of them to laugh. Loudly. *My punishment continues.*

'Alright?' she said, handing him a pint whilst taking a sip of foam from the top of hers. 'Find it okay?'

'Yeah. My wife's from near here, so we did a fair bit of courting round this way.'

'Courting?' Jenny said laughing and shaking her head as she

pointed to a small, copper-topped table in the corner. 'That's another blast from the past. Are you sure you're not related to my dad?'

'What's up with the word courting? It's a good Manchester expression is that.'

'In 1965, it quite possibly was, yes.'

'Never thought I'd be lectured on the modern way of doing things by someone from Glossop. You lot still stop and point at the planes when they're flying over to Ringway Airport.'

'Manchester International Airport, grandad. It's not been called Ringway since 1975.'

'Don't start…I come in peace.'

'Sorry.'

They sat quietly for a moment. The jukebox kicked in. Someone had selected '*How Long*' by Ace. Smithdown smiled - Jean loved this song - and he instinctively reached for his cigarettes but then thought better of it.

'The girl's boyfriend coughed to the murder then?' DC Seddon asked.

'Jimmy Todd? Yes. He was in court first thing this morning. Special sitting. Back again on Tuesday,' Smithdown replied.

'Did you talk to him?'

'I did.'

'And?'

'He was scared shitless. Not of me. Not of being charged. Not even of going to jail. He was a wreck, but beyond admitting he'd killed her with the bare minimum of detail, it was no comment all the way. But a confession is a confession as far as the boss is concerned. All sorted now, I suppose.'

'I get the feeling you're still not happy,' Jenny stated.

'Not especially,' Smithdown offered, being cautious with his responses. 'The scene up at the Mermaid's Pool - you weren't happy about that either, were you?'

'No. I wasn't. But it's GMP's case not ours. It's not for me to say.'

'Well, I was interested in what you said afterwards. "Stage-managed bollocks" - that was the expression, I believe?'

'That was the expression, yes,' she agreed.

Smithdown waved his hand in a rolling motion: 'Care to elaborate?'

Jenny put down her pint: 'It looked like the pool had been dressed by the local amateur dramatics' society. Other than hang a big sign up saying HERE LIES THE BODY OF NAOIMI WELLS - HER HAND IS IN A PLACCY BAG IN THE BOATING LAKE IN OLDHAM TOWN CENTRE… I don't know what more they could have done. I mean it must be her – obviously it's her - but why go to all that bother?'

Smithdown made a "hmmm" noise and took a drink of his bitter.

'What do you mean, "hmmm" what does "hmmm" mean? Don't start being a pillock again, or I'll set the lads on you.'

Smithdown looked at the giants standing at the bar. 'No need for that. You're right. It stinks. Why take her across the border into another county and then kill her? It would have been far easier to do it the other way around. Why all the attempts at spooky bollocks by dumping the body at this Mermaid's Pool - on Easter Eve as well. Someone's been doing their Kinder Scout shit-we-tell-the-tourists research, haven't they? Why dress the scene? It was properly over the top.'

'It really was, wasn't it?' DC Seddon said. 'Also, why go to the bother of making sure her teeth were burned to avoid identification if you're then going to leave a pile of identifying personal effects lying about the place? It…'

'…makes no fucking sense,' Smithdown agreed.

'Exactly!'

Silence for a moment. 'I had to go and tell the daughter that her mum had died,' he said. 'Not nice.'

'No. It's never nice isn't that,' Jenny agreed.

'Didn't cry. Said nowt. Just took it. Tough little kid.' Smithdown reached into his pocket and took out the photo of Naomi Wells that he'd had since his first visit to the children's home. He showed it to DC Seddon. 'She gave me this. I forgot to give it back to her.'

'That's Naomi? She looks like she's having such a great time,' she said. 'Poor, poor girl.'

'Indeed,' confirmed Smithdown. 'Here's a thing, see what you think.' Slightly self-consciously, the detective raised his left arm into the air and made a fist, imitating Naomi's pose in the photo. Jenny Seddon looked at him, looked at the photo, then glanced around the bar to see who was watching.

'Bit inappropriate, under the circumstances, DI Smithdown. Can't say I approve.'

Smithdown held his pose. Other people in the pub were staring at him now. Slowly he put his arm down. He pointed at the photo. 'The hand we found - Naomi's hand - was a left hand. Naomi was kippy-handed. Look at the way she's punching the air.'

'Kippy what?'

'An old Manc expression. Kippy-handed. She was a lefty.'

'It's probably been a while since you were out clubbing…'

'…I was in one the other night, actually…'

'… but people in nightclubs have been known to punch the air with either hand, DI Smithdown.'

'You're right. Of course you are. Thing is, I've been in her flat. I looked in her kitchen. She had a left-handed tin opener in her drawer. Unimaginative people give them to kippies as presents when they don't know what else to give them. Every kippy-hander has one. My daughter is left-handed. She has one. I gave it to her before she left for uni.'

'Okay,' said Seddon not quite sure where the conversation was going. 'But that matches, doesn't it? You found a left hand in the lake at Oldham and the left hand was missing from the body at the pool.'

'Yes, but that poor creature up at the pool was reaching out to the pool with her right hand.'

'Hate to spoil your flow, but it was the only one she had, Detective Inspector,' Jenny pointed out.

'I know, I know. Hear me out. With her last breath - on fucking fire, mind - she instinctively reached out with her right arm.'

This time, Smithdown stretched his right arm out in front of him, again generating a few looks from the pub regulars. 'I don't know. That just doesn't feel right. Naomi was kippy-handed, but that I think that poor soul up at the pool was right-handed. Maybe whoever did that to her wanted us to think it was Naomi.'

Jenny took a drink. Then she took off her glasses and cleaned them.

'Go on. I'm listening,' she said.

'That body up at the pool was torched beyond recognition,' Smithdown continued. 'Yet the hand we found - it's definitely Naomi's - had been selectively burned to leave a usable fingerprint. That's handy.'

'Poor choice of words Mr Smithdown…'

'I can only apologise,' the detective offered. 'The way the scene was dressed is one thing. That's weird in itself. The thing with the hand, that's potentially weird too. Both together? I'm not having it, Jenny. You don't mind if I call you Jenny, do you?'

She shook her head. 'As long as you don't ask me to call you John. I'm not quite at that stage yet.'

'Fair enough. Here's a thought: maybe they want us to think it's just one murder. But what if it's actually two.'

'Buy one murder, get another one for free?' Jenny said.

'Exactly - I fancy some nuts,' Smithdown said, getting up from the table. 'Do you want some?'

'Go on then.'

Smithdown rummaged in his pocket for change. 'Right then, two packs of Big D coming up. So, here's the plan. We need to get back on Jimmy Todd's case and find out what really happened in that flat. We need to work out where the rest of Naomi's body is; and we need to find out who the fuck is really in that smoky body bag in the morgue at Stepping Hill.'

'How do you mean,' DC Seddon asked. 'We?'

CHAPTER EIGHTEEN

8.45pm Saturday 2 April 1988

It was dark now at Strangeways Prison in Manchester. Lights out soon. The 19th century red brick jail, with its imposing balconied ventilation tower, dominated the skyline just north of the city centre, close to the border with Salford.

The jail currently housed five hundred more prisoners than it was originally designed for. Earlier in the day that figure became five hundred and one.

That morning, one of the more puzzling elements in the murder of Naomi Wells had been summoned from his cell at Oldham police station and taken via an underground corridor to the magistrates' court next door.

Head down, he had quietly answered 'yes' when asked to confirm his name, address and date of birth. He had then been asked if he understood that he was being charged with murder. Again, he'd given a quiet 'yes'. Then he'd been told by the chairman of the bench that the charge was too serious to be heard in a magistrates' court, so he was to be remanded in custody until it could be dealt with at the City Police Court on Minshull Street after the Bank Holiday Weekend.

He'd then been taken from the court and driven through Failsworth and Collyhurst to Strangeways. There, he'd been processed and told that although, as a remand prisoner, he had different rights to a regular prisoner as he was presumed innocent, there was currently no room in the remand area of the jail. So, he was to be housed in the main body of Strangeways as a provisional Category A prisoner.

Next, he was taken across the jail's noisy, clanking stairwells and shown his cell. There was another prisoner already there, who greeted his new cellmate by name. The new inmate couldn't understand how the other prisoner could possibly know who he was. When the cell door shut, Jimmy Todd became very afraid indeed.

'BBC Manchester News at ten, this is Richard Hemmingway. An investigation is underway after the death of a remand prisoner at Manchester's Strangeways Jail earlier today. Jimmy Todd was facing a murder charge after his girlfriend's body was found at a Derbyshire beauty spot in the early hours. Vince Hunt has more.'

'This morning, 28-year-old-Jimmy Todd had appeared in court in Oldham, charged with the murder of Naomi Wells. The 26-year-old mum of one's body had been found next to the Mermaid's Pool near Kinder Scout at Hayfield. It's believed she'd been set on fire - her body burnt so badly that a positive identification was deemed impossible, until Todd himself confessed to the killing.

The previous day, Naomi's severed hand had been discovered in Alexandra Park boating lake near Oldham town centre.

Todd had been sent to Strangeways straight after his court appearance and had only been at the jail a matter of hours before his body was discovered. It's thought there are no suspicious circumstances in connection with his death and that no one else is being sought in connection with the incident. Vince Hunt, BBC Manchester News, Strangeways.'

CHAPTER NINETEEN

10.05pm Saturday 2 April 1988

After leaving Jenny Seddon in the Star Inn, Smithdown had headed home via the town of Mossley. The road hugged the hills through the small towns and villages that peppered the route home to Oldham. '*Born to Be With You*' by Dave Edmunds was on his cassette player. Edmunds' *Subtle as a Flying Mallet* was one of the detective's favourite albums.

As he drove, cigarette sparks flying out of the barely open window as he flicked his ash, Smithdown noticed that the sky to the east of his route looked odd. There was normally an orangey glow to the view from here - the kind of hazy, urban hum of light that would be expected to hover over a town the size of Oldham. But tonight, the sky seemed to flicker and dance like the fake coal effect of an old gas fire. It looked alive.

The detective took a slight detour via Grasscroft and drove down Oldham Road towards Grotton, an area, he always like to note, that was far more pleasant than its name suggested. As he travelled through the village, he saw dozens of people standing outside their houses. They were pointing, talking and shaking their heads. As he rounded a bend that had the advantage of a small layby, Smithdown pulled in and stopped. He stood at the gentle ridge edge that swept down towards Oldham town centre. Several other drivers had also parked up. One of them, a man of a similar age to Smithdown, looked at the detective and nodded down the valley. 'Absolute fookin' madness,' he said.

Smithdown had to agree. The intermittent illumination of

orange was fire. Oldham was burning.

'D'ya know who I blame?' the man asked. 'Do ya? I'll tell ya exactly who I blame…'

Smithdown didn't wait to hear the answer. He got back in his car and headed for the town centre. Noisy bursts of trouble flashed past his window as he drove: a fistfight here, a restaurant window put through there. The level of aggravation - and the sour, frightening atmosphere it generated - got stronger as he neared the south east corner of the town. The road ahead was blocked; a car had rammed into the side of another and had attracted a crowd. The jeering mob managed to look both jubilant and angry at the same time. Smithdown turned off into the terraced side streets and weaved his way through the tightly packed houses. He slowed right down until he was driving almost at walking pace.

More and more people, many carrying improvised weapons, dashed in front of him as they crossed Glodwick Road. Their movements and voices suggested they were young; many of their faces were masked in balaclavas. *The owner of that army surplus store over in Royton must have sold more balas than Soft Mick today. He's probably retired.*

A stone cracked against the driver's-side window of his car and Smithdown instinctively flinched and swerved slightly away from the direction it came from. Hunched over his steering wheel and moving slowly forward, he looked left and right. Ahead of him, on the flat roof of the Turn of Luck pub, half a dozen people were throwing stones, bottles, and half bricks down at a gang of youths at street level. They were returning fire with anything that came to hand. Not all them wore masks: the detective noted that most of the youths at ground level were South Asian. Most of the people on the roof were white.

Smithdown watched as another group of teenagers carried a large wooden dining table above their heads like a rowing team carrying their boat. They picked up speed as they got to the pub's main window and then shoved the table through it. A cheer went up. Then the pub missile throwers responded by rolling a huge metal beer barrel to the lip of the roof and tipping it off, scattering the youths below in the process. It bounced erratically as it hit the ground and rolled across the road, adding to the debris that had already made the road impassable.

The detective pulled his car into the quietest looking side street he could find, locked his car and continued on foot. On the corner across the road from the pub were two men in their 20s with a video camera. It didn't look like the kind that the local television news crews used. He'd seen them many times and knew most of the local BBC and Granada TV cameramen by sight or by name. This camera was smaller, less substantial - the kind you could rent from most high street TV shops or even buy if you had the money. One of the men was filming, the other was directing him towards individual pockets of rioters. He didn't recognise the cameraman - wiry, nervous and aggressive looking with an angry-looking rash on his neck - but the 'director' was clearly Tom Lennon.

Smithdown approached them. 'Documentary maker now, are you Tom?' he shouted over the noise. 'Don't strain your poorly eye, will you?'

The cameraman muttered 'wanker' under his breath and pointed the lens at the detective and took a few steps towards him. 'We're in a public place and we're not causing any obstruction, Mr Smithdown,' Lennon said. 'Surely your time would be better spent on tackling the feral Asian youth over there who are committing criminal damage and public disorder under your very nose.'

'Any comment to make about the feral Asian youth, Mr Smithdown?' the cameraman asked.

The detective pointed his finger at the directly at the lens. 'What's your name, lad?'

'Hitchcock,' the cameraman replied, smiling and scratching at his face. 'Alf Hitchcock.'

'Is the camera running, Mr Hitchcock?'

'Yeah, it is,' the cameraman shouted, causing the camera to tilt up and down slightly as he nodded.

‘Good. Then stick this in your documentary. Turn the camera off and fuck off home or I’ll do you for being a pair of shit-stirring twats.’

Lennon smiled at the detective. He had a light, nut brown suntan and his teeth were unusually white and straight. He was smartly dressed in a black jeans, t-shirt and Harrington jacket. He towered over Smithdown. ‘We’re going to get a few close ups first, I think,’ he said. ‘Then we’ll be on our way.’

The pair walked towards the Turn of Luck pub. ‘Give my regards to your mum, Tom,’ Smithdown shouted after them. Lennon began pointing and directing again. Smithdown noted that they weren’t filming any of the white rioters.

The detective wound his way through the back streets towards the town centre. Every few seconds a half-brick or bottles clattered against the pavement or a wall. There were shouts and whoops all around him as rioters filled the ginnels and walkways that spread in all directions.

As he walked, he stopped and spoke to pockets of youths dotted around the streets. He identified himself as a police officer, showed his warrant card and advised them to go home and stay off the streets for the rest of the night. He didn’t linger or argue - there was too many of them for that - he spoke quietly, listened if needs be, then moved on to the next group. Some took what he said on board and walked away. Others told him in no uncertain terms that they had no intention of going anywhere.

He saw a fresh set of masked youths appear from a block of flats; they were carrying plastic trays, the kind favoured by milkmen. All the trays had a dozen milk bottles in, each with a rag stuffed into its neck. They set them down just as several uniformed officers appeared. The PCs immediately came under fire from a stream of Molotov Cocktails that splattered fire across the pavements around them. One officer’s tunic caught fire briefly before his colleagues were able to beat it out. They seemed panicky and ill-prepared for what they’d encountered and began defending themselves with improvised dustbin lid shields.

Smithdown shouted some advice to his colleagues: 'Fuck off out of it before you get barbecued, you dozy twats,' he said. They followed his words of wisdom to the letter and fell back through a patch of wasteland next to a second-hand shop.

The detective crossed the ring road and worked his way around the side of the Town Square shopping centre. Bollards to stop cars entering the area had been smashed and the entrance to a Rumbelows electrical shop had been rammed with a Ford Escort. The double doors hadn't quite given way. Smithdown was heading over to speak to the youths buzzing around the car - they were trying to force the shop's doors open with staves of wood when they suddenly froze, let out shouts of warning and scattered. Smithdown turned; he had more sense to think they were running away from him. He spotted a battered Peugeot 205 heading his way and at considerable speed and managed to turn away just as the wing mirror hit his arm, sending him spinning to the ground. From his vantage point lying on the pavement he saw the Peugeot crash into the back of the Escort, pushing the first car fully through the doors with a metallic crash. There was a rousing cheer as a gaggle of young men dashed forward, clambered over the two cars and entered the store.

Within a matter of moments, a selection of video recorders, radios and cassette players had been liberated. Smithdown noticed that - rather incongruously - one youth had opted for a kettle. *That'll be for his mum, nothing if not considerate that lad.*

A steady stream of people now entered the shopping centre in their wake as the detective got to his feet. *Fair to say things are getting a bit out of hand here, where the fuck are the police?*

Smithdown immediately got his answer; a squad of riot officers in full protective gear headed up the high street, banging their shields as they went. *About fucking time.* A second squad stomped past him from the other direction and formed a barrier across the entrance where the bollards had been. *Right, now I won't have to single-handedly defend the shopping centre, shame really, I could have done with a new telly.*

Then, GMP Tactical Aid Group officers - bigger, stronger-looking and sporting even more protective gear than their colleagues - appeared seemingly from nowhere and began chasing the escaping youths down. One TAG van whizzed past Smithdown; it sent a young man flying by following him at speed down a side street and clipping him with the expertly timed opening of the vehicle's passenger door. He was snatched and bundled into the van by a huge TAG officer. *That lad's going to get a right shoe-ing before he gets to the cells.*

Smithdown - his elbow throbbing with pain - made his way through an alleyway between the shops. He rested against the wall for a moment, the heat of his injury making him feel momentarily faint. The detective heard a voice: 'Hey… It's you… Are you alright, Mr Smithdown?' Uddin Rahman said, running down the alley to where the detective was standing.

'I'll live, lad. What the hell are you up to? After a telly for your mum?'

'That's borderline racist in my opinion, Mr Smithdown,' Uddin pointed out.'

Fucking Nora. 'I'm just sightseeing. Nothing more. There was a bit of trouble here last night, but nothing like this. Unbelievable. Everyone is taking the chance to have a crack at this - white lads, Pakistani youth, Bengali youth. This is an equal opportunities riot, I'll say that.'

'Well, can I suggest that you get out of here as soon as you can, Uddin? Those TAG lads will be delighted to have you in the back of their van, then you'll be in the bed next to your brother at the Oldham Royal all cosy like with a fractured skull. I mean it, lad. Go home, right now.'

'What about you?' Uddin asked. 'You're hurt.' He seemed genuinely concerned.

'I'm fine. Now go.'

Uddin nodded and ran down the alley away from Town Square. 'No heroics, Mr Smithdown,' he shouted as he went. 'You are not a young man.'

'Cheeky twat,' Smithdown muttered and headed towards the rising tide of noise as the alley up ahead opened out into another row of shops. A tight knit gang of youths, most with balaclava masks or bandanas covering their faces, were staging a stand-off in the pedestrianised street. Missiles ricocheted around the high street as the police riot squad spread out across the walkway and began advancing forward. Their presence seemed to have the desired effect almost immediately - Smithdown could see that some of the younger, more slightly built rioters quickly lost heart at the sight of the riot shields and began to slip away down the side streets. TAG officers were there to grab them with only the quickest and most agile rioters able to make their escape.

The detective could see that as quickly as it had flared, the heat was being taken out of the situation. He was now in a position to take in the extent of the damage: every second or third window on the high street was either cracked or smashed; rocks and bottles littered the street and a few fires - the residue of Molotov Cocktails - were being stamped out.

There was one spot on the High Street that seemed to have escaped almost entirely unscathed: the entrance to the Kingdom nightclub. A double semi-circle of men - all of them white, most of them shaven-headed and many carrying baseball bats - had formed outside the club. Richard T. King stood at the heart of the semi-circle; Tom Lennon and 'Alf Hitchcock' were by his side. Lennon spoke to King then smiled and nodded in the detective's direction. The nightclub owner - who was wearing an ornate Oriental dressing gown - gave Smithdown a cheery wave. 'Evening Mr Smithdown. What a night… the atrocious crime of being a youth! Your guys seem to have the situation in hand, though. Very firm. Very fair. About time too, if I may say. What a night!'

'Knowing you're safe and well is a real weight off my mind, Mr King,' Smithdown said. 'You should get yourself inside before you get a chill.'

'Bless you, Detective Inspector,' King said. The detective watched as the nightclub owner rubbed his hands up and down his upper arms with a smile, tied his dressing gown with a flourish and went inside his club. Tom Lennon followed;

'Hitchcock' carried on filming. The guard of protectors outside the club stayed exactly where they were.

You cocky twats, what the fuck are you up to?

'Welcome to Granada News, I'm Hazel Barrett. Our main story this Sunday lunchtime. A major clean-up operation is underway in Oldham after rioting broke out across the town late last night. Gangs of Asian youths - some throwing bricks and bottles - fought pitched battles with police for several hours in what's been described as the worst outbreak of civil disorder Greater Manchester has ever seen. Tim Wyatt was following events for us last night and sends this report from the scene.'

'At the height of last night's violence, as many as 250 youths took to the streets of Oldham town centre. In this exclusive footage, they can be seen fighting pitch battles around the Turn of Luck pub. Bottles and stones rain down and a beer keg is thrown from the roof - narrowly missing the rioters below. Elsewhere the Town Square shopping centre was ramraided, with several shops being looted.

This morning Greater Manchester's Chief Constable James Anderton visited the scene to see the scale of the damage for himself. He's been talking to people from the business community including nightclub owner Richard T. King, who says he believes the police aren't doing enough to stamp out trouble caused by rival Asian gangs:'

> *"Sadly, the growing tensions between various communities and factions in this town just aren't being tackled by the police or the council. We saw it with revenge attacks over the last few days and we've seen it again here overnight. Perhaps they're afraid thatit's too much of a hot potato, I don't know. I'm not a politician, I'm a businessman. But it's businesses that are counting the cost of the inaction this morning, I know that much. But we won't be beaten - we'll be open tonight, in defiance of the trouble-causers who are out to spoil this amazing town."*

'Police say that 63 arrests have been made following the disturbances - mainly for public order offences and criminal damage. They're now urging community leaders to call for calm to avoid another night of trouble. Tim Wyatt, Granada News s, Oldham.'

'In other news, concern is growing over the whereabouts of Oldham Councillor Sharmeen Chowdhury.

Councillor Chowdhury - who represents the Coldhurst ward - hasn't been seen since the council closed for the Easter weekend break on Thursday. Colleagues say that for her not to leave word as to where she was going is completely out of character. They're urging Councillor Chowdhury to get in touch as soon as possible to let them know she's safe and well.'

CHAPTER TWENTY

12.15pm Sunday 3 April 1988

Detective Superintendent Pym, motioned DC Donaldson into his office with friendly gestures of hand and head and closed the door behind him. 'Bob, take a seat,' Pym said. 'I won't keep you.'

'No problem, sir. What's it about?'

'It's about DI Smithdown, Bob.'

'Oh yes? Right. And?'

'I'm worried, Bob.'

'I suppose that's understandable, sir.'

'Where is he - I mean right now, where is he?'

'Out and about, as usual. He took it upon himself to get involved in the rioting last night. He was on the streets advising the local youth to go home to their mams. Not all of them took his advice, as the head count in the cells clearly shows.'

'Exactly, Bob,' Pym said, leaning back in his chair. 'That's my point. The Naomi Wells murder, the machete attacks between the Asian communities, now the riots. He seems to be grabbing every ongoing case on our patch, calling them his and then trying to link them all together. I wouldn't be surprised if he starts taking an interest in this missing councillor too. Plus, there's Jean to consider. Any normal person would be off on compassionate leave. Not him. I'm concerned, Bob. Genuinely concerned.'

'He can handle it, I've no doubt,' Bob replied. 'He knows what he's doing and if he stays in holding Jean's hand all day, he'll go mad. More importantly, he'll send Jean mad too. He's better off out and about, doing his job. Getting things done.

Just my opinion, sir.'

'Noted, Bob. But I don't want things slipping through the net, do you understand what I mean? His focus should be on these race attacks. The Chief Constable wants results. Barring the inquests, the Wells murder is all boxed off. The post-mortem on Jimmy Todd will tell us what we already know then he'll be off to Hollinwood Crematorium. All sorted. Yet I know for a fact John's been mooching around Glossop with that DC from Derbyshire, still wasting time on the Wells case. None of us is going to get any medals for poking around a murder that's done and dusted.'

'I suppose not, sir.'

'How about you keep an eye on this missing councillor, get a grip of it before he does. Sharmeen Chowdhury - she's well-connected, fronts up the Scrutiny Committee on the council. High profile but no family around here. Workaholic apparently. Future council leader some say. It'll play very well for you if you track her down. You sort her out and that'll be one less thing for John to worry about.'

'Are you sure?' Bob asked. 'He won't be happy. He doesn't like things going on behind his back.'

'No question of it going on behind his back. I'll tell him. It'll be official. There'll be an Orange on his desk ASAP,' Pym said reassuring DC Donaldson by promising to deliver an official memo in an orange GMP internal envelope. 'Don't worry, there'll be no comeback on you. I just want to lessen his load. I know full well he won't be told how to do his job. And I never would. But I want to help. I've just got to be a bit subtle about it, that's all.'

'Subtle. Right you are.'

'Thanks Bob. Knock on some doors at the council, see what turns up. And keep me informed. Got it?'

'Got it.'

CHAPTER TWENTY-ONE

12.25pm Sunday 3 April 1988

Give it to me. Take it out of her, open me up and give it to me. Then pump all this shit into my veins, not hers. They assumed their usual positions in the Christie chemo unit: Kate sitting next to her mother as the tube was fixed onto the semi-permanent canula in her hand, the DI in a nearby chair, close to his wife and daughter yet slightly distant.

'What's on your mind, love?' Jean Smithdown asked her husband.

'Sorry?' he asked. 'I was miles away.'

'Mind… Yours… What's on it?' his wife said.

'Work, probably,' offered Kate. 'How to single-handedly stop Oldham descending into anarchy and chaos.'

'Something like that,' the detective replied. He had no intention of telling them what he'd actually been thinking.

'I've got an idea,' Kate said. 'They could build a big wall around Oldham town centre, like *Escape From New York*. All the nutters in one place. Sorted.'

'I'll get straight onto Chief Constable Anderton and we'll swing that plan into action,' Smithdown said and pulled a face at his daughter. *Smartarse.*

'Seriously,' Jean said. 'What's on your mind?'

'No place for shop talk, this.'

'I'd appreciate it - something to think about other than this,' she replied, nodding towards the chemo going into her.

'Sure?' he asked.

'Sure,' his wife reassured.

Smithdown pulled up his chair so he was closer to them. He dropped his voice so the other patients couldn't hear him.

'Right. Okay. Obviously, there's been a fair bit going on at the moment...'

'What with the chopped up, burned-to-buggery bodies and the machete attacks and the rioting and all,' said Kate.

'Yes,' agreed Smithdown. 'All the above...'

'A reasonable few day's work,' Jean added.

'Quite,' the detective concurred. 'And that's what's bothering me. Six months of mither just happens to have kicked in over the space of one Bank Holiday weekend.'

'TFC,' offered Kate.

'Exactly,' agreed her father. 'Added to that, Jimmy Todd's mysteriously topped himself and now some councillor has gone missing.'

'Totally TFC,' Kate said.

'TFC?' asked her mother.

Father and daughter said the words in unison: 'That's a Fucking Coincidence.'

'Charming,' Jean said, straightening the blanket she had over her frail legs.

'The riots will keep everyone occupied for months,' Smithdown continued. 'Years even. There'll be inquiries and recommendations and all sorts. It was absolute carnage last night.' Smithdown rubbed his elbow - he hadn't told them that he'd been hit by a car. No need to add to their worries. 'Yet it all felt a bit... orchestrated. Richard T. King seemed well prepared - I'll give him that. No one got near his place. Plus, I saw Maureen Lennon's lad Tom filming it all last night too. The big bastard who works at King's club. Absolutely bizarre. But he was only interested in filming the Asian lads.'

'Maureen Lennon's lad?' Jean said. 'Not seen her for years. I hear she's not been so well.'

'I presume you've spoken to Tom about Naomi Wells?' Kate asked.

'Why would I do that?' her father said.

'Because she used to knock around with him before she hooked up with Jimmy Todd.'

'I don't know why I bother sending DCs out to do house

to house enquiries, I should just get them to ask you. Go on then…'

'I told you she was "Party Girl Number One" - they say it was her who first brought E up from Manchester.'

'E? Oh ecstasy - that's what we're calling it now, is it? I'll let the drugs squad know. When did they split up?'

'Start of the year, I think.'

'Any idea why?' the detective asked his daughter.

'Because Tom found out she was mixed race. And that's a no-no as far as he's concerned.'

Smithdown looked at his wife. She'd dozed off. He dropped his voice to a whisper: 'That's nice. He's got no record, I've checked, but the more I find out about this lad, the more I don't like him. Maybe I should go and pay him a visit. I don't suppose you know where he lives, do you?'

'As it happens, I do,' Kate replied, also whispering. 'I'll tell you if you let me come too.'

'Why the hell would I do that?'

'I need a good story for when I leave uni. A calling card to help get me a job. This could be it.'

'You're not coming along. No chance.'

'Then I'm not telling you where he lives.'

'Fucking Nora,' Smithdown sighed, then turned to see the other patients and their families staring at them. 'Sorry,' he mouthed.

CHAPTER TWENTY-TWO

4.35pm Sunday 3 April 1988

'I thought you knew Tom's mum?' Kate asked as they headed back into Oldham after dropping Jean Smithdown off at home and making sure she was comfortable. She was immediately suspicious about her normally warring husband and daughter going out together but had been too tired to ask too many questions.

'From years ago, yes,' the detective said. 'Schooldays. It's that weird thing of knowing someone yet not really knowing them. I'd often say to Tom: Say hello to your mum. It's just one of those things you come out with, isn't it?

'Why don't you ask her where he lives?'

'Like your mum says, she's not so well. Cancer. Like mum. But her's is terminal I believe. She's in a hospice.'

'Christ, I fucking hate cancer, Dad.'

'I fucking hate cancer too, love.'

On his daughter's instruction, Smithdown turned his car into a terraced street. It was bustling with activity: people chatting on doorsteps, going in and out of each other's two-up two-down houses, pushing prams down the street, small groups of residents standing in groups. *Proper community this, makes a change, these days.* In his heart, he knew there were plenty of officers at the police station that would view this part of Oldham very differently. He loved being a policeman, but he hated some of the words and attitudes he heard in the station. The language some of them used about the South Asian community made his skin crawl.

Smithdown pointed at an end terrace that led to a local green space known as Snipe Clough. 'Do I take it that's Tom's house?'

'It is,' his daughter confirmed. 'How did you guess?'

Lennon's house had metal grills covering both windows, upstairs and down. Underneath each window was draped a flag of St George. The front door had been painted white with a red cross - it was also protected by a metal grille. 'I thought all that bollocks had died a death,' Smithdown said to his daughter.

~

The mill towns around Manchester had seen wave after wave of interest from Far-Right political groups over the years. They'd rise. Then fall. The National Front - seemingly so powerful and dangerous in the 1970s - had worn itself out with ideological infighting and then split into two. The British National Party had emerged as the dominant force. Smithdown remembered seeing their first march in 1982 on the news; it was on St George's Day. *Of course it was.* The following year they'd had enough of a surge to warrant a Party Political Broadcast on TV.

'I see these twats are back again,' Smithdown had commented to his wife, before she'd told him off for swearing in front of Kate.

'Dad's right though Mum,' Kate had replied, 'they are twats.'

Rise.

Then fall.

By 1987 the BNP had decided to sit out the General Election. Their influence seemed to be on the wane, but the attitudes still bubbled under. There'd been talk - second hand, sometimes third - that officers from Oldham Police had links to some of the parties. If that was true, then they'd been very careful to hide their tracks. If Smithdown had found any evidence he'd have reported them in an instant.

~

In the meantime, here was Tom Lennon; claiming he'd been

attacked by a South Asian gang, filming South Asian rioters and sending it to TV stations, dumping a girl after he'd found out she was mixed-race whose body parts start appearing in lakes. Tom Lennon, with his house festooned with English flags, on an almost entirely South Asian street, three weeks before St George's Day.

DI Smithdown's desire to talk to Lennon had just gone up another notch. 'That's weird,' said Kate, staring at the house as they pulled up outside. 'It wasn't like this last time I was here.'

'Can I ask, what exactly were you doing here, last time you came?' Smithdown said as he rang the doorbell next to the metal door grille. The small terraces on the street had no driveways or footpaths - only a small red step separated the doors from the street.

'What's that supposed to mean?' Kate said. 'I'm not supposed to come here because it's a South Asian area? One of my best mates at school lives across the road. Just because the police don't come around here, doesn't mean the rest of us can't.'

'I didn't mean that - and it's not true by the way - I meant what were you doing at Tom Lennon's house?'

Before Kate could answer, the white and red inner wooden door was opened. Smithdown recognised the blotchy face immediately. 'Ah, Mr Hitchcock,' the detective said, speaking through the metalwork. 'Fancy meeting you here. You're a home help now as well as a film director. Well done. Is Tom in please?'

'Nope,' the young man said, itching his neck and yawning. 'He's elsewhere.'

'I see. Sorry, what's your actual name? And think on - if you give me the name of the "Master of Suspense" again, I'll do you.'

The young man hesitated for a moment. 'Griffin. Adam Griffin. Pleased to meet you.' He looked at Kate. 'And you. Especially you.'

Smithdown made a point of finding his notebook, finding

a fresh page and then writing down the name Adam Griffin… laboriously checking the spelling too. He looked over Griffin's shoulder; the house had bare floorboards and no wallpaper. There were cardboard boxes piled up in the hallway and all the way up the stairs. 'I know you,' the detective said. 'I've got a very good memory for suspicious-looking fuckers. Almost perfect, in fact.'

'Well, I sometimes work at Kingdom if they're short,' Griffin replied. 'I know you like hanging about there.'

'Nope, that's not it,' Smithdown persevered. 'Where do I know you from? It'll come to me...'

'I mean, this is fascinating, obviously…'

'Hospital! You work at the Royal Oldham Hospital, don't you?'

Griffin's cocksure persona dimmed a little. 'Yes, I do. I'm a porter. Well done. Quite the gift you have there. Anyway, if that's everything…'

Smithdown waved a finger side-to-side, informing him that he hadn't finished yet. 'I see your footage made Granada Reports yesterday,' the detective said. 'Thank goodness you were there to record things. Very civic minded of you. A cynic might think you were deliberately shit-stirring, but luckily I'm a very charitable sort of person.'

'So I'd heard,' Griffin said, again looking at Kate.

'Could we come in and wait?' she said, staring right back at him. *I'm the police officer here, thank you Kate.*

'Ordinarily, I'd have you in as quick as a flash,' Griffin grinned. 'But it's not my place. Sorry. Maybe come back another time?'

'Definitely,' confirmed Smithdown. 'Can I ask where you were between 9.30 and 10.30 on the evening of Friday the 1st of April. A teenage boy was attacked quite near here - Mustafizur Rahman. He was hit with a machete and beaten with baseball bats. Loads of them.' Smithdown took a very deliberate look over Griffin's shoulder at the boxes in the hallway.

'So I believe,' Griffin replied. 'Pakistani lads did over a

Bengali I hear. Nasty business. I was here all evening, just relaxing with Tom. Watching videos, chatting. That kind of thing. Nice quiet night in.'

'All night?' the detective asked.

'All night.'

'Sounds idyllic,' Smithdown said. 'Can I leave you my number, so Tom can give me a ring?'

'Of course. I'll make sure he gets it.'

'If I don't hear from him, maybe I'll come down to Kingdom and find him. Maybe see you, as well?'

'Be lovely to see you,' Griffin said. 'We'll get the DJ to play you a request. Something appropriate.'

'That's be nice. Do you like pub rock?'

'What?' asked Griffin.

The detective leant in, pressed his face between the bars so his nose stuck through and spoke to Griffin as if he was stupid: 'Do you like pub rock? I do. I love it. How about *Police Car* by Larry Wallis? Do you know it? "I sit in the shadows waiting for a fight…" Crackin' tune. See you later…' he looked at his pad again, '… Mr Adam Griffin.' Smithdown tapped his pad on the metal bars. Then he and his daughter walked back to their car.

'Are you normally that melodramatic?' Kate asked.

'When required, yes,' her father replied, opening his car. 'What a little turd.'

'Absolute skin crawler. Never seen him before. Did you clock the house? All those boxes?'

'I did. You were about to tell me about how you ended up at Tom Lennon's.'

'Was I?'

'Yes, you were.'

'We were out clubbing last year,' Kate said, reluctantly. 'He offered me a a lift. We stopped off at his house to get something. Didn't invite me in. Off we went, then true to his word, he dropped me off at ours - said he was off up to the hills going camping or some such outdoor bollocks. Nothing happened. Don't get all weird about it.'

'I'm your dad. It's my job to get all weird about things like that. So, no indication he was going off the deep end - with all the Nationalist stuff?'

'He seemed perfectly normal last year. Until he finished with Naomi.'

'Because she was mixed race?'

'That's what I'd heard.'

'You never mentioned it.'

'If I was to tell you about every time I met a racist in Oldham, Dad, I wouldn't have time to do anything else.'

'Point taken.'

'Maybe that's my story for my uni course,' she said. 'About how this town is divided with parallel communities. Whites. Bengalis. Pakistanis. All the fear and suspicion and how it changes people.'

'Tall order,' Smithdown said. 'Stay well away from him in the meantime, okay?'

'Okay.'

'Promise?'

'Promise.'

They got in the car and were quiet for a moment. 'Dad?' Kate asked. 'Is Mum going to be okay?'

'I don't know, Kate. I wish I did. But I don't. Shall I drop you in town?'

'Yeah - I want to see the damage for myself.'

Smithdown opened the glove compartment and rifled through the cassettes.

'Do we have to listen to bloody pub rock?' his daughter groaned.

'Yes. We do,' he replied, fast-forwarding the *Live Stiffs Live* album until he found '*Police Car*' by Larry Wallis.

'Manchester Radio News at five - this is Beth Hall. Council officials say Oldham will need a multimillion-pound re-building programme after rioter's wreaked havoc in the town centre overnight. Many businesses remain closed after rival gangs of Asian youths took over the town last night, fighting with police - and each other - over the course of several hours. But at least one businessman has vowed he WILL be open tonight, in defiance of the rioters. Robert Crane has more.'

'As the clean-up continues and community leaders call for calm, the true cost of the violence is now becoming clear. Insurance assessors have given police and local councillors a provisional report - it's thought that the repair bill will run into tens of millions of pounds. Not to mention the loss of income for businesses that cannot, or will not, re-open today.

Meanwhile Oldham entrepreneur Richard T. King - owner of the Kingdom nightclub - says he definitely plans to open his doors this evening. Mr King wants the gangs to know that he won't be beaten:'

> *"What happened last night was terrible for Oldham, terrible for the town centre and terrible for the way we're seen in the wider community. We don't normally open on a Sunday, but it's a Bank Holiday and we're going to make an exception. In fact, we're going to make a point of opening. To stay shut would be like saying that the rioters have won. So, our doors will be open tonight. We won't let them win."*

'Tomorrow, assessors will turn their attention to the Glodwick area, where several roads were badly damaged by firebombs. It's now thought that many houses, possible even entire streets, will have to be demolished after the riots. Robert Crane, Manchester Radio News, Oldham.'

CHAPTER TWENTY-THREE

5.05pm Sunday 3 April 1988

Smithdown was planning on popping into work and going straight out again but the sound of loud voices from DS Pym's office caught his attention. He changed direction and casually walked past.

Sitting on the edge of Pym's desk, looking at a framed photo of the DS with Chief Constable James Anderton, was Peter Jeffries, Member of Parliament for Oldham North. The Conservative MP was, in Smithdown's opinion, someone to approach with extreme caution. A notorious self-publicist, Jeffries had carved himself a niche as a populist show off, always available to the press if some rent-a-quote outrage about society's latest turn for the worse was required. His apparent fascination with child abuse - he had a weekly column in a Sunday tabloid which he regularly used to sound off on the subject - had earned him the nickname "Paedo Pete." Despite this - or more likely because of it - the people of Oldham seemed to love him. The fact that the town wasn't a traditional Tory heartland didn't seem to matter, the voters of Oldham normally returned Jeffries election after election with a thumping majority. Until last year, that is. He'd won comfortably by most politician's standards, but his majority had been reduced dramatically. The local paper - the *Oldham Messenger* - had been running a series of editorials about the MP, saying he'd lost touch with the issues the town cared about: jobs, housing, unemployment, hospital waiting lists.

Dressed in his usual slightly-too-tight three-piece suit and sporting a "three glasses of wine at lunch" complexion, Jeffries was holding forth to DS Pym and to Bob Donaldson. All three had drinks in their hands. Pym looked annoyed when Smithdown appeared at the doorway.

'John, Mr Jeffries is here to talk about Councillor Chowdhury, one of our missing-from-homes. Her colleagues are very concerned about her. Mr Jeffries here has taken an interest in the matter - she's a C onservative councillor - and wants to know what we're doing about it. I've asked DC Donaldson to oversee the investigation. I was updating Mr Jeffries about all the other matters that are keeping you busy this Bank Holiday weekend.'

Jeffries stuck out his hand and gave Smithdown a ludicrously firm handshake. 'Of course,' Smithdown said. 'It's very worrying. There's so much going on in this town right now, Mr Jeffries, none of it good.'

'It's like there's something in the water,' Jeffries said, his manner theatrical and showy. 'Utter madness. And now this. You know, it's only people like Councillor Chowdhury who keep this town from tipping right over the edge. She's a real public servant, Mr Smithdown. With all the trouble last night, you can understand why we're so concerned about her.'

'As I say, DC Donaldson will be dealing with it,' offered DS Pym.

'Sorry Bob,' Smithdown said. 'Don't mean to tread on your toes.'

DC Donaldson raised his open palms in a 'it's nothing to do with me' gesture. 'What can you tell me about her?' Smithdown asked, ignoring DS Pym.

'Well,' the MP said. 'She has no family in Oldham. She's from Leicester. She isn't married. Work, work, work that's all she does. When she didn't appear at the council offices on Thursday, that's when people became concerned. Totally out of character. She practically lives at the Town Hall.'

'What does she do at the council, Mr Jeffries. Sorry, local politics isn't my strong point.'

Pym tried to interrupt again: 'John, I'm sure you've other

things to occupy yourself with other than a missing person...'

'She represents the Coldhurst ward,' Jeffries continued. 'She's also Chair of the Scrutiny Committee. She makes sure things are done by the book. You've got to keep an eye on these councils Mr Smithdown. Regardless of their political colours, everyone needs to be accountable. And that's what she does. In spades.'

'Could that be connected with her disappearance, do you think?' Smithdown asked.

'We're right across this now, John, thanks,' said Pym. 'I've assured Mr Jeffries that we'll stop at nothing to trace Ms Chowdhury's whereabouts. Bob will be reporting directly to me. I'm taking personal charge of the matter now. I just thought it was a courtesy to let you know.'

Classic Pym. Like flies around shit if there's some sucking up to be done. He'll make Assistant Chief Constable yet.

Still ignoring the DS and his reassurances, Smithdown kept his attention on the MP. 'Is she popular within the council?'

'Oh, our lot think she's wonderful,' Jeffries replied. 'She's an absolute workhorse. It's traditional to have an opposition councillor as head of scrutiny. It keeps the Labour lot on their toes and avoids any whiff of cronyism.'

'How was she seen within the community?'

'Which one? There are many, many communities in Oldham, Mr Smithdown.'

'Any of them,' Smithdown said. 'All of them.'

'John, I think you've taken up enough of Mr Jeffries' time,' DS Pym interjected.

'No Jim, it's fine,' the MP stated. 'Good to talk these things through. Get a fresh perspective. Like I say, the Tories loved her. Nothing got past her. The Labour and Liberal lot begrudgingly respected her. Within the Bangladeshi community she was seen as a role model. The business community thought that she was too harsh on them.'

'Any issues with her race?'

'Oh yes. The usual crowd thought she was an uppity Asian gobshite who had ideas above her station.'

'Which usual crowd?'

'Mr Smithdown,' Jeffries said, putting his glass down. 'I shouldn't have to be telling an officer of Oldham Police that the Far-Right is on the rise in this town. They've been licking their wounds, lying low, but they're re-charging their batteries. Going legit. They've got their sights on winning Council seats. Maybe even getting places in the European Parliament. Quite easy to sneak in and win elections that hardly anyone votes in. We've got to be vigilant, Detective Inspector. History teaches us that. I wrote a piece for the *News of the World* about it the other week. You should read it.'

'Yes. I probably should.'

'And you should probably also get on your way, John,' interrupted DS Pym once again. 'I promised to introduce Mr Jeffries to some of the Tactical Aid Group officers who proved so effective the other night.'

'Of course. Nice meeting you, Mr Jeffries.'

The MP crunched the detective's hand and gave him a business card. 'Give me a call if I can be of help, Mr Smithdown.'

'I will. Thank you.'

'What's your next move, John?' DS Pym asked, clearly annoyed.

'Think I'll grab a bite to eat. And then go clubbing.'

CHAPTER TWENTY-FOUR

7.45pm Sunday 3 April 1988

Many police officers based in Oldham liked to drink and unwind at the private bar and social club situated on the top floor of the police station. It was called, somewhat unimaginatively, The Bar. Smithdown had gone off the place since the Oldham Borough Force had merged into Greater Manchester Police in 1974 and the licensing hours had become a little less flexible than he'd liked.

Other officers preferred the somewhat better-named Old Bill bar and restaurant at the side of the police station - the interior was decked out with police memorabilia. Some ventured across the pedestrianised shopping area outside the station to the Three Tunnes, a straightforward town centre pub favoured by the uniformed officers and civilian support staff.

All of these places had one key drawback for John Smithdown: there were too many cops in them. He preferred his own company - or at least that of people who didn't talk about police work all the time - so he preferred to drink in The Raj restaurant just up the hill.

Most of Smithdown's colleagues knew this, so they tended to avoid the place, unless it was to pick up a takeaway and give the detective a quick nod. Kate Smithdown also knew her dad liked to drink at The Raj, so that's why she headed there.

The front window had a shatter mark in it and was being held together with tape - other than that it was business as usual. 'Pint of lager please,' Kate said, pulling up the one remaining high stool so she could sit next to her father at the tiny bar.

'Aren't halves a bit more ladylike?' her father asked.

'Fine, I'll order two halves then.'

'Hilarious. Pint of lager and another bitter for me.'

The drinks arrived. Smithdown sipped his and took a handful of Bombay Mix from a bowl placed next to his pint. He offered some to his daughter: 'No thanks,' she replied. 'I don't want to deprive you of your evening meal.'

'Very gracious of you,' Smithdown replied, saluting his daughter with his pint.

'This is a restaurant you know,' she pointed out. 'You could order some actual food.'

'Not hungry. Maybe later.'

'What's on your mind, Dad?'

'Everything. Everything is on my mind. How about that?'

'Come on. Might work with Bob and the lads at the station this, but it doesn't work with me.'

Smithdown pushed the last of the Bombay Mix around the bottom of the bowl with his index finger. 'I've just been given a lesson in things-I-should-have-been-aware-of by Peter Jeffries. Peter Fucking Jeffries! The Member of Parliament for Self-Promotion. The guy everyone dismisses as a buffoon knows more about what's really going on in this town than the cops do. We should have been across this Far-Right, neo-Nazi stuff but we've missed it by a mile. I feel embarrassed about how little I know about the different communities in this town. Just because I'm matey with Mr Aleem so I feel like I'm doing my bit. It's all bollocks. I know nowt. And what's worse, I believe there's cops in that police station who are out and out racists and that's a disgrace.'

'You're doing your best, Dad.'

'No, I'm not. I'm doing enough to get by. Enough to keep up appearances. It's not on.'

They were quiet for a moment. Father and daughter, drinking at the tiny bar of a restaurant with a smashed window. 'So, what's the plan?' Kate asked.

'I need to find Tom Lennon. And you need to go home.'

CHAPTER TWENTY-FIVE

11.15pm Sunday 3 April 1988

Walking into the Kingdom club to the clicks and pulses of '*151*' by Armando, Smithdown noted that security was considerably tighter than the last time he'd visited. There seemed to be at least twice as many shaven-headed young men dressed in black outside as well as in. The detective quickly tired of getting a shake of the head and a shrug from the security staff as he asked: where's Tom Lennon? Plus, the noise level as he entered the main body of the club was so intense, he could barely hear anyway. So, he thought he'd head straight for Richard T. King's office instead.

He got as far as the end of the bar when he noticed that King wasn't in his office, he was in the main body of the club. Dressed in a baggy, psychedelic hooded top and very roomy jeans, he was standing by a plastic bin filled with ice and bottled water. King was handing the bottles out to the young clubbers. One, a young woman about the same age as Kate Smithdown, touched King's face and smiled at him. She stood for a moment and stared at the bottle, then danced away, shaking her head as if the gift was the single greatest act of generosity the world had ever seen.

The thunderous volume meant it was easier for the detective to mime at King rather than attempt to speak. He pointed to the nightclub owner, pointed to himself, made a talking motion with his hand and pointed upstairs. King smiled; he touched a bouncer on the shoulder, pointed to the water, then at the crowded dance floor. He then indicated that Smithdown should follow him.

Adam Griffin was already in King's office, standing almost

to attention as if he'd been expecting them. 'Good evening Adam', Smithdown said as he passed. 'Lovely to see you earlier. Hope that house is spic and span.' The young man scratched at his face and silently mouthed 'fuck off' at the detective. Smithdown pulled a face at Griffin as if he was mortally offended, then winked at him.

'Water, Mr Smithdown?' King asked.

'I will, thank you. It's baking in here.'

King tossed a bottle to him and Smithdown drank half of it in one go. 'You're giving it away, I see. Not like you.'

'Well I'm concerned about what some of these kids could have taken before they arrive in my club,' King said, taking a seat behind his floating table. 'There's a lot of ecstasy about, no one knows where it's coming from and it can cause severe dehydration. Although, ironically, we can't be handing out too much water because over-hydrating can cause brain damage, apparently. You can't win, can you? Anyway, I've put my admission charge up to cover any costs, so don't feel too sorry for me.'

'I wasn't planning to. Down to business then. Tom Lennon - I want him. Where is he?'

'He's on a rest day,' King said in a helpful voice. 'Do you know Mr Smithdown, that guy gave his all protecting this place during the riots. Literally put his life on the line. So, he's taking a well-earned break.'

'I've been to his house and the only person there was Syd Little here,' Smithdown sighed, nodding towards Griffin, who held his ribs and silently mimed uproarious laughter, before his face dropped to a blank canvas again.

'Why so keen to track down Tom, may I ask?' King said.

'I want to talk to him about Naomi Wells.'

'All stowed away that case, isn't it?' asked King, casually rubbing an invisible mark off his snow-white trainers that now rested on the suspended desk.

'There's a few blanks I'd still like to fill in,' replied the detective, resisting the urge to give the desk a good kick.

'Jimmy Todd's the only person who could do that, I fear,'

said King. 'And he decided to take the other route. The thought of suicide is a powerful solace, Mr Smithdown.' He left a few beats of silence. The bwomp-bwomp of the music downstairs filled the space. 'Nietzsche,' King added.

'Tell Lennon to present himself to Oldham police station, Mr King,' replied the detective. 'Or I'll close you down until he does.' A pause. 'And that's a direct quote from me. Same goes for you, Little Ern,' he added, giving the side of Griffin's face two gentle taps as he passed. 'Front desk by 10am. Clear?'

'Absolutely,' King responded. 'Thank you so much for coming.'

As Smithdown left the office, another one of the seemingly interchangeable security staff passed him on the stairs: shaved head, black clothes, powerful build, just like all the others. He smiled at the detective, adding a cheery wink too. *Don't know what you're so jolly about - you'll be out of a job tomorrow.*

King and Griffin waited until they heard Smithdown clear the stairs and open the door to the dancefloor, momentarily increasing the noise level ten-fold. The door closed and the noise dropped.

'I will fookin' do that cunt,' Griffin said. 'Swear to God.'

The bouncer who'd passed Smithdown on the stairs spoke. He was still smiling. 'His daughter's in.'

'Whaaaat?' Griffin said, clapping his hands. 'The little brunette. Serious? Oh man!'

'She arrived a few minutes ago asking for Tom. Says she wants to interview him for a journalism project. I don't think Columbo there knows she's here. She even asked if her dad had been in.'

'Fook me!' added Griffin, raising his fists as if he'd just scored a winning goal. 'I mean seriously, fookin' fook me.'

'Perfect,' said King, taking a bottle of water from a small metal filing cabinet near his desk and tossing it to Griffin. 'Just perfect.'

CHAPTER TWENTY-SIX

1.25 am Monday 4 April 1988

Smithdown was at home when he got the call that Kate had been taken to hospital. He was just sitting quietly with his wife, holding her hand as they read and listened to a radio phone-in show when DC Bob Donaldson rang.

'Boss. Is Jean there?' the DC asked.

'Yes,' Smithdown replied. *That's an odd question, even by your standards, Bob.*

'Take the call in another room, will you?' the DC asked.

'Okay.' He went through to the hall then asked his wife to put the receiver down when he'd picked up the extension, making it seem like he didn't want to disturb her listening. The radio host - James Stannage - was taking a caller to task about his opinions on repatriation after the weekend riots. Smithdown waited for the sound of the other line being closed until he spoke: 'I'm here, Bob.'

'Right. Straight to it. Kate's in the Royal and she's in a bad way. She was taken in after being found collapsed in the street.'

'Christ Almighty. Where?'

'Outside Kingdom in the town centre. They think its ecstasy-related.'

'No fucking chance,' Smithdown responded, manging to shout and whisper at the same time. 'Absolutely. No. Fucking. Chance. That's not Kate. We both know that.'

'All I know is you better get down to the Royal quicksticks,' Donaldson said. 'I'm sorry, boss. I really am.'

Jean Smithdown was so used to her husband getting late night phone calls and slipping out of the house that she didn't question why he was putting on his shoes and coat. She just asked him to take care. 'I will,' he replied.

With no thought to speed limits, one-way systems or red lights, Smithdown was at the Royal Oldham Hospital within 20 minutes. He left his car on a space reserved for doctors, found out where Kate was from a receptionist in double-quick time by flashing his warrant card and headed straight to the ward she'd been taken to. He grabbed - literally grabbed - the first doctor he came across: 'Smithdown. Katherine Mary. Date of birth: ninth of November '67. Brought in after a suspected drug overdose. I need an update. Can you give it to me? If you can't, then I need you to take me to someone who can. Right now.'

'She's in ICU,' the doctor said. He looked so young to Smithdown's eyes. The detective had to gulp in air to stop the overwhelming need to cry. *Not my girl. Not my Kate. Not you, too.*

'What can you tell me?' asked the detective. 'I'm her dad but I'm also a police officer - a crime may well have been committed here.'

'She was brought in unconscious,' the doctor said. He had a similar haircut to Jimmy Todd - same blonde good looks. 'Temperature and blood pressure were sky high. Seen a few like this in recent months - looks like MDMA overdose. Ecstasy. Probably laced with LSD too for a bit of added bite. She'd been drinking too, so that didn't help. Quite the mixture. She has a swelling on the brain - looks like she worked out what was happening to her and was trying to counteract the dehydration that comes with ecstasy by drinking a huge amount of water. Too much water, as it happens. The water did as much harm as anything. You know that old tale that you can die by drinking too much water? It's true.'

'You know what I'm going to ask…'

'Is she going to be okay? I don't know. I'm sorry I can't be more positive. We're bringing her temperature down and the swelling seems to be subsiding - but I really can't say yet. We're still feeling our way with MDMA but it's fair to say she had enough in her system to stop a double-decker bus. She's very lucky. Tough girl.'

'When can I see her?' Smithdown asked.

'Soon. Wait here. I know it's frustrating but bear with us for a little while.'

'Okay. Sure. I understand. Please let me know as soon as you can. Thank you.'

Smithdown sat down in the waiting area and saw a young girl about Kate's age in the chair opposite him. She was wearing dayglo, baggy clothes and her hair was in two high bunches on her head. She was quietly crying. It took him a few moments to recognise her: 'Sandra? Christ, I didn't recognise you.'

Sandra Charles was a girl from Kate's school. The detective hadn't seen her for several years and still had a mental image of her as a ten-year-old at Kate's birthday party. He'd always made sure that, despite his job, he'd never missed any key moments in his daughter's life. *Looks like you've got yourself another key moment right here, John lad.*

She caught the detective's eye; for the briefest moment he thought she was going to run away. But she didn't. She stayed still, shook her head and wept. Harder this time.

Smithdown crossed over to the chair next to hers, put an arm around her and was about to say a few comforting when she spoke first: 'Oh, Mr Smithdown, I'm so sorry. So very, very sorry. You've got to believe me, nothing happened. She did nowt wrong. We'd just had a few drinks, that's all. A few pints, I swear to God. You've got to believe me.'

The detective held her as close as the scooped back plastic chairs would allow.' Of course I believe you Sandra. It's okay. Trust me. Everything will be alright. But you've got to tell me exactly what happened. Don't leave anything out, even the tiniest detail. Not a single thing, do you understand?'

Sandra wiped her eyes with the back of her hand. A smear of glitter was left behind. Smithdown pulled a small packet of Handy Andy tissues from his pocket - he nearly always carried them - split the cellophane wrapping and gave Sandra several sheets. 'Everything. You must tell me everything. Okay?'

She nodded. 'We went to the Turn of Luck. The damage from all the trouble was still pretty noticeable but they were open. She was asking people questions about the riot and the trouble they'd had. We had two drinks - two, I swear. Then she said she wanted to go to Kingdom. They were having a Ravers Versus Rioters night. Never misses a trick that Richard T. King, does he? Anyhow, she wanted to talk to Tom Lennon about...

'Christ Almighty, she promised me she'd stay away from him,' Smithdown interrupted. 'Sorry, love. Carry on.'

'Tom's gone proper weird since his mam got cancer, draping his house in flags. Dumping that girl... the dead girl... when he found out she was mixed-race. Filming stuff around town. Kate thinks he got it in his head that his mam would have been treated quicker if they weren't so many Asian people in front of her on the waiting list. Pretty out-there shit. Sorry, Mr Smithdown. I know Kate's mum is proper poorly with cancer too.'

'Yet, strangely enough, we aren't draping our house in the flag of St George,' Smithdown pointed out. 'It's bollocks, love. It was bollocks in the 70s and its bollocks now. What else?'

'So, she wanted to talk to Tom and sure enough he was at Kingdom...'

Fucking Nora.

'... but not on the door. He wasn't in uniform, neither. He was just hanging about, handing out water. It was baking in the club last night. Absolutely sweltering. The radiators were on full blast too.'

'Go on.'

'They talked. That was it. He didn't seem to want to know. He was smiling, like it was all a big joke. Like what she was saying was the daftest thing in the whole world. Then he left. We stayed in the club and talked a bit, then that's when Kate started... whooshing.'

'How do you mean, whooshing?'

'She went to the toilet and she said… Sorry. It's a bit embarrassing.'

'Please. Tell me.'

'She told me she'd just had the best shit she'd ever had. Sorry Mr Smithdown. Such a weird thing to say, but that's what she said. The best ever. Then she kept saying… I feel like I'm whooshing. I'm coming up. I'm really whooshing. She was grinding her teeth - her jaw was jittering so much she pressed her head against the wall of the club to stop it from going side to side. When she started hugging people and crying and telling me how much she loved me, that's when we figured she'd been spiked. She was panicking then; necking water like there's no tomorrow, frightened she was going to die of dehydration. She'd researched it for uni. She was burning up. That's when we went outside and called an ambulance from a phone box. She'd made me carry a load more water out with us. Bottles and bottles of it. She went unconscious just before the ambulance arrived. And that's it. I heard the doctor say he didn't know if she's going to make it. They wouldn't tell me owt. Oh, Mr Smithdown. This is mad.'

'It is, Sandra,' the detective conceded. 'It really is. I'm sorry to keep asking questions…'

'It's fine, honestly.'

'Did you drink anything else in the club? Another few pints?'

'No, just water.'

'Did you leave the drinks unattended?'

'No. They were in our hands the whole time.'

'Was the water identical?'

'Yes. I think so. I don't know. Oh God, I'm not sure. We both got them from Tom Lennon. I didn't really check. I'm sorry. It was so hot. It was just water.'

'Looks like it was a bit more than just water, love.'

'But we both drank it Mr Smithdown. How come I'm okay?'

'Because fortunately for you, Sandra, you're not my

daughter. This was targeted against my Kate - they used those drugs like a weapon against her.'

'She was just asking questions, Mr Smithdown. For her uni project! Why would someone dose her just for that?'

Smithdown squeezed the girl tightly. 'Because this town is going mad, love. That's why. Absolutely mad.'

'Manchester Radio News at eight, this is Beth Hall, good morning. A young woman is fighting for her life in hospital after being found unconscious in Oldham Town centre. The 20-year-old, who hasn't yet been named, is thought to have collapsed after taking the drug ecstasy. Robert Crane has more.'

'An ambulance was called to the scene at just before midnight after a friend of the woman raised the alarm.

They found the 20-year-old in the street close to the Kingdom nightclub, though a spokesman for the club says they believe that neither of the women had actually visited the nightspot.

She was treated first at the scene and then taken to the Royal Oldham Hospital, where she's believed to be in an induced coma.

It's thought that she may have taken the drug ecstasy, which is becoming increasing popular among revellers involved in the dance music scene in clubs across Greater Manchester.

If toxicology tests show that she did take ecstasy, it could prove to be the first case of its kind in the Oldham area. Robert Crane, Manchester Radio News at the Royal Oldham hospital.'

CHAPTER TWENTY-SEVEN

9.10 am Monday 4 April 1988

Smithdown slept in Kate's room until a new doctor came on shift. He quizzed the doctor relentlessly about his daughter's condition *no change… a good sign… keep hoping for the best* then he headed for Oldham Police Station.

Officers and support staff quietly gave him their best wishes, shared their hope that everything was going to be alright or just placed a hand on his shoulder as he passed them. He acknowledged each with a thin smile or a nod of the head as headed for DS James Pym's office. He went straight in, closed the door and sat down without being asked. His lit up a cigarette, despite knowing that Pym didn't care for smoking in his office. 'John, I'm very sorry to hear about what happened to Kate. We've made sure her name has been withheld from the press. In the meantime, if there's anything we can do…'

'I want to raid the Kingdom nightclub and Tom Lennon's house as soon as possible,' Smithdown said, staring out of the window at the ring road traffic. 'Simultaneously, obviously, so word doesn't get out. They dosed my daughter with ecstasy, used it as a weapon just as much as someone used machetes against Mr Aleem and Mustafizur Rahman, that lad over at Coldhurst. I want Lennon in custody before lunchtime. I want to question him about what happened to Kate and about all the other shit that's been stirred up around here over the last few days.'

'John, there's no way I can allow you to do that,' Pym said.

'There's no evidence that Lennon's involved. There'll be a dozen members of staff at Kingdom who'll swear blind he wasn't even there last night. Even if we arrested him, your involvement will have his brief rubbing his hands with glee. Lennon would be out before teatime. I'll get a different team to look at what happened with Kate, but it can't be you. It's got to be separate.'

'That's what they want, Jim,' Smithdown responded, quietly. 'Separate everything. Different teams looking at different things. A murder here. Maybe another there. The machete attacks, the riots, that missing councillor. Our lot scurrying around on different treadmills instead of seeing the bigger picture. Everything smells like Tom Lennon and he's away somewhere laughing at us. Laughing at what he did to my Kate.'

'John, I know you're upset. I totally understand. But I need you as far away from this as possible. You shouldn't even be here. You've barely slept since Thursday. Kate needs you. Jean needs you. Go home.'

'No. You don't see it do you? It's more than my Kate. More even than the machete attacks and the riots. It's bigger than all the parts put together, Jim… and Tom Lennon is at the fucking heart of it. Christ Jim, he tried to kill my girl…'

'You cannot be involved in any investigation into what happened to your daughter while you're still on this force, John,' the DS stated. 'It's as simple as that.'

The detective continued to look out of the window. Then, without a word he got up and left Pym's office. He headed straight for the photographic unit. The red light was on outside the dark room; the detective ignored it and walked in. The bright white harshness of the fluorescent strip lights in the corridor flooded the dark room, cancelling out the dim red glow in the tiny room and getting an immediate reaction from Paul Rees. 'Fuck me! The red light's on! No fucking entry, it says so on the bastard door,' the photographer shouted.

Smithdown put a hand on the photographer's slim shoulder and led him out of the darkroom as if he was being arrested.

'Sorry Paul. I need you. Now.'

'What do you want, Mr Smithdown?' the photographer said, rubbing his eyes as they adjusted to the shift in brightness.

'I want you to tell the truth, lad. Nothing but. Trust me. It'll be right.'

Smithdown led Rees up the stairs and back to Pym's office. 'Right Paul. Take a seat. I want you to tell Detective Superintendent Pym here exactly what happened the other night - just before you photographed the domestic injuries on that young girl. Do you remember? Dark hair? She was called Becky Wells. Little thing with plastic sandals on.'

'Yes, I remember her,' Rees said, speaking cautiously, clearly concerned he was about to do wrong whichever way this went.

'Tell Mr Pym what happened,' Smithdown said reassuringly. He was looking straight at the DS as he spoke.

'I really don't know what I'm supposed to say…'

'Just tell him,' Paul. 'It'll be fine. I promise.'

Still wary, Rees began to speak: 'Mr Smithdown asked me to snap the little girl's injuries. She'd been in some sort of incident at home. Mum's boyfriend I believe, the guy who topped himself in Strangeways.'

'That's right Paul,' coaxed Smithdown. 'I did ask you that, didn't I? How would you describe her injuries?'

'She'd been knocked about a bit, that's for sure. Bit of bruising…' Paul hesitated for a moment.'

'Go on,' the detective encouraged.

'Split lip. She had a split lip.'

'And what did I ask you to do before you took the snaps, Paul?'

The photographer looked back and forth between the two detectives, baffled as to what to say next. 'Mr Smithdown, I don't understand.'

'It's fine, Paul. What did I ask you to do?'

'You asked me to turn around and look at the wall, Mr Smithdown.'

'I did. But you sneaked a peek, didn't you? It's okay. Tell the truth, that's all I'm asking.'

A pause. 'Yes. I did.'

'And what did you see, Paul?'

'Mr Smithdown, please…'

'Paul. It's very important that you tell DS Pym exactly what you saw.'

'I saw you pull the girl's lip open to make it worse,' Rees said, quietly. 'There was blood everywhere.'

'Christ Almighty,' sighed DS Pym.

'That's right, Paul,' agreed Smithdown. 'I split her lip right open, didn't I?'

'I know why you did it,' the photographer said. 'It was to stop the girl going back home and getting more of the same. You might have saved her life. I completely understand why you did what you did, Mr Smithdown. Completely.'

'Much appreciated, Paul,' Smithdown said. 'Sorry to interrupt your work. That's all I need. On your way.'

DS Pym waited for the photographer to leave. 'You'll be suspended on full pay pending further investigations, DI Smithdown,' he said, making notes as he spoke. 'You're to have no contact with anyone involved in this case, or anyone from the Greater Manchester Force. You'll receive notification shortly about when you'll be interviewed under caution by the Y Department.'

Smithdown allowed himself the tiniest of smiles on hearing the name of the dreaded Y Department. Every officer despised GMP's internal complaints division based on the 11th floor of the force's headquarters at Chester House in Old Trafford. Such was the stigma attached to being summoned to see them, there was a separate staircase so other officers didn't have to look at you as you entered their interview room. It was known as the Walk of Shame. It wouldn't be the first time John Smithdown would do that walk. It might be the last though.

'I need your warrant card and I need you off the premises immediately,' Pym continued. 'Don't go back to your office.

Just go. I'm very sorry John.'

'Right you are, Jim.'

Smithdown did as he'd been asked and left the building. He walked to the nearest phone box, pulled out a handful of two pence pieces and made a neat pile of coins on the phone box casing.

First, he rang his wife and explained what had happened to Kate. There were tears.

Then he rang directory enquiries for the numbers of all the local hospices.

Finally, he rang DC Jenny Seddon of the Derbyshire Constabulary.

'BBC Manchester News at noon, this is Richard Hemmingway. A senior Oldham police detective has been suspended over allegations of assaulting a child. Detective Inspector John Smithdown was relieved of his duties earlier today after the alleged incident at the town's police station. Vince Hunt has the details.'

'The young girl, thought to be aged nine, was being cared for at Oldham Police station after an apparent domestic incident.

While she was there it's claimed that she was deliberately injured by an officer who was supposed to have been looking after her. Greater Manchester Police has declined to name the person involved, but senior sources within the Oldham division have confirmed that the officer is in fact Detective Inspector John Smithdown.

He'd recently been involved in the investigation into the murder of 26-year-old Naomi Wells. The Oldham single mum's body was found at a Derbyshire beauty spot on Saturday. Her hand had previously been found in a plastic bag in Oldham's Alexandra Park. It's thought that the injured child may be her daughter.

DI Smithdown has been suspended and will now face a disciplinary inquiry into what happened. That could be followed by criminal charges. Vince Hunt, BBC Manchester News, Oldham.'

PART TWO

CHAPTER TWENTY-EIGHT

2.30 pm Monday 4 April 1988

Working his way through his pile of two pence pieces, Smithdown got what he wanted. The third hospice that he rang had reluctantly confirmed to him that they did indeed have a Maureen Lennon in their care. It was in neighbouring Rochdale and the detective was there within half an hour.

Maureen Lennon was sitting up in bed chatting to a woman in a tabard who was pushing a drinks trolley; it was fully stocked with beer, wine, mixers and sprits. Maureen was debating whether to have a Bacardi and Coke or a vodka and orange. She was pointing a finger - a grey, desperately bony finger - at a bottle of Vladivar when she spotted the detective: 'Johnny Smithdown. Good God. Will you take a drink? Or is it not allowed when you're on duty.' There was Irish in her accent but there was a lightness to it. Some words were from across the water, others were pure Oldham. Smithdown had known her from primary school but they'd lost touch when he had gone to Oldham's Blue Coat School and she had gone the more traditional comprehensive route. Their lives had intersected lightly over the years - in the street, at a christening or wedding - but being a policeman meant that some people kept him at arm's length. He knew this and accepted it.

He leant in and pressed his cheek against hers. Her skin felt like baking paper and there was a sour smell in her hair. 'I'm not technically on duty, Maureen' he replied. 'So, why not?' He scanned the cans of beer on offer. 'I'll have a Long Life, please.'

'Wish I could fookin' have that too,' Maureen said. There was a beat of silence, then she and the woman staff member wailed with laughter.

Smithdown had never been in a hospice before, but it's fair to say that this wasn't what he was expecting. *Let them have a drink, why not? No harm at this stage of the game, is there?*

The hospice assistant passed Smithdown a small can of the unfortunately named light ale and handed Maureen her vodka and orange. She held the glass in both hands; it seemed to take all of her strength to just lift it to her lips as she took a tiny sip. Then she settled the drink back into her lap. Smithdown leant over, tapped his can against the rim of her glass and pulled up a seat. He could see her skin stretched hard and tight against the roundness of her cheekbones; the outline of her eye sockets was clear and stark. There were only a few light strokes of her old features left - Maureen Lennon was almost unrecognisable. 'How's your Jean?' she asked. 'Still the best-looking woman in all of Oldham?'

'I can confirm that she still is. No question about that, Maureen. Not so well at the moment, though. She's been pretty poorly, in fact. But she'll come through,' he regretted the insensitivity of his words immediately they'd left his mouth.

'I'm sure, Johnny. I'll be praying for her.'

'Given where we are, I feel daft for asking,' Smithdown. 'But, how are you?'

'I'm close, Johnny. I'm very close to it now. Remember when we were kids? We never thought of the future, did we? Never ever. Now all I think about is the past. I was thinking of you the other day too. How strange is that? Probably seeing all this mither on the telly news and thinking… Johnny Smithdown will need an extra-large mop to wipe all this shite up.'

'It's this shite I want to talk to you about, actually, Maureen. Maybe you can help me mop a bit of it up.'

There was silence. Maureen took another sip. 'It's not about my Tom, is it?'

'It is about your Tom, Maureen,' the detective said. 'I need to find him and I don't think I'll get an honest answer from anyone else - but I might just get one from you.'

'Maybe. Maybe not.'

'I don't want to upset you, Maureen. Really, I don't. Let's just say I need to find Tom as soon as I can.'

'What do you want with him, Johnny Smithdown?' she asked. 'What has he done that's brought you all the way out here?'

'It's best if I don't say…'

'You'll have to say, I'm afraid Johnny.'

'Maureen, my daughter Kate is in hospital and I think Tom helped put her there. She's in intensive care. Please.'

She heaved the glass of vodka and orange to her lips, took a bird-like sip and let it rest again. 'For God's sake, Johnny. I'm so sorry. I didn't know. How could I know?'

'Please, you need to help me, Maureen. All the recent trouble - all the shite - seems connected to him. I've got a smashed-up town, people missing, people in the hospital, people dead. Things are bad in Oldham, Maureen and it feels like they could very easily get even worse. Please. You must help me.'

Maureen thought for a while, rubbing the rim of her glass with a stick-like finger. For a moment the detective thought she might nod off; her eyes dropped for a moment, then she jumped slightly. 'They never bothered me,' she said, finally. Quietly.

'Sorry?'

'The Pakis. The Asians. They never bothered me. I know what it's like to be discriminated against. No Irish, no dogs and all that. No, they never bothered me. But by God they seemed to upset our Tommy. Him and his mates take to the hills anytime they can, to get away from 'em. He said they couldn't bear the sight of them anymore. Like I said, I've no problem with them, but our Tom, well that's a different matter altogether.'

'Could he be up in the hills right now, Maureen? Is that where he could be?'

'Sure. Anytime he can, him and his mates head up there.

It's an old hunting lodge out near Hayfield. Right out in the sticks. Do you know where it is?'

'No,' Smithdown said. 'But I know someone who will.'

'There's a group of them. The Wolves they call themselves… The English Wolves, that's it. Daft name, isn't it? Irish Wolves would be better, don't you think? They get lads from Stockport, Salford, Huddersfield, all over joining them some weekends. I don't know what they're up to and I don't ask. But they're better off up in the hills than causing trouble down here, I suppose.'

'Maureen. I've got to go,' the detective said. 'If you hear from Tom, I want you to get one of the staff here to call me. I'll leave a number.'

'I'm not stupid, Johnny. I know he's been up to no good. But, my God, if he's harmed that beautiful girl of yours, I'd never forgive myself. Or him.'

'I'll be in touch, Maureen and I'll come back when I can,' Smithdown said, finishing his drink and then touching Maureen's hands, still clasped around her vodka and orange. Her fingers felt deathly cold and as he looked in her eyes he could see they both knew that this was probably the last time they'd meet.

'Right you are,' she replied. 'There's always a drink and a welcome here for you, Johnny. You know that, don't you?'

'Yes, Maureen. I do.'

'Wish Jean all the best from me,' she said. There were tears in her eyes now.

'I will, Maureen. Bye. And thank you.'

CHAPTER TWENTY-NINE

4.50 pm Monday 4 April 1988

'Mum, where's my football kit?'

'In your drawer - all washed and nicely folded,' Jenny Seddon shouted up the stairs. 'Wonder who did that?' she added - a little more quietly - to her unexpected guest. 'Come through to the kitchen, Mr Smithdown. Tea? Wine? Beer? Bit early, but it's a Bank Holiday, isn't it? These things are allowed.'

'I'll take a beer please Jenny, thank you,' the detective said, removing his wet mac and folding it over his arm. 'Please, call me John.'

'I'll try, might be tricky, you're just such a... Mr Smithdown,' she explained, placing a tin of Thwaites beer and a dimpled pint glass in front of the detective.

'Wine, love?' asked Brian McIntyre as he stirred a large pot of chilli on the stove. He was wearing running gear, very similar to the outfit he'd been wearing at the mountain rescue centre. *Bet he doesn't actually own any other kind of clothes.*

'Yes. A small vase-full please,' Jenny replied, standing on her tiptoes, kissing her partner on the cheek and then taking a seat at the large pine table that dominated the kitchen. Jenny and Brian's three-storey terraced house was in the Old Town area of Glossop and was exactly what Smithdown had expected it to be: noisy and messy with a huge pile of muddy walking boots in the porch. The kitchen had a huge collection of children's artwork covering every available space. Two children - or maybe three, it was hard to tell - ran in and out of the kitchen, grabbing snacks and drinks as they went. All were boys aged ten and under, all said HI! to the detective in loud, confident voices and all had bright red hair. 'Right you horrors,' shouted Jenny. 'Go and watch a video in the front room and leave us to talk to Mr Smithdown.'

All three children did as they were told and dashed to the next room in a blur of red hair and biscuits. Smithdown could hear them arguing about whether to watch *Ernest Goes to Camp* or *Spaceballs* as Jenny closed the kitchen door.

'So,' Jenny said, taking a seat next to Smithdown and making very deliberate direct eye contact with him. 'First things first. Serious question.' She matched it with a serious expression and glanced at the closed kitchen door. 'Can I pinch a cigarette, please?'

'Jenny!' Brian cried, waving his wooden spoon in her direction. 'I thought we agreed!'

'From the look on Mr Smithdown's face I'd say this was an emergency,' she replied, pulling a JPS from the detective's battered packet and sharing a light with Smithdown from the equally worn box of Bryant & May matches. 'Fire away, Mr S.'

'I'm not one for big, long speeches,' he said. 'So, this is the state of play: I reckon I've got two murders on the go; one suicide that might not be a suicide; two… sorry three probable attempted murders. I've got missing-from-homes and so many public disorder and criminal damage charges that the magistrates court won't know what's hit them after the Bank Holiday. It's madness. The connecting factor is one Thomas Robert Lennon, aged 26 of Snipe Street, Oldham. Occupation: security supervisor. Current whereabouts, unknown. No previous convictions but has all the hallmarks of extremist, possibly neo-Nazi beliefs. I think he is, at the very least, involved in some way. At worst, he's behind the whole fuckin' lot.'

'Is that it?' Jenny asked. Her eyes wide as she inhaled luxuriously on her cigarette, then wafted away the smoke with quick, guilty movements of her hand.

'Almost. One of the attempted murders is on my

daughter… she's in hospital right now. Oh, and I've just been suspended from GMP. I think that just about covers it, yes.'

'Fucking hell…' Jenny responded, looking at her partner and blowing smoke from the corner of her mouth to send it in the other direction. 'Is that why you're this side of the border, because you've been run out of Oldham?'

'I sort of banished myself, in a way,' admitted Smithdown.

'We heard about your suspension on the radio,' Brian said. 'Nice of someone at Oldham nick to provide the press with your name. It's almost as if someone's got it in for you, isn't it?'

'Looks that way, doesn't it? To be fair, that's the least of my worries. The reason my girl is in an intensive care unit is because someone spiked her with ecstasy and LSD. They targeted her to get at me. Now I want to get at them. It's going to be easier to do that without my boss breathing down my neck. So, I decided to go freelance for a bit. Now… this is where you two come in. I'm told Lennon and his mates are in the habit of heading for the hills near an old shooting lodge close to Hayfield. Do you know it?'

Brian McIntyre came away from the stove, reached up to a shelf and pulled out an Ordnance Survey map from dozens that were stashed there in a disorganised pile. He unfolded the Dark Peak map and spread it out on the table. The satellite towns of Uppermill and Diggle on the outskirts of Oldham were at the top left of the map, along with the Pennine Way route past Black Moss reservoir close to Smithdown's house. Brian's hand traced a line across Stalybridge, Tintwhistle and Glossop before finding Hayfield.

The detective saw the flat moorland plateau of Kinder Scout; it was rendered white on the map because of its lack of contour lines. 'There's two that I know of,' said Brian, plucking the cigarette from Jenny's hand, taking a drag and handing it back to her. 'One's here at White Brow - it's marked on the map. You can see it from the Glossop to Hayfield road.' He pointed to a black dot marked Shooting Cabin in an area designated for grouse shooting.

‘Seems a bit obvious to be a hideout, love,’ Jenny said. ‘You’re a massive hypocrite by the way,’ she added as she smoked the cigarette down to the filter.

‘Absolutely,’ Brian agreed. ‘But there’s another lodge here.’ His finger circled an area of moorland called Burnt Hill. ‘It’s not on the map. Maybe that’s what you’re looking for.’

‘Jesus Christ,’ said Smithdown. ‘Burnt Hill. There’s another one for the weird name list…’

‘Maybe that’s your spot, John?’ Brian said.

‘Could be,’ the detective agreed. ‘I’ll go and take a look. Thank you. Can I borrow the map?’

‘You’d never spot it at the best of times,’ Jenny said popping her cigarette end into an empty wine bottle with a sizzle. ‘It’ll be dark soon and it’s raining pussycats. You’ve got absolutely no bloody chance of finding it. I’ll take you.’

‘I can’t ask you to do that,’ Smithdown said.

‘I know you can’t,’ Jenny said. ‘Because you’re a stubborn old sod. That’s why I’m offering. Brian? Get some boots and waterproofs for our guest - we’re going for a yomp.’

CHAPTER THIRTY

7.55 pm Monday 4 April 1988

Brian McIntyre's boots almost fitted Smithdown. But not quite. Barely a hundred yards up the farm track from the Glossop road the detective could feel them pinching his heels and digging into the top of his feet. It didn't help that he was walking at least 20 per cent faster than he normally would as he tried to keep up with Jenny Seddon. She strode seemingly without effort up the incline as it took them up onto the moors. The orangey glow of Hayfield began to fade behind them as the dark slopes and bends of the landscape began to make themselves known. So did the noises: the bird cries, the wind across the coarse grasses, the sounds of multiple brooks and streams in all directions filling with light, misty rain. This was the second time that Smithdown had been in the shadow of Kinder Scout at night and he had come to a conclusion that he didn't like it - not one little bit.

As they progressed up and through the clough, there was an added atmospheric touch that seemed almost designed to unsettle them: a faint waterfall of smoke that tumbled down the sides of the narrow valley and snaked towards them like a white magic carpet. It smelled like steamed vegetables. 'What the fuck is that all about?' Smithdown asked, as the smoke approached them and began to curl around their boots.

'This is grouse country,' Jenny replied, maintaining the pace up the track. 'The moor managers will have been burning back the sphagnum moss - the stuff you see on top of the peat. They control the moorland vegetation to make it easier for the knobs to shoot the grouse. It's getting pretty cold now. The smoke that's been rising all day is falling back and it's making its way down the moors. Bit spooky, isn't it?'

Their head torches lit up the top of the smoke as they watched their footing; the path began to give way to open moorland. 'I fucking hate this place,' Smithdown muttered. "It's like fucking Scooby Doo. When this is all done with, I'm never, ever coming back to Derbyshire ever again.'

'You big soft get,' Jenny laughed. 'It's just a bit of smoke.'

'I mean it. There's too much weird bollocks going on around here for my taste.'

As they crested the brow of the next hill, Smithdown could see the lights of Stalybridge and Oldham in the distance across the top of the next ridge. Then they dropped down, the detective slipping a few times but just about managing to keep on his feet. In the tight valley below, he could see the murky outline of a single-story brick building. The two windows and the doorway at the front were covered in metal shutters and there were signs warning that this was a DANGEROUS BUILDING and that people should KEEP OUT. Smithdown looked around. The smoke from the moors rippled slowly past them, following the contours of the route they'd just taken. 'I was here a few years ago,' Jenny said. 'I don't remember it being like this.'

Smithdown touched the nearest shutter and ran a finger around it. He did the same on the second front window and the door. 'All the fixings look pretty new,' he said.

The two detectives circled the lodge. There were more shuttered windows behind the building and a plastic barrel of builders' debris. Again, Smithdown touched the windows - one was fitted slightly less snugly than the rest. He kicked over the barrel and, without prompting, DC Seddon began to dig through the contents. Her search produced several pieces of two by four wood and some metal offcuts from the shutters. Smithdown worked the metal piece behind the loose shutter and bent it back far enough to slip the wood inside. They both pulled back and down, hanging their combined weight onto the wood; the metal shutter's fixings popped off and the window covering clanged against the side of the lodge as it tumbled down. 'Nice one, DC Seddon,' Smithdown said. 'I'll be putting you forward for a commendation.'

'Unlikely,' she pointed out. 'You're on suspension.'

Smithdown emptied the remaining bits of rubbish from the barrel onto the ground and upended it, placing it near the exposed window to act as a step. He went first, putting his hand through the window frame as he took a quick glance around the inside. The light from his headtorch scoured the interior: some boxes, a barrel with wood in it, nothing much to a report. He climbed in then turned his back to the inside of the lodge and helped DC Seddon through the gap. He felt a shudder of discomfort - fear - as he did so.

With the combined light of both head torches they could see a little better. The detectives started to look slowly around the inside of the lodge, their sweep starting just to the right of the main door. The inside was clean - as if it had been recently swept. Thirty or forty folding metal chairs were stacked neatly in one corner. In the next corner were the boxes. Very similar to the one's at Tom Lennon's house.

They continued to turn their heads slowly in unison, trying to keep their light beams together. The light dimmed as it went far into the lodge. Then the light seemed to stop suddenly as it hit the broad figure of a man, standing so close they could touch him. 'Fuck me!' cried Smithdown, instinctively pushing both hands out and stepping back sharply, almost losing his balance.

The figure rocked backwards, then lunged at them. Then back again. Then silence. It was broken by a whispered voice: 'Dummy,' DC Seddon said, holding the yellowy gaze of her head torch onto the dark, inanimate figure on a sprung stand. 'It's a martial arts practice dummy. Try and keep it together Mr Smithdown.'

The DI stared at the figure. It wobbled slightly where he'd struck it and the spring below the main torso squeaked. It was pitted with dents and marks and the head was being held together by electrical tape. 'Try to swing your punch a bit more from the hip next time, she added.

'I'm going right off you, DC Seddon,' whispered Smithdown.

In the third corner of the lodge was a tub of wood, similar to the one they'd found outside. Their headtorches revealed the wood to be baseball bats, a dozen or more. Finally, their torches came full circle and illuminated the door. Painted on the inside of the metal shutter was the white face of a wolf. It was a simple design that looked like it had been spray-painted with a stencil - two pointy ears, a triangular face and two slits for eyes. Underneath the face, two long-handled machetes had been mounted on the wall, so the blades crossed. 'Oh, look,' sighed DC Seddon, 'they've got a logo. Very important to have an easily recognised symbol to represent what you're trying to do. It's good for your brand; increases sales.'

'And what exactly do you reckon is being sold here, DC Seddon?'

'Being a racist dickhead, I'd say, Mr Smithdown,' she replied. 'Being a very dangerous racist dickhead, to be precise.'

'I think you're probably right,' he replied.

They approached the plastic barrel; Smithdown pulled out a baseball bat. It was dented and chipped. A closer look revealed that they all were. Then to the boxes. Some were small and shallow, others larger and deeper. 'I saw boxes like this at Tom Lennon's house,' Smithdown said. 'Loads of them.'

The detective pulled at the brown parcel tape that held one of the smaller boxes shut. Inside were stacks of A5 flyers. Smithdown held one up so it connected with the beam from Jenny's headtorch.

ST GEORGE'S DAY UPRISING!
ARE YOU SICK OF IMMIGRANT GANGS RUNNING RIOT IN OUR TOWN? ATTACKING EACH OTHER WITH MACHETES!?
DO YOU FEAR FOR OUR MOTHERS, SISTERS AND DAUGHTERS AFTER THE RECENT SPATE OF SEX ATTACKS ON WHITE WOMEN AND YOUNG GIRLS IN OUR COMMUNITY?

THE RACIST INTIMIDATION OF WHITE, WORKING CLASS PEOPLE (WHO ARE THE BEDROCK OF OLDHAM) MUST END!
THIS IS OUR TOWN... OUR COUNTRY!
FOR TOO LONG WE HAVE BEEN TREATED LIKE SECOND CLASS CITIZENS!
THAT ENDS ON SATURDAY APRIL 23rd
ST GEORGE'S DAY!
JOIN US AT 12 NOON OUTSIDE OLDHAM TOWN HALL!

(Security by English Wolves)

'Christ Almighty,' Smithdown. 'That's what that bastard Lennon's trying to provoke. A full-on fucking race war.'

'I hadn't heard about this spate of sex attacks in Oldham,' said DC Seddon. 'When did they happen?'

'There's a reason you haven't heard about them,' Smithdown replied, causing the light from his head torch to dance back and forward in the dark as he shook his head. 'That's because they haven't happened yet. Because that's the final outrage Tom fucking Lennon has up his sleeve. That's still to come. Kick things off with a few machete attacks to get things going - get the communities turning on each other. That's a cracking start, isn't it? Then some murder. Got to have some murder, haven't you? Then a bit of rioting - film it, obviously, and make sure the telly people get their hands on the footage. Then organise sex attacks on white girls to really stoke things up. Once you've got everyone close to boiling point, put them in one place on St George's Day, then... Boom.'

Smithdown opened one of the larger boxes. Inside were Styrofoam chips; he brushed the top layer aside. Underneath were Stanley knives - sixty at least in the first box. Smithdown pushed out one of the blades then clicked it back into place. 'That's nice,' the detective said quietly. 'Just in case the whole starting-a-race-war thing doesn't work out, they're doing a bit of carpet-laying on the side.'

DC Seddon pulled the boxes away from the wall. Tucked

behind them was a folded up Black and Decker Workmate. She pulled it out. The main clamping section was covered in what appeared to be blood. 'And a bit of DIY surgery on the side,' she said.

'Fucking Nora,' Smithdown said. 'Naomi - that poor girl.'

'So, it really was her, then… At the Mermaid's Pool?'

'Maybe. Maybe not. There are so many missing persons on the go, who knows? This thing gets messier by the minute. And I reckon that's exactly what Tom Lennon and his mates want. Mess. Chaos. The more messy and chaotic the merrier. The more he muddies the water, the harder it is for us to see what he's really up to. But now we know. It's war.'

The two detectives stood quietly for a moment. Jenny put several flyers and a Stanley knife into the pocket of her jacket.

'That's great,' Smithdown said. 'But we need more evidence. We need to show the scale of this. But we can't drag this lot down the moors, can we?'

'No, but we can photograph it,' Jenny replied, producing a Boots instamatic camera and a cube flash from her jacket. 'I've got a few frames left from my holidays.'

'Good thinking, DC Seddon. We're just like *Dempsey and Makepeace*, you and me, aren't we? My wife loves that show.'

Jenny attached the flash cube to the camera and checked the counter to see how many frames she had left. 'Mind your eyes,' she told Smithdown.

He took her advice. She took a picture of the bats, then the knives, then the wolf logo on the door. Finally, she took a picture of the bloodied Back and Decker. Each flash dazzled Smithdown despite him covering his eyes with his hand. 'Let's go,' DC Seddon said, as the final frame was taken.

The blinding light from each photo had burned a round shape on the detective's retinas that took a while to shift as they made their back down the valley. The four flashes from the camera had been efficiently contained by the walls of the shuttered lodge, except for the window they'd removed. The light from each of the flashes had escaped through that window, bounced against the side of the clough behind the building and ricocheted across the moors. Four ultra-bright signals that cut through the night.

Tom Lennon and five of his fellow English Wolves saw the flashes from their tents on the other side of the valley. They immediately broke camp and headed towards the lodge.

'BBC Manchester News at seven this is Richard Hemmingway. Firefighters have spent the night tackling a blaze on moorland in North Derbyshire. Fire crews from two counties were called to the scene at around 10 o'clock yesterday evening in an area known as Burnt Hill close to Kinder Scout, as Vince Hunt Reports.'

'Burnt Hill lived up to its name last night as emergency crews from Glossop and Hyde converged on the fire which started on moorland near the village of Hayfield.

The heart of the blaze - which centred on an abandoned hunting lodge - was too far from a water source to use fire hoses, so it had to be dealt with by hand by firefighters using beaters to extinguish the flames inch by inch.

An investigation is now underway into the exact cause of the blaze, but it's thought that it may been started deliberately.

In the meantime, fire chiefs say that during wildfire season - the middle of March to the end of May - the public should take extra care while visiting the moors. And they're advising people to stay away from the area around Burnt Hill. Vince Hunt, BBC Manchester News, Hayfield.'

CHAPTER THIRTY-ONE

7.45 am Tuesday 5 April 1988

Smithdown grabbed an uncomfortable few hours' sleep on Jenny Seddon's sofa before he was woken by all three of her children. They were standing close - very close - to his face and giggling as he opened his eyes. 'He's awake!' they cried, triumphantly. 'He's awake! Mum! The old copper man is awake!'

Sensing that their work here was probably done, the children ran off. Smithdown heard a kettle click on and fire up. A mug of tea appeared on the coffee table close to the detective without comment. He took it and - fully dressed - hauled himself upright.

'Guess what?' Jenny said.

'Go on.'

'There was a fire last night out near the lodge. Must have started after we'd gone.'

'Well that's a fucking coincidence,' Smithdown said, causing a ripple of giggles from Jenny's children. 'Good job I suggested we take some photos, isn't it?'

'What would we do without you?' Jenny offered dryly. 'So - what's the plan then?'

'Shouldn't you be in work?'

'I wish I was. School holidays. This lot are going to my mum's in Buxton for the day.'

Smithdown took another glug of his tea and popped a cigarette between his lips. He noticed that all three children were watching him from the other side of the door frame, so he put the cigarette back in the packet. 'I'd better go home before my wife reports me missing.'

Smithdown took his tea into the kitchen, tipped a quarter of it down the sink, topped it up with cold water and drank the lukewarm brew down. DC Seddon held out the instamatic film cartridge from her camera. 'You'll be needing this,' she said. 'Please excuse the swimwear shots. I might be a bit pissed on some of them, too.'

'I'll get the pics sorted asap,' Smithdown said, smiling. 'Then I'll meet you down at Oldham nick at one o'clock and we'll take them to the DS. I might have to wait outside to start with as I'm not supposed to enter the police station. Then I'm sure the DS will immediately see the light, give me a promotion and a huge pay rise and say no more about it.'

'Hmmm - will he though?' Jenny asked. 'Didn't you rip some kids lip open?'

'Technically, yes, but let's try to look forward rather than dwelling on the past.'

'Didn't it happen, like, a few days ago or something?'

'I'll see myself out,' he offered, heading for the door. He opened his wallet and stuck a ten pound note into the hand of the eldest of the children as he passed, making a circular motion with his finger to indicate it was for all three of them. They cheered their approval and took off up the stairs like a trio of ginger rockets.

'I saw that, DI John Smithdown,' Jenny said as he was leaving. 'Adding bribery to your list of crimes isn't going to help matters. I'll see you at one.'

~

During the drive back home to Oldham, Smithdown ran through the way he wanted things to pan out over the next few hours. He made a mental list:

Return to lodge - anything left worth salvaging?
Stage simultaneous searches of Tom Lennon's house and Kingdom club.
Eliminate King from enquiry?
Public appeal to capture Tom Lennon.

Arrest TL - multiple counts of murder and attempted murder, abduction, offences under 1986 Public Order Act for inciting racial hatred and of riot. Criminal damage? Probably not worth it but see if it sticks.
Missing-from-homes - poor lad that disappeared after Mustafizur was attacked seems to have got lost in all this. TL connection? Ditto missing councillor. What's Pym doing? Enough? Anything?
Question TL over abduction and murder of Naomi Wells and possibly of Councillor Chowdhury.
Question TL over three attempted murders (including Kate).
Pray. Pray. Pray that Kate is okay.
Check on Jean.

When he arrived home, he could smell toast. *I'm famished. I could murder some toast.* He heard his wife's voice from the living room: 'John!' she shouted. She sounded far cheerier than he was expecting, joyous almost. 'In here,' she cried again, impatiently. 'Quick, quick. Great news from the hospital, love.'

Jean Smithdown was sitting in her favourite armchair, facing the morning sunshine. Her pale face was alive with energy and excitement. The detective knelt by her side. 'It's our Kate,' she explained, grabbing her husband's hand. 'She's conscious. She's talking. She's going to be alright. Oh John, she's going to be alright.'

The detective felt the heat of tears in his eyes. He put a hand around the back of his wife's neck, pulled her to him and kissed her cheek. 'I was going to go and visit her on my way to the station,' he said. 'Did the hospital ring?'

'No,' she said with a smile and a nodded across the room. 'Tom was there this morning. He came straight here to tell us, bless him.'

Standing next to their living room window, with its commanding view across the moors, Tom Lennon saluted Smithdown with a half-eaten piece of toast and popped the remainder in his mouth. 'Cracking toast, Jean,' Lennon said with a grin. Smithdown outwardly returned his smile. *I will fucking kill you, Tom Lennon. I swear to fucking God, I will.*

'So good of him, John,' Jean said in a quiet voice. 'With Maureen being so ill and all.'

'Least I could do, Jean,' Lennon said. 'Mr Smithdown took the time to visit my mam at the hospital, didn't you? I thought it was only right and proper for me to keep an eye on Kate after what some piece of shit did to her. Sorry for the language, Jean.'

'I've said considerably worse over the last 24 hours, Tom,' Jean replied, pushing herself up from her chair. 'Considerably.'

'Tea and toast for you too, John?' she asked. 'Tom can fill you in. Then you can let me know what's happening with you and James Pym. I'm sure you said some things that you didn't really mean in the heat of the moment. Doubtless it can all be sorted out. You two are like a pair of kids, honestly. They've been like this for years, Tom.'

Jean Smithdown walked carefully to the kitchen, occasionally touching pieces of furniture for support as she went. Smithdown waited for her to leave the room and heard the click of the kettle and the twin rattle of two pieces of bread going into the toaster. Smithdown paused for a few seconds until the kettle began to noisily whoosh, then he rushed across the room with a speed that seemed to take the younger man by surprise. The detective put his face as close to Lennon's as the height difference would allow. The younger man reeked of smoke. Smithdown had never felt such hatred for any other human being in his life. He could feel it in his bones. His hands shook and he had difficulty speaking.

'No need to thank me, John,' Lennon whispered, with a wink.

'What is it you want, lad?' Smithdown asked. 'What is all this for?'

'An end to new Commonwealth and Pakistan immigration, a properly financed system of repatriation, voluntary to start with; the repeal of the so-called Race Relations Act and the abolition of the ludicrous anti-white organisation known as the Commission for Racial Equality.' Lennon almost chanted the words as if he'd said them many times before. 'We want Oldham back. And then we want our country back.'

'How much of this is you?' Smithdown asked. 'The murders, the attacks, the missing people. Most of it? All of it?'

'Haven't you heard the news?' Lennon whispered. 'All that stuff is waaaay down the running order. Asian-on-white violence. Asian-on-Asian violence. It's really kicking off but all anyone cares about is the riots and the way immigrant filth are destroying this town. Damage to property outweighs damage to people every time. I did a media degree, John. Did you know that? Or did you just think I was just another bull-necked thicko fired up by what they've read in *The Sun* or heard down the pub? I think not. I've studied the way news cycles work. How they need to be fed. If it bleeds it leads. If it burns, it earns.'

Smithdown pulled a leaflet from his pocket - one of the A5 flyers he'd found with DC Seddon at the abandoned lodge. He pushed it into Lennon's face, then tucked it into the neck of his Fred Perry polo shirt. 'Sex attacks? Is that what's next? Raping girls and then blaming it on other communities?'

Lennon grabbed the flyer and looked at it. He smiled and tutted with mock disapproval at the contents. 'Looks like people are very upset, Mr Smithdown. You and your mates in the police haven't been looking after this town properly. Well, some of your mates have. There are a few good souls in Oldham police. Some genuine people who want what's right for this town. They're alright. In the meantime, thank goodness for the English Wolves. They'll provide protection when and where it's needed.'

'You're fucking thick, lad,' Smithdown spat. 'We saw what was up in that lodge. Saw what you're planning. It's over.'

'No, Mr Smithdown,' Lennon countered. 'You're fucking thick. There's nothing to tie me to the lodge, or the Wolves, or any of it. That lodge was cleaned out spic and span after you left. Then torched. Which leaves you with what? My word against yours. My word against some old soak who's on suspension for abusing a little girl. Some bitter old fuck who's not right in the head over his sick wife and his druggie daughter. No mate. The only person it's over for is you. We're just getting started.'

Lennon pushed his Harrington jacket lightly to one side and put his hand to his hip. He had a leather sheath strapped to chest. In it was the biggest knife Smithdown had ever seen. Lennon wobbled his head and winked at him. 'If you go near my mother again,' Lennon said. 'I'll gut your wife and then your daughter, understand? It's simple. Stay away from me, stay away from the town centre and stay away from the Wolves until after St George's Day. All you need to do is potter about your garden for a few weeks on suspension. That's it. Watch some telly. Go for a walk or two. Take Jean for a nice pub lunch. Keep the fuck out of the way. That's all. No one's going to listen to some mad old cop who abuses children anyway.'

'We've got photos, lad. A detective from Derbyshire saw it with her own eyes.'

'Have you now,' Lennon smiled. Again, the wink. The knife that Lennon had shown him had rattled the detective. But it was the wink that really worried him.

'Will you have another cuppa, Tom?' Jean Smithdown said as she re-entered the living room. The two men stepped slightly apart.

'I'm alright Jean. I'll get on my way. Things to do. People to see. Take care Mr Smithdown. And think on.'

Jean Smithdown touched Lennon's arm as he passed. 'Give my best to your mam, Tom. I'll be thinking about her. And you. All the best.'

'That's very kind, Jean,' Lennon said. 'Will do. All the best to you. I hope your Kate makes a full recovery. I know she will.'

Lennon leaned in and kissed Jean Smithdown lightly on the cheek. 'I'll be seeing you,' he said with a smile.

Jean and John Smithdown watched as Lennon walked briskly up their driveway. Moments later a motorbike whizzed past their front gate. Lennon was still putting his helmet on in the pillion position. The couple watched the bike fade into the moorland road towards Oldham town centre.

'I'd better ring the hospital,' Smithdown said. 'Just to make sure Kate's okay.'

'Yes, you'd better,' she replied. 'Oh, and John?'

'Yes love?'

'Could you also make absolutely sure that piece of shit gets everything that's coming to him?'

'I will indeed, love. Everything.'

'Good. Because he's a bloody wrong 'un.'

~

Once out of sight of the Smithdown's house, Tom Lennon instructed Adam Griffin to take the road to Uppermill then head for Glossop.

Lennon knew exactly where he wanted to go - before he'd arrived at Smithdown's house a friend of the English Wolves in the Derbyshire Constabulary had given him the address of DC Jenny Seddon's house.

CHAPTER THIRTY-TWO

8.50 am Tuesday 5 April 1988

There was no way that Smithdown would ever let Bob Donaldson see him with even the hint of a tear in his eye. But the sight that met him as he walked into Kate's hospital room made it very difficult for the detective to keep his emotions in order. Kate was awake and she gave him a woozy smile. Next to her, slumped in an uncomfortable looking hospital chair, was DC Donaldson - fast asleep.

"I think he's been here all night," Kate whispered to her dad.

He leant in and kissed her cheek. Her hair seemed to have absorbed that smell that only occurs in hospitals. Smithdown breathed it in like it was the most addictive perfume ever. *Thank you, thank you, thank you for giving me my little girl back.*

Donaldson's head popped up in a way clearly designed to give the impression he hadn't been asleep at all. 'Morning, sir,' he said. 'Nothing to report here. All quiet. Mind you, I'm not supposed to be talking to you at the minute, am I?' He winked at Smithdown. ' This guy is mad, bad and dangerous to know Kate.'

'Bob, what the hell are you doing here,' Smithdown said. 'My God, I appreciate it, but I didn't expect you to be here, let alone be here all night. I'm sure the staff had things under control.'

'Well, you never know, do you?' Donaldson said. 'Open spaces, these hospitals. Anyone could be coming in and out. And we can't have that, can we?'

'You're right. We can't. Have you seen anyone that had no business being here?'

'Tom Lennon was sniffing about early doors. I saw him off, the cocky twat.'

'Thank you, Bob. I mean it. Thank you. You won't believe what that shit's been up to. Now's not the time. I'm hoping to get in to see the DS at lunchtime to show him what I've got. It's chilling. Absolutely fucking chilling.'

'Okay. Christ - the madness continues. I'd better get myself down the road, then. Take care Kate.'

'Thank you, Bob,' she whispered as he headed out of the room. Her eyelids began to close with tiredness.

Smithdown handed the DC the film cartridge he had in his jacket pocket. He whispered, so his daughter couldn't hear: 'Take this to Paul Rees in photographic.' Smithdown checked his watch. 'I need two sets of the last four or five frames by one o'clock. I've got that DC from Derbyshire coming over to back me up. Tell Paul to ignore any holiday snaps. What I'm interested in is the weapons stash we found up at Hayfield. Not to mention the fucking Black and Decker torture chamber they had set up there, too.'

'Just gets worse and worse this, doesn't it?' Bob said. 'Okay. Will do.'

'I'll sit with her for a while,' Smithdown said. He put out his hand. They shook. 'Thanks again for what you've done, Bob.'

'Not a problem. All I did was keep an eye on things. You'd do the same for me, I'm sure.'

'I would, Bob. No question. Though I hope you never find yourself in a situation half as bad as this.'

CHAPTER THIRTY-THREE

9.35 am Tuesday 5 April 1988

'Just a minute,' Jenny Seddon shouted as she put on her dressing gown and ran down the stairs. After rushing to get the children ready to be picked up by her mum, she'd showered quickly and was getting ready for the 25-minute drive to Oldham when the doorbell rang. She could see the outline of the delivery man though the frosted glass of her front door. Bloody nuisance she thought as he rang the bell for a second time. 'JUST A MINUTE!' the DC cried, then stubbed her toe on the small hallway table. 'Christ Almighty,' she muttered as she got to the front door and turned the lock. 'Sorry,' she said, looking at the spilt in her toenail *thanks to that stupid bloody table.* 'I was upstairs. It's not for those lazy buggers across the road again, is it?'

As she opened the door fully, a fist shot forwards, hitting her square on the nose, knocking her glasses from her face. The blood had already begun to pour by the time the second and third blows came in. She saw them land in the reflection framed in the visor of her attacker's motorbike helmet.

Right, left, right. Boxer. Well-trained. Oh shit. Oh shit, shit, shit.

She fell backwards and the back of her leg caught the small table that supported the phone, a few directories and several framed photos of her family.

I'm always banging into that, should have moved it years ago. Too late now.

As Jenny hit the bottom of the stairs the man was on top of her, his hands around her throat. She had trained for situations similar to this many times, but her options right now were severely limited. She couldn't move back because of the stairs and his weight. Left and right were closed off because of the walls either side of the narrow staircase. The cold black helmet meant attacking his eyes was a waste of time. The high-collared leather jacket that he wore protected his neck, collar bones and Adam's apple.

Fuck. This is bad. So very, very bad. Thank God the kids aren't here. Oh Christ, my kids.

Again, DC Seddon's training held firm. She tried to bring her knee up, hoping to connect with his groin. Once, twice, a third time. But he was so close the best she could manage was a few glancing blows against his hip. She felt for the pressure points on the back of his hands and between the thumb and forefinger. The thick biker gloves he wore stopped her getting a firm hold.

Think.

She tried to grab one of his fingers to wrench it back; his hands were quite far around her neck. It was difficult, but she managed to connect with the forefinger of his right hand and pulled hard. He let go of his grip briefly only to punch her again, fracturing her eye socket. Both hands went straight back to Jenny's neck - she knew she was about to pass out.

Last go. Last chance.

The DC grabbed below the lower part of his helmet, her fingers skittered around the strapping until she found the release catch and yanked it. She slowly pulled off the helmet to see the blotchy face of a man in his 20s. Adam Griffin was laughing at her, sticking out his tongue and crossing his eyes, making fun of her distress. 'Like I give a shit that you can see my face,' he whispered. 'Too fucking late now, love.' His grip around her neck tightened.

DC Seddon smashed the back edge of the helmet against his nose as hard as she could. It took a second blow to break it. The hands loosened as he screamed in pain. Griffin pulled slightly away from her; the space this created allowed her a better upward swing and she hit him twice more, the full weight of the helmet creating two small compression fractures either side of his head. He fell backwards.

Yes! Thank you. Yes.

Her training told her that she was far from being free of danger. Was she prepared to kill her attacker?

Abso-fucking-lutely.

She managed to get to her feet, took two shaky steps forward, raised the helmet above her head and was about to drop down and pin his arms under her knees when he rolled to one side, got to his feet and took a few steps back. They looked at each other for a moment. A few beats of silence apart from their matching heavy gasps for air. Then Jenny Seddon looked straight at him, crossed her eyes and stuck out her tongue. Her teeth were covered in blood. 'I will FUCKING DO YOU,' the DC shouted as she ran towards him. With both hands she heaved the helmet at his face. Griffin's head bounced off the wall and then re-connected with the helmet generating a satisfying rat-a-tat sound.

Jenny collapsed onto the muddy hall carpet; she looked up and saw him grab the instamatic camera from the table.

It's empty, you daft fuck.

Then Griffin dragged himself through the door before she lost consciousness.

Good job, Jenny love. Proud of you.

Then, with no more fight left in her, she let go.

It would be nearly an hour before she was discovered by the postman.

CHAPTER THIRTY-FOUR

10.45 am Tuesday 5 April 1988

Kate remembered nothing about what happened to her at the Kingdom club and Smithdown knew that now wasn't the time to push her for more information about it.

Sitting in his car outside the hospital the detective weighed up the options. He had time to kill while he waited for Jenny Seddon and having assaulted a minor, engineered his own suspension and carried out some low-key breaking and entering, Smithdown took the view that he now had very little to lose. He didn't want to cause Bob any more problems by being seen with him as he wasn't supposed to have contact with any officers from GMP while his suspension continued, but no one said that he couldn't go and knock on a MP's door.

Everyone in Oldham knew where Peter Jeffries MP lived. His farmhouse stood high on a hill overlooking the village of Alt, to the south-east of the town centre close to the Tameside border. The slope underneath the house featured a billboard pointing in the direction of Oldham that could be seen for miles. Against a vivid Tory-blue background was a head and shoulders shot of Jeffries, his round face set in a stern frown. One eyebrow was raised in a challenging manner; the photo matched the catchline emblazoned on the poster in white, capital letters:

PETER JEFFRIES: FIGHTING FOR OLDHAM,
FIGHTING FOR YOU.

Jeffries' dogs - two rottweilers and a red setter - came galloping up the driveway to meet the detective. Smithdown waited until the MP shooed them away before he got out of his car. Smithdown's Ford looked rather tatty parked next to Jeffries' collection of classic cars; the MP had been polishing a sky-blue vintage Jaguar as Smithdown arrived. Despite this task he was wearing two-thirds of a three-piece suit. He put down the polishing cloth he'd been using, put on his jacket and set about crushing Smithdown's hand. 'Come in Detective Inspector - though it's just plain John at the moment, isn't it? Until that small matter of child assault is cleared up…'

'Look, there is an explanation behind that,' Smithdown said as he dipped his head to avoid the beam over the doorway and entered Jeffries' country-style kitchen.

'I know there is. You caused that girl a little bit of pain to save her from a great deal more pain. I understand. And given that her mum's now been murdered, and her abusive boyfriend is dead, it looks like you did the right thing. Tea?'

'I could murder one, thanks.'

Jeffries provided Smithdown with tea in a Margaret Thatcher mug. The MP took a seat at the rustic pine kitchen table and gestured for the detective to join him. 'What's on your mind, John?'

'The Far-Right.'

'There's plenty of people in Oldham that would call me the Far-Right, John.'

'You're a hang 'em and flog 'em Tory, Mr Jeffries. I'm talking about neo-Nazis. What do you know about the English Wolves?'

'I don't know a great deal,' the MP said, choosing his words with care. 'But I've heard quite a bit. All of it bad. Very bad.'

'What have you heard?' the detective asked.

'When we spoke yesterday, I told you the Right were on the rise,' Jeffries said. 'People thought they'd faded away because they didn't fight the last General Election, but they're back under a different guise. They're seeking legitimacy, challenging the mainstream parties for political power. They're shredding the old look - the classic skinhead and bovver boots - and putting suits on. But the new men in suits still need protection. If they're going to go out on the campaign trail, they'll be targeted by Left wing agitators at every public meeting, every speech, every attempt to engage with the public. So, the Wolves are their protection squad.'

'How do you know all this, Mr Jeffries?'

'John. Please. I'm a politician. It's in my interest to know where my next political rivals might be coming from. What do you know about the English Wolves?'

Smithdown rubbed his unshaven face: 'It's more what I think I know,' he said, cautiously. 'I think they've been stoking up trouble between the Pakistani and Bangladeshi communities; I think they're using it to bait the white working class population and stoke up racial tensions; I think they're feeding video footage to the media that backs up their version of events. I think the murder of Naomi Wells - the girl at Kinder Scout - and your missing councillor are tied in too. I reckon these English Wolves have soaked this town in their own brand of racist petrol and I think they're planning to throw a match on it by using rape as a weapon on the run up to St George's Day.'

'My God,' Jeffries said. 'That's insane.'

Smithdown showed the MP the flyer he'd taken from the lodge at Hayfield. 'I also think they dosed my daughter as a warning to me and I've just found their top lad Tom Lennon at my house with a knife as long as the Huddersfield Road.'

'Tom Lennon? I see.'

'Yes, Mr Jeffries. Tom fucking Lennon. Mate of yours, is he?'

'No, Mr Smithdown. No friend of mine. He volunteered as a helper in my office a few years ago. Stuffing envelopes, making tea. That's all. But you could tell he was there to watch. To learn. We let him go when we found out he'd been doing the same thing with the other political parties too. He was spying, of course, but not for anyone else. He was spying on behalf of himself.'

'What, so he could get into politics?'

'No. Not politics as it stands. Something else. He was angry at the apathy of voters, especially what he called the indigenous population. The white working class. He believed that many problems could be traced back to their inaction. He was like any young person who flirts with politics, they always want to do things differently. And it looks like he's found a very, very different way of doing things.'

'I think what's happened so far has just been the warm-up act,' Smithdown said. 'Come St George's Day, with everyone stoked up after these targeted sex attacks, that's when it'll really kick off. A full-on white riot. Then good old Tommy Lennon can stroll in, like the Great White Saviour, and legitimise the Far-Right so they can get a handful of actual political power.

'No, no John. I don't think so. He's too clever for that. There's nothing to link him to the Wolves, I imagine?'

'Not directly, no,' the detective admitted.

'Of course there isn't. I imagine he'll drop the Wolves like a stone once St George's Day is done. He'll step forward as the appeaser, Mr Reasonable, the man who can understand how tensions can boil over but would never, ever condone violence. No - I think he'll stand as an independent in the upcoming council elections as the genuine voice of working-class Oldham and play the man-of-the-people card. He could win by a landslide. Then he'll be onhis way.'

'Didn't you think about coming to the police with your suspicions, Mr Jeffries?' the detective asked.

'They're just that. Suspicions. If I were to head to your police station every time I had concerns about racists in Oldham, I might as well move in.'

'You sound like my daughter,' Smithdown said.

'I heard about what happened. How is she?'

'She's on the mend,' the detective replied, feeling himself getting upset and angry all over again. 'Thank you for asking. And thank you for your time, Mr Jeffries. And the tea. And the information. I'll be back to take a statement from you. If they let me back on the force, that is.'

CHAPTER THIRTY-FIVE

1.20pm Tuesday 5 April 1988

DC Seddon was already 20 minutes late. *Not like her - not her style at all.* Smithdown leant against the metal railings that led to the Oldham Police station entrance and smoked a JPS.

He'd been there since 12.45 and he wasn't particularly enjoying the experience. Colleague after colleague, people he'd known for decades, had passed him with the merest of nods. Some had avoided eye contact with him altogether; several had clearly turned on their heels and gone another way so as not to breathe the same air as him.

One person didn't: Bob Donaldson waved then jogged down the slope from the main entrance towards Smithdown. 'Hi Bob. Is the DS free?' the detective asked. 'I'm still waiting for DC Seddon.'

'Pym won't see you. He says it's for your own good. If you're spotted in the building you've had it when it comes to your disciplinary. It's bad enough that half the force has already seen you hanging around here.'

'Did you show him the photos?' Smithdown asked.

'I didn't.'

'Could you go back in and put them under his nose. That'll change his mind.'

'I wish I could.'

'Bob, please.'

'I can't because there's nothing on them. Some nice snaps of your mate and her kids on the beach but that's about it. The last few frames didn't come out. The lad in photographic says he's tried his best, but they've come out blank.'

'Fucking Nora. Are you sure?'

'Positive.'

'Jesus wept - we're being nobbled here, Bob. Fucking Pym. I knew it.'

The two men stood in silence for a moment: 'Is it true that you got yourself suspended on purpose?' Donaldson asked.

'Who told you that?'

'The lad in photographic says you forced him to grass you up about that Wells kid.'

'He's got a lot to learn that lad.'

Bob put an arm on Smithdown's shoulder. 'Permission to say something that you probably won't like?'

'Go on then.'

Donaldson pointed to the Oldham Borough coat of arms above the door to the police station. The scroll at the bottom said: *Sapere Aude.*

'Dare to Be Wise. Very good, Bob. Never had you down as a Latin scholar.'

'Good advice, though, innit? Clear off, boss. Go back to the hospital. Spend time with Kate. Take Jean out for lunch. Get away from here. You've got more on your plate than anyone should have to deal with at home, let alone all the shit that's been going on here. We're on it: the attacks on the Asian lad and Mr Aleem; the missing-from-homes, all of it. Half of Oldham is already in custody for rioting and as soon as Kate's well enough I'll be round to take a statement from her personally to see if there's anything in this cstasy business.'

'That twat Tom Lennon did it!' Smithdown shouted, attracting attention from passing shoppers.

'You're not going to like this either then…' sighed Bob.

'This should be good…'

'There's half a dozen witnesses that say they saw Kate buy the gear from a dealer outside Kingdom and then necked it herself.'

'Fuck off, Bob. That's bollocks and you know it.'

'I don't know it,' the DC said, raising his voice for the first time. 'I wish I did, but I don't. I'm trying to help you here but you're making it very difficult. Back off, let us do our jobs. For once, do as Pym asks; I know he's a dick, but it's for the best.'

'What about the missing councillor?'

'He's on it. He's got a DC in Leicester as we speak talking to her family. House to house is happening with her neighbours. Media appeals have been done. I think he sees the brownie point possibilities now Peter Jeffries has stuck his oar in. Police work does actually happen in your absence, you know.'

'Of course, I'm not saying it doesn't…'

'Go. Now. Give my love to Jean. And to Kate.'

'I will, Bob.'

'Straight to the hospital, now. I mean it.'

'I will, Bob. You're dead right.'

The two men exchanged a half salute/half wave as DC Donaldson walked back into the police station.

Smithdown thought for a moment as he finished his cigarette, then he got in his car, put on some Dr Feelgood and headed straight for Tom Lennon's house.

CHAPTER THIRTY-SIX

1.45pm Tuesday 5 April 1988

Smithdown decided that the time for subtlety had long since passed, so he made no effort to disguise the fact that he was tying a rope to the metal window grille protecting Tom Lennon's front window. He made even less of an effort to gloss over the small matter of attaching the other end of the rope to the towing hook of his car.

As he went about his work, Lennon's largely South Asian neighbours began to take an interest in what was going on. Net curtains twitched and were pulled aside; some residents came to their red front doorsteps and debated with their neighbours about what the man in the grey suit was up to. A passing postman lay down his bag of letters and parcels, took a seat on the kerb, lit a cigarette and waited. There was a sense that something worth watching was about to happen.

Smithdown didn't disappoint them.

Pausing a moment to advise a young boy on a bike to stand clear, he got in his car, turned over the engine and accelerated. '*Roxette*' by Dr Feelgood whirred into life from the stereo as he eased the Ford Escort forward. There was a satisfyingly loud pang-pang sound as two sides of the front window grille came away from the wall. As a crowd began to gather, the detective got out of his car, calmly untied the rope from the half-removed grille and tied it to the other side.

He nodded at the postman, who seemed largely unfazed - although clearly fascinated - by what was going in. 'You the police?' the postman asked from his prime position on the kerb.

'For the purposes of this exercise, yes,' Smithdown

confirmed.

'No need to call them then, is there?' the postman observed.

'None whatsoever.'

'Best crack on, then.'

'Will do,' the detective said with a smile as he got back in his car and again eased into the accelerator. The final two fixings came away more quickly this time and the window was exposed. The detective reversed then parked his car. One of the many reasons Smithdown preferred to use his own vehicle was the easy access it provided to a variety of household items and tools that he stored in the boot. He took out a small axe, a crowbar and a picnic blanket and walked over to the window. A young mum walked by with a pram: 'Afternoon,' he said, placing the blanket on the ground in front of the window. He waited until she'd passed before jamming the blunt, top end of the axe straight into the glass, resulting in a very loud noise from the glass and an ooh of surprise from the crowd. The blow sent most of the glass tumbling inside the front room of the house. The rest went onto the blanket. He then used the edge of the axe to chip away at the remaining fragments sticking out of the frame and tipped the debris from the blanket through the window.

'You're very tidy, aren't you?' offered the postman.

'Can't have glass on the pavement with kiddies about,' Smithdown pointed out.

'Fair dos,' the postie agreed.

Smithdown placed the blanket over the frame to protect himself from the remaining shards and climbed in, pushing aside the thick curtains. He stepped into a sea of empty beer cans, takeaway boxes and crumpled cigarette packets. All of the smells those items generated were joined by an undertow of vinegary, male sweat - as if someone had set up a bar in a boxing club.

The stencilled wolf logo he'd seen in the abandoned lodge was on the chimney breast above a 1970s style gas fireplace. He trudged through the debris and got to the living room door, which was slightly ajar. He touched the door frame with the head of the axe with the intention of pulling it towards him; then he stopped. There was a sound - maybe heavy steps, maybe banging - from elsewhere in the house. Then a whining sound, the kind a fox might make on the moors at night. Then silence again.

Smithdown yanked the door open, using his axe like a hook, and stepped sharply into the hallway, leading the way with the crowbar in his outstretched arm. Again, there was a bang. More whining. *It's coming from the cellar.* The detective knew the layout of these terraced houses. He'd grown up in one. The cellar door was between the back room and the kitchen. The stone stairs would be steep, the headroom low, the light dim and the room to manoeuvre almost non-existent. *No choice in the matter, down we go.*

The back room of the house was a similar mix of cheap furniture and ankle-high rubbish. It was dark, the heavy blackout curtains at the rear window were open but only slightly apart. The graffiti on the walls was bolder than the front room: alongside the wolf stencils the detective had seen before there was also hand-painted NF and BNP signs as well as several swastikas.

Smithdown stood at the doorway to the cellar. It had three bolts holding it shut at the top, middle and bottom. He could still hear whining and banging. There was a mirror attached to the cellar door and Smithdown looked at himself as he hesitated. He saw a grey-faced, tired looking man with an axe in one hand and a crowbar in the other. *This is mad. Absolutely fucking mad.* He tucked the crowbar into his belt and slid back each bolt as quietly as he could. Then, he stretched out his hand to touch the door's handle. Another bang. Smithdown had to admit to himself that he was scared.

The detective decided to count down in his head before yanking open the door.

Three

Two

Then a figure appeared behind him and Smithdown

jumped, turned and pulled back his axe ready to swing. Fortunately, he didn't, otherwise he would have put Uddin Rahman in hospital alongside his brother. 'Fucking Nora, lad! I nearly brained you. What the fuck are you doing here?'

'Half of Oldham is standing in the road watching what's going on,' Uddin pointed out. 'I live nearby, and I thought I'd take a closer look. Good to the see the police finally taking a bit of action. Although I heard on the news that you've been binned off.'

'Let's just say I'm acting in a freelance capacity at the moment and leave it at that, shall we?'

'I thought so - axes aren't normally standard police issue, are they?'

'They might be soon, the way this town's heading. I don't suppose there's any point in asking you to fuck off and leave me to it, is there?'

'None whatsoever,' Uddin confirmed. 'This is the best show in town. Plus, this is Tom Lennon's house - and if you're here that means he's probably got something to do with the attack on my brother. If that's the case, I want to be the first to know about it.'

'How do you know it's Lennon's house?' asked the detective.

'Oh my God! Are you the only person who doesn't know what's going on? Have you seen the outside of this house?'

'Okay. Fair point,' Smithdown conceded.

'He's feeling better now, by the way. My brother. Thanks for asking.'

'That's great. Can we discuss it later? I'm a touch busy. Here, grab this, will you?' Smithdown handed Uddin the crowbar and - without the aid of a countdown this time - opened the cellar door. The grating hinges produced a long, loud screeching sound like air being released from a balloon.

'This is just like being in a film,' Uddin said to the detective.

'Shut… Your… Trap,' Smithdown whispered back as he flicked his lighter to provide some light. It gave enough of a yellowy glow for them to see to the bottom of the steps. The detective was surprised to see another door there. *The cellars in these terraces are open plan. There's no door here normally. Not right at all, this.*

The whitewash on the walls crumbled to the touch as the pair made their way slowly down the cellar steps. It seemed to get colder as they got nearer to the door. The only sound was the scrape of their shoes against the stone steps.

Though the entrance to the cellar was old and untouched, the door at the bottom was clearly new. The wooden frame was fresh pine and the padlock and heavy sliding bolt that accompanied it looked like they'd come straight from a hardware shop.

'It's locked,' Uddin pointed out from halfway up the steps.

Smithdown shooed him back and hit the door with the axe three times around the latch: above it, to the left and below. 'No. It. Isn't,' he said, a syllable for each strike. A fourth blow landed straight onto the bolt and separated it from the door. It lurched open, clattering against the wall behind it.

The smell inside the cellar room was harsh and sour - sweat, bleach and urine hit Smithdown and Uddin as the air from their side of the door rushed in. They heard the noise again. Thud-thud. The whine was louder and more insistent now.

The detective stepped into the cellar room and slowly moved his lighter around. 'Let's see what we can see, Uddin,' Smithdown said.

The detective wasn't too surprised to see boxes and tubs of weapons; they were probably the same knives, bats and machetes he'd seen at the lodge. He was quite surprised to see bags of multi-coloured pills piled up on metal shelving units pushed up against two sides of the room. There were a dozen units with four shelves each - and every shelf had twenty or thirty bags of pills, each one the size of a crisp packet.

He was, however, very surprised indeed to see Naomi Wells handcuffed to the frame of a bare metal bed, banging her head against the wall behind her and trying to shout through the thick strip of electrician's tape across her mouth. The handcuffs - which looked to Smithdown like they were police issue - were attached to both of her ankles and to her right wrist. It would have been pointless putting handcuffs on her left wrist, because her left hand was missing.

CHAPTER THIRTY-SEVEN

1.50 pm Tuesday 5 April 1988

'Shitting, shitting, shitting hell, Tom,' said Adam Griffin as they watched Smithdown climb through the front window of Lennon's house. 'He's going to find her then we're fucked. I mean really fucked. We can't grab them, there's too many people about. What the fuck are we going to do?'

Griffin had two swollen eyes that were starting to purple up. He had blood-speckled toilet paper sticking out of both nostrils. The two stood in a ginnel between two rows of terraced houses that faced Lennon's. 'We're going to stop acting like a big mard girl with bog roll up her conk and we're going to get a grip of ourselves and then of the situation,' Lennon said. 'That's what we're going to do.'

The two stood in silence. They saw Uddin follow the detective through the window, then they heard the banging of Smithdown's axe against the cellar door. 'We need to send someone to see his daughter. Right now,' Lennon said.

'I'll go,' Griffin said. 'I'll fucking do her, right there in the hospital. I done that cow of a copper in Glossop, I'll do her and all. Makes no odds to me.'

'I think you'll attract too much attention, looking like that,' Lennon pointed out. 'We need to be a bit more low-key, for once. Someone else can go. Then we'll see how keen Mr Smithdown is to help out our Naomi. He might just rethink his priorities.'

CHAPTER THIRTY-EIGHT

2pm Tuesday 5 April 1988

'I will fucking kill the bastard lot of them,' screamed Naomi Wells as Smithdown took away the gaffer tape, releasing a toyshop bouncy ball that had been put in her mouth. It made a bizarre poing-poing sound as it hit the harsh stone cellar floor and rolled under an old table. 'Dirty, bastard fuckers,' she added.

Naomi's left arm was neatly bandaged between the elbow and the end of the stump. She was wearing jogging bottoms, a t-shirt that had once been white and her jet-black hair was plastered to her face. 'I know you!' she shouted. 'You're that DI fucking what's-his-face, aren't you?' What are you going to do me for this time? Loitering in a cellar in possession of one fucking hand?'

'I wasn't expecting that response, if I'm honest,' muttered Smithdown as he inspected the handcuffs. 'It's DI Smithdown, that's right, Naomi. We've lots to talk about, but right now we need to get you out of here as quickly and as quietly as possible. Emphasis on the quietly. Do you think you can walk?'

'I'd rather fucking run,' she replied. 'But I'm every-so-slightly handcuffed to this bleeding bed.'

'Uddin,' the detective said. 'Run up to my car and get my bolt cutters out of the boot. If anyone ask you what's going on, say nowt. If anyone asks you who's in the house, say nowt. If anyone…'

'…I get it, I get it. Say nowt,' he confirmed, tucking the crowbar Smithdown had given him through a belt loop on his baggy jeans.

'Correct.'

The young man took a step backwards then hesitated: 'What happened to your hand?' he asked Naomi.

'I sold it,' she said. It was said in a straightforward, matter-of-fact tone. Smithdown remembered it from when he'd arrested her in the past.

'Sold it?' Uddin shouted in response. 'Sold your hand? For money?'

'Yes.'

'Quietly,' Smithdown reminded them both. 'We're supposed to be doing this quietly.'

'You sold your actual, real-life hand? I'm in shock here. Genuinely. Are you being serious? Oh wow - a second-hand hand! That's just... wow. I mean, who buys hands? Serious question. Who buys hands?'

'Richard T. King,' Naomi said. 'He buys hands.'

CHAPTER THIRTY-NINE

2.25 pm Tuesday 5 April 1988

Detective Constable Bob Donaldson gave a friendly nod and a cheery smile to the reception staff as he walked into Oldham Royal Hospital. He chatted briefly to a hospital porter he vaguely knew; his son was applying for a job with the police and Donaldson wished him the best of luck. He jokingly told an elderly man in a wheelchair to slow down as he passed him on the corridor, winking at the nurse who was pushing him. Then he made his way towards the ward where Kate Smithdown was being treated. He waited until the corridor was clear then opened the door of the private room and quietly stepped inside.

Kate was asleep, her normally spiky hair flattened and pressed against her head. It made her look much younger. Donaldson watched her for at least a minute, making sure she was fully asleep. Then he took the sterile mini scalpel that he'd taken from another ward on his earlier visit from his pocket. It was tiny - the kind they used for cutting away stitches or bandages when a patient had recovered.

In his head he ran through the picture he would paint when he filed his report.

Kate must have pinched it when one of the nurses wasn't looking. Only a little thing, but sharp as anything those blades. The shame of it all was just too much for her, I reckon. Plenty of people saw her buy those drugs but she denied it and denied it. You can't blame her, I suppose, being a copper's daughter. But I never thought for a moment she'd do herself in. Terrible. Just terrible. I've known her since she was this big. Watched her grow up. Just awful to find her like that. Blood everywhere. There was nothing I could do. I called for help straight away but it was too late. It was the way she did it that got me. You don't cut up the arm if you're messing about. You mean it. I blame myself. If only I'd stayed longer to keep an eye on her, maybe it wouldn't have happened. I'm so, so sorry.

Donaldson was about to peel open the scalpel, reminding himself to keep the thin, flat handle inside the foil wrapper to avoid getting his fingerprints on it, when he heard a voice from the corner of the room: 'Hello Bob.'

'Fook me Jean, you nearly had me in coronary care.' The blade went back into his pocket.'What are you doing here?'

Jean Smithdown pushed herself up from the chair in the corner of the room and stood deliberately close to the alarm button next to Kate's bed. For someone so thin she looked incredibly strong. 'I'm on mum duty, that's what I'm doing, Bob. Keeping Kate from harm's way. How about you?'

'I promised John I'd swing past. Have you heard from him?'

'I have. He told me to get myself down to the hospital and keep an eye on our little girl. He said there's a lot of trouble right now and that you've got to look out for your loved ones. Keep them close. Keep them safe. Just in case.'

'He's not daft, your husband.'

'He's not, Bob. And neither am I.'

'So, you won't be needing me?' Bob asked, his hand still on the scalpel in his pocket.

'Definitely not. If there's a problem I just need to press this alarm here and a nurse will come running. I tried it the other day. It's amazing. One press and someone was here in an instant. The staff here are wonderful, they really are. So quick. So attentive. God bless the NHS I say, Bob.'

'Can't disagree with you there, Jean.'

They stood for a moment. Both assessing the situation. Weighing it up. Both knowing, yet not saying. 'I'll be off then,' Donaldson said.

'Goodbye Bob.'

'Bye Jean.'

Jean Smithdown stood perfectly still, her hand still hovering close to the alarm button. She waited until the door was closed and Donaldson's footsteps faded away into the general noise of the hospital. Still she didn't move. It was a good three minutes until she allowed herself to sit down. And weep.

CHAPTER FORTY

2.40 pm Tuesday 5 April 1988

'The police station isn't this way,' Uddin said from the passenger seat of Smithdown's car. 'It's literally the other way. I'd have thought that you, of all people, would know where Oldham Cop Shop is.'

'We're not going to the police station,' the detective pointed out. 'I need somewhere safe, somewhere away from anyone who means Naomi harm. And, unfortunately, that isn't the police station right now.'

'Why is he even here?' Naomi asked the detective from her position lying flat on the back seat of the car. 'He's fucking annoying.'

'That's not very nice,' Uddin said.

'He knows you're alive,' Smithdown pointed out. 'Not many people do. I want him near me. He's got a proper gob on him.'

'Again, not very nice…' Uddin muttered.

'Plus,' the detective added. 'I'm not sure I could have carried you up those stairs on my own.'

They'd created quite a stir in the street when they'd emerged from the house. Smithdown imagined someone giving a description to the police about what they saw: a middle-aged white male, grey hair, moustache, wearing a white shirt and grey trousers… Accompanied by an Asian male, early 20s, wearing a brightly-coloured top and loose-fitting jeans. They were helping a third person into a car - possibly female. The third person had a grey suit jacket covering their face. Some eyewitnesses say this person was holding their arm as if injured.

Smithdown hadn't been sure what to do in the street. Despite how suspicious the scene looked, the people stood and watched in near silence. One elderly man even helped them get Naomi into the car by holding the door open. As they'd lifted Naomi into the car, a plastic bag of pills had fallen from the detective's trouser pocket and hit the kerb. The two men's eyes met for a moment, then the older one picked the bag up and handed it back to Smithdown. There had been a ripple of noise through the crowd when this had happened. It was as if the people in the street knew that despite the strangeness of what they were witnessing, there was good at play not evil. Once the young woman was in place, the detective had stood for a moment and looked at the crowd. He'd nodded his appreciation and then driven off.

'I could have walked,' Naomi said from the back seat. 'I didn't ask to be carried. Can I sit up now? It smells bad back here. Have you been eating chips in this car? I'm starving by the way.'

Smithdown was astonished by her resilience. She'd complained about many things since they'd broken open the door in Lennon's basement, but she hadn't once mentioned the pain she must have been in. *Tough woman. Fuck knows what she's been through.*

'No, you can't sit up - stay put,' the detective instructed. 'Not long now.'

Smithdown's car reached eastern edge of Alexandra Park and turned into Queen's Road. He stopped, told his two passengers to wait - particularly when Naomi swearily complained about the indignity of lying on the chip-scented back seat for a moment longer - and knocked on the door of an impressive, three-story red brick town house.

A minute later, the detective was back. 'Let's go,' he said. 'Quick as you can. Naomi, keep your head covered.'

She did as she was asked as Smithdown and Uddin helped her up the steps and into the roomy hallway of the house. Like a soldier on manoeuvres, the younger man swept the air around them with his crowbar as they walked. He hadn't let it out of his sight since Smithdown had handed it to him in Tom Lennon's house.

Naomi took Smithdown's jacket from her head and looked at Mr Aleem. 'Hello, Naomi,' he said with a smile. His face was purple and bruised and looked as if the smile hurt him. But he did it anyway.

She looked at Aleem's bandaged arm - then looked at her own: 'Snap,' she said. 'Do you have anything to eat? I'm absolutely famished.'

CHAPTER FORTY-ONE

3.15 pm Tuesday 5 April 1988

'Mr Aleem?' Smithdown asked. 'Do you have a recording device of some description that I could borrow?'

'Yes, I do.' He went to another room. The detective heard what sounded like the contents of a drawer being turned out. The house was quiet. Aleem's family had moved out of the house, fearful of more attacks. They'd gone to Longsight to stay with relatives and he was due to follow them but had changed his mind when Smithdown appeared at his door. The detective was glad he was there but concerned about his friend's bruised and battered appearance. *Another tough customer. Not one complaint about his injuries.*

'I bought it a while ago,' Mr Aleem said, returning with a small Dictaphone. 'I planned to fill it with great ideas that would make me a millionaire. I've barely used it.' He tested it with a one-two, one-two and then played it back. Satisfied that it was working, Mr Aleem put it back into record mode and placed it on the kitchen table in front of Naomi. He put two spare micro cassettes next to the recorder. 'You may need these as well,' he offered.

'You might be right there,' Smithdown replied. The recording light on the Dictaphone winked on and off as he spoke, reacting to the detective's voice. He waited until Naomi finished the last piece of a pile of toast that Mr Aleem had put in front of her. Uddin pulled up a chair and leant forward, as if he were about to listen to a master storyteller weave a fantastic tale. Mr Aleem took a chair and leant in too.

'So,' the detective began. 'First things first Naomi. The hand. Tell us about how your hand ended up in the boating lake at Alexandra Park.'

CHAPTER FORTY-TWO

3.30 pm Tuesday 5 April 1988

'I'm just doing what Mr Smithdown told me,' DC Bob Donaldson told Brenda Graham in a quiet, conspiratorial voice. 'He was very particular. Speak to Brenda, get little Becky well away, do whatever it takes to make the kid safe, because she's not safe there. Those were his very words.'

'Okay,' Brenda acknowledged, taking one of Donaldson's Rothman's and lighting it as the pair stood at the back doorstep of the care home.

'Don't let me down, Bob. That was the last thing he said. Don't take no for an answer and don't let me down.'

'But why?' Brenda asked. 'No one knows she's here but the police and social services. I'm here day and night. We're well out of the way here, to say the least. Surely, Becky's best left here? She's had enough to-ing and fro-ing to last a lifetime.'

'I agree with you,' Bob said, his arms outstretched. 'I really do. But he was adamant. There's something going on that's for sure but he's not sharing it with the likes of me.'

She thought for a moment. 'Poor girl. She's been through so much. Now more disruption for her. Bloody John Smithdown. What's he playing at?'

'Who knows? I'm just a foot soldier, doing what I'm told.'

Brenda grumpily tapped the cigarette out against the back wall so she could smoke the rest of it later. A mini waterfall of sparks tumbled down the red bricks. 'I'll get her stuff together,' she muttered. 'Bloody John Smithdown.'

CHAPTER FORTY-THREE

3.35 pm Tuesday 5 April 1988

'Me and Jimmy owed King money,' Naomi began. 'A lot of fookin' money. He'd been flooding the town with E and everyone wanted it. We couldn't shift it fast enough. Actually, we could shift it fast enough… in fact we started shifting it faster than we were getting it. People were eating them like sweets. But then there was a break in supply. Some gangster-shit in Ibiza. The pill heads of Oldham were not happy. We had their money; they had no Es and King had no profit. Probably didn't help that we were necking it ourselves like there was no tomorrow. Any road - we owed King ten grand. That's what he told us, anyway. So that's when he offered me a deal - I give up my hand and me, Becky and Jimmy disappear off to the coast.'

Uddin couldn't help himself: 'Ten grand for a hand? Wow. I mean... wow. That's just off the scale mad that is.'

'Just to be clear,' Smithdown said, holding up a hand to temper Uddin's excited curiosity. 'Richard T. King chopped your hand off in exchange for cancelling your drug debt?'

'The money was a side bet to be honest,' Naomi admitted. Then she let out a long breath. There was a pause. The detective waited. He knew from years of interviewing people that creating silence was a good way of getting someone to say more. 'They came to the flat and that shit Adam Griffin belted my little Becky,' she continued. 'They had Jimmy pinned down. He couldn't stop them. Griffin proper knocked her about. Tom Lennon was there too. Just watching. He said she'd get worse if I didn't go along with the hand thing.'

She paused again. For a moment Smithdown thought she

might cry. She didn't. 'Poor Jimmy. He was a good guy. Kind. Great with Becky. She really liked him. Now he's dead and everyone thinks he beat up a little girl.'

'No wonder he didn't want to talk to me when he was in custody,' Smithdown observed.

'He couldn't.' Naomi said. 'He let everyone think that he'd done that to our Becky, and he said nowt. Then he goes to Strangeways and suddenly hangs himself? I don't fookin' think so.'

'Christ. Becky said nothing either, not a word,' the detective said.

'I hear you got her put in care by ripping half her face off.' Naomi responded. 'You're a twat but you probably saved her life.'

'How did you know about that?' Smithdown asked.

'It's amazing what you hear when you're handcuffed to a bed in a cellar,' she replied, pointing to the ceiling. 'Is she okay?'

'She's in a children's home over at Alt,' the detective said. 'She's absolutely safe. So, Jimmy had nothing to do with Becky's injuries?'

'They said they'd kill her if we didn't do what they said. In fact, they said she'd get worse. King said them racist pricks… the White Wankers or whatever they're called... could have her first. Then they'd kill her. My hand was by way of a swap for no more harm coming to Becky. The drug debt was just a bonus. What would you have fookin done? They could have taken both me arms as far as I was concerned.'

'But what did they want with your hand?' asked Mr Aleem. 'Sorry, John. This is your interview, apologies.'

'Not at all,' Smithdown said. 'That was exactly what I was going to ask, to be honest.'

Smithdown, Mr Aleem and Uddin all looked at Naomi, not wanting to seem too eager but all - for their own reasons - wanting to know the answer: 'They wanted it so that your lot would think it was me up at that Mermaid's Pool.'

'So, who was it then?' the detective asked. 'At the pool?'

'That councillor woman.'

'No, no, no,' said Mr Aleem. 'Sharmeen Chowdhury. My God.'

Smithdown thought about the scene at the Mermaid's Pool. The twisted, smoking thing that had once been a person. He remembered what DC Seddon had said: What had she done to generate that kind of hate? 'Because she was Asian?' the detective asked.

'King didn't give a fook what she was,' Naomi said, almost laughing. 'Though it was probably a nice tease in getting Tom Lennon and his mates involved. Nah. Nowt to do with it. She was just in King's way. She was of Head of Stopping Cunts Getting Away With Shit for the Council. And old Richard T. King is literally King of the Cunts Who Try To Get Away With Shit.'

Smithdown and Uddin both looked at Mr Aleem for an explanation. 'I wouldn't quite put it in those terms myself, to be honest,' Aleem sighed. 'But, put another way, Sharmeen was Chair of the Scrutiny Committee. She was one of us...'

Smithdown looked puzzled. 'A Tory, John. It's traditional to have an opposition councillor in charge of overseeing what the Council does. So, Labour-led council, Tory Chair of Scrutiny. Most of her time was spent knocking back housing proposals, particularly ones that involved the mass development of ex-council house stock. Like all those boarded up houses to the east of the town. People tend to think of council houses as being newer houses, built in the last few decades. But a lot of council stock is older mill workers' terraces. A lot of them were badly damaged in the rioting.'

'That's handy,' Smithdown said. He was fairly certain he heard Uddin snigger, but he let it pass.

'Quite,' Aleem continued. 'Now, I'm all for a bit of gentle social engineering via home ownership. You've got a Conservative for life if you've sold someone their council house and they've made thousands of pounds on it - but putting it all into one person's pocket is a no-no.'

'Was King behind all the applications?' Smithdown asked.

‘Possibly,’ Aleem conceded. ‘There’s been a flurry of these lately - made in a variety of names not normally known for their interest in housing development. Councillor Chowdhury was making it her business to find out who was behind them. Then she went missing. Caught up in the riots was the way it looked.’

Smithdown was quiet for a moment, processing what he was hearing. Naomi cut in: ‘King makes millions on damaged council houses,’ she said, as if it was completely obvious. ‘Tom Lennon gets to act like a hero and become a fookin’ councillor or some such shit…’ She glanced at Mr Aleem. ‘No offence. And the White Wankers get to fire up a race war and kill some brown people. Everyone’s a fookin’ winner, aren’t they? Is there any more toast?’

‘On its way.’ Aleem said. He indicated to Uddin that it was his turn to make toast. Reluctantly, the young man headed for the kitchen.

‘Did you honestly think they’d let you go?’ the detective asked. ‘Didn’t you think someone would want to know more about what happened to you?’

‘You know full well Mr Smithdown, nobody gives a shit about people like me being cut up and burned. Ten a penny we are. Barely gets reported when some no-one like me goes missing. But someone like Councillor what’s-her-face? Different matter. So, they do her in. It looks like it’s me and then she’s just an unfortunate missing person after the riots. No one can prove anything. Bingo.’

‘I gave a shit, Naomi,’ Smithdown said, quietly.

‘Yes,’ replied. ‘You did, didn’t you?’

‘We can’t prove any of this,’ Smithdown pointed out. ‘I know you’re right and I know that bastard Lennon targeted my Kate too, but we can’t prove any of this.’

‘Yeah you can,’ Naomi corrected. ‘That councillor’s hand will do the job. Bang that on the front desk at Oldham nick and you’ve got them by the goolies.’

‘But we don’t have her hand,’ Smithdown pointed out.

‘Not yet, you don’t…’ Naomi said, raising her eyebrows

conspiratorially. 'But I know where it is. That sicko Griffin kept the fookin thing. Until Tom found out and made him get rid of it.'

'So where is it now?' Aleem asked.

'It's in that pool.'

'It can't be,' the detective pointed out. 'It was dredged top to toe after the body was found. There was nothing in it apart from a load of old pop bottles.'

'They waited until your lot did their stuff then went back and dumped the hand in it,' Naomi said. 'Pretty clever really. What's the one place you wouldn't think of looking? The place you've already looked. They watched you from that lodge. That hand is still in the pool right now as far as I know. There's your proof, right there.'

Uddin returned with more toast. So far, he'd taken Smithdown's request to heart and kept silent. Now he spoke: 'I don't mean any disrespect by this, I'm not saying I don't believe you, I'm really not. But why keep you alive? Why tie you up in that cellar? It would have been easier to do you in when they were taking your hand. Why keep you alive?'

Smithdown remembered the leaflets at the lodge. The promise of justice after what the Wolves described as 'a spate of sex attacks' in the town. Attacks that, to the best if his knowledge hadn't happened. He realised then why they had kept Naomi alive. And it sickened him. 'Leave it lad,' the detective advised.

Uddin pressed on: 'No, sorry. It doesn't make sense…' he continued.

'Leave it, I said,' Smithdown repeated.

'If I was them, right,' the young man continued, 'I'd have killed you at the earliest possible opportunity. Probably when I was doing your hand. That's when I'd have done it. But they kept you in that cellar. Why would they do that? I'm just asking. Why would they?

'Practice,' Naomi said flatly. She gave Uddin a hard, direct look. 'They knew that attacking young white girls in town and blaming the South Asians would really kick things off, yeah?

But they needed someone to practice on. Yours truly…'

There was quiet now. 'I'm so, so sorry,' Uddin whispered.

'Next time I ask you to leave it, just leave it, right?' Smithdown said.

'Sorry. I just. Right. Okay. Sorry.'

Mr Aleem had tears in his eyes. He spoke quietly: 'Naomi. Who cut your hand off?'

'Adam Griffin did it. He's a porter at the Royal and apparently, pushing people around a hospital qualifies you to perform surgery. I can assure you that it don't. It really don't.'

'Mr Aleem, you've helped us no end,' the detective said. 'I appreciate it. I really do. I wonder… could you possibly help a little more?'

'Of course, John. Anything.'

'Naomi here needs medical attention...'

'I'm fine...' she interrupted.

'Christ Almighty! You've been locked in a cellar for days and your hand has been chopped off. I think that's worth a once over with a stethoscope at the very least, don't you?'

'Spose so...' she conceded.

'We can't trust the hospitals around here, especially if the Wolves have mates at the Royal. Can you take Naomi over the border to the hospital in Glossop? While you're there, find Detective Constable Jenny Seddon from the local police. She knows the deal. I trust her, but she didn't show up to the meeting we'd arranged earlier today, so she needs updating.'

'John, of course I want to help, but I can't drive,' Aleem pointed out, lifting his bandaged arm as if proof were needed.

'Good point. Take a taxi.'

'Shall we go now?' Aleem asked.

'No. Sit tight here. Tell no one about Naomi. Wait until we've found what we're looking for at the pool, then I'll call you.'

'*We've* found what *we're* looking for?' Uddin checked. 'I'm coming too?'

'Yes, you are,' Smithdown said. 'Can't have someone with a gob as big as yours, knowing what you know, wandering about. Might as well put it on the news...'

'So rude, honestly,' Uddin muttered.

'Plus, I need a witness. It's my word against half of Oldham at the moment. Being a witness will require you to keep your eyes and ears open and your trap shut.'

'Of course,' Uddin said, 'Mr Discreet. That's me.'

'We need to put Tom Lennon and his mates on the back foot,' Smithdown told them. 'Naomi here - back from the dead - plus Councillor Chowdhury's hand should do the trick. About time too. Our town's gone very, very wrong this last week or so. We need to start making things right.'

CHAPTER FORTY-FOUR

4.05 pm Tuesday 5 April 1988

'King here…'

DC Bob Donaldson punched three two pence pieces into the payphone and spoke once the beeps had cleared. 'Mr King, it's Mr Donaldson here. Bit of an update, a bit of news, plus a bit of a suggestion. Which do you want first?'

'I want you to tell me what the fuck is going on and what the fuck is being done about it,' King said. 'That's what I want.' His legs swung gently left to right as he rested them on the suspended table in his office. Lennon and Griffin were there too. 'I've had enough surprises for one day, thank you very much.'

'The daughter was a no-go at the hospital,' Donaldson stated. 'Couldn't be done. Maybe another time. So, I improvised and grabbed the little 'un from the care home instead. Told the woman in charge that I was acting on Smithdown's orders. She seemed happy with it. I've tipped off the press to that effect and that'll link her name to his. So, everything is being pushed nicely in his direction now.'

'I thought you weren't supposed to name kids in care…?' King queried.

'Children and Young Persons Act 1933, Mr King,' Donaldson pointed out, in a bad-tempered voice. 'The welfare of the child is paramount. She's under a care order with anonymity, but her safety overrides that. We'll use the law in our favour to link Smithdown to the kid. He's done for. You stick to showbiz - leave the law to me.'

'So where is she now?' King asked.

'Young 'un? In the boot of my car with half a bottle of your electric water down her trap.'

'Well, that's one less thing to worry about.'

'Funny you should say that -we do actually have another problem,' Donaldson said, tapping one his spare coins on the telephone box window. 'According to your man Lennon it turns out that dickhead Griffin kept a bit of Councillor Chowdhury as a keepsake. Is he there?'

'Yes, he is,' King confirmed.

'Tell him he's a fucking tool from me.'

King put his hand over the receiver and caught Griffin's very swollen eye: 'DC Donaldson says you are - and I'm quoting here - a fucking tool.'

'Her hand is in the water up at Kinder Scout,' Donaldson continued. 'And if Naomi knows about it, then you can be pretty sure they'll be headed that way. If Smithdown gets hold of it, we're all fucked.'

'An absolute mess, this is,' King said, staring at Lennon and Griffin.

'No, I reckon it's perfect,' Donaldson corrected. 'We get them all together in the same spot and sort it out in a one-r. Smithdown, Naomi, the Paki lad and the daughter. Bang. Job done and everything lands on Smithdown's plate.'

'That sounds grand but there's one small problem - I DON'T KNOW WHERE THE FUCK NAOMI IS,' King shouted.

'Luckily, I do. I had them followed from Tom's house, she's at Aleem's. Two uniform lads - both true to the cause - are outside the house now waiting on instructions. I suggest the instructions should be to take out Naomi properly. She's already dead as far as everyone's concerned anyway and I'll say Smithdown told me to deliver little Becky to him. Out of his mind with grief over his missus, and all that - ashamed of what his daughter had done. So, he's taken the little 'un up the moors and done her in. There are plenty more good soldiers back at the station who'll back me up and say he was going round the bend. Then it's done.'

'What about Aleem?' King asked.

'Easy. Pakis came back to finish the job, didn't they? More fuel for the fire. As it were.'

'You make it sound so easy,' King sighed.

'It is easy,' Donaldson said. 'It always was. Councillor out of the way, use Naomi as the diversion, stoke up the trouble in town, get a foothold on the council. Easy-bastard-peasy. Too many dickheads with their hand on the tiller - that's been the problem. Not anymore. I'm taking charge now. Tell Cannon and Ball there to meet me up at Kinder. I'll make sure things are done right. I appreciate that you're seeing all this largely as a way of making a fuckload of money. But to us, this is a fucking war. God's on our side. So are a good portion of the Oldham police. So, it's a war we cannot - will not - lose.'

'Manchester Radio News at six this is Beth Hall. There's growing concern this evening over the whereabouts of a nine-year-old girl who's gone missing from a care home in Oldham. It's believed that Becky Wells may be with a middle-aged man who has recently been suspended from Greater Manchester Police. Robert Crane has more.'

'Oldham Police and council social workers say that Becky Wells may in real danger after going missing in the Alt area of Oldham earlier today.

The child is thought to be in a very distressed state after the recent death of her mother.

Police investigating her disappearance believe that one of their colleagues may have vital information about Becky's whereabouts. They want Detective Inspector John Smithdown to contact them immediately. He has been suspended from his job after an incident at Oldham Police station where a child was injured while in his care. Sources within Oldham Police say that Becky Wells is the child that was hurt.

Now an appeal's gone out asking local residents in Alt and surrounding areas to look out for the pair. Mr Smithdown is described as white, in his 50s with grey hair and a moustache. He's wearing a grey suit and white shirt. Becky Wells is slightly built and has dark hair. When last seen she was wearing a t-shirt, jeans and sandals. Robert Crane, Manchester Radio News, Oldham.'

CHAPTER FORTY-FIVE

6.10 pm Tuesday 5 April 1988

'If I'd have known we were going climbing, I wouldn't have worn these trainers,' Uddin said after Smithdown parked close to the dam end of Kinder Reservoir and they took the path up towards the moor. The warm evening wind followed them, pushing the pair lightly along. The sun was dropping now, getting closer to the ridge of Lantern Pike behind them. Soon, the moorland underneath Kinder Scout would be in shadow, then darkness - and so would the Mermaid's Pool.

'I don't think this is technically classed as climbing,' Smithdown countered. 'Though it will be technically classed as bloody dark in about an hour, so we'd better get a shift on. Been here before?'

'Absolutely not,' Uddin replied. 'I don't do countryside. Too many variables. You know where you are in a town.'

'I think your brother might disagree with you there,' Smithdown muttered as they walked past the reservoir overflow. The lack of rain over recent weeks had reduced it to a weedy trickle over the top of the shiny green moss that lined the concrete funnel running from the top of the dam. What little water there was then joined the River Kinder which stretched away down the valley back towards Hayfield.

The detective looked up at the Kinder Downfall as they walked: 'Do you know what's weird about the waterfall up there?' Smithdown asked, waving a finger in the direction of ridge above them. He was trying to make conversation as they walked. He felt awkward with the young man, out of his depth.

'I must confess I don't, Mr Smithdown,' Uddin replied. 'Do

I need to?'

'No,' admitted the detective. 'But I'm going to tell you anyway. One of the mountain rescue lads told me about it last time I was here. It'll pass the time.'

'Brilliant,' Uddin said, wiping his trainers on a clump of grass for the third time since they'd started. They passed through a kissing gate - taking turns to swing the wooden gate back then forwards to step through - then began their walk across the open upper moor.

'It's unusual because sometimes the water goes up, instead of down,' Smithdown said.

'Yeah, right.'

'It's true.'

'Absolutely.'

'See that?' the detective asked, pointing up towards the ridge of Kinder Scout. One section had a deep groove cut into it several hundred feet across, bookended by huge slabs of rock. 'It's called the Downfall. It's a waterfall that sometimes goes backwards when the wind is just right. A waterfall that goes up not down. Weird, isn't it? The wind rattles in and if it's stronger than the downward force of the water, the waterfall goes up instead of down.'

'As if things weren't freaky enough right now - what with the whole let's-fish-a-hand-out-of-the-Mermaid's-Pool stuff, you're pointing out further local spots of weirdness. And this one just happens to be called the Downfall. Thanks for that, Detective Inspector Metaphor.'

'I'm not being metaphorical. I was just making conversation. Did it sound like I was?'

'Potentially,' Uddin sighed. 'I can't work you out.'

'Likewise,' the detective grunted. 'Sorry. Just thought it was interesting. You think too much, mate, that's your problem.'

'Okay then - seeing as though you are clearly steeped in local legend… tell me this: why do they call it the Mermaid's Pool?'

Smithdown thought about the story he'd been told about the mermaid legend… and her propensity for killing people she didn't like. 'It's just mumbo jumbo bollocks courtesy of the locals,' the detective said, keen not to pursue the line of conversation any further. 'It's getting dark and as we're about to go paddling looking for the severed limb of a murdered woman… so it's probably best if we skip that one.'

'Shall we just walk in silence, then?' Uddin asked, somewhat sarcastically.

'Of course not. Sorry. Any other non-weird questions?'

'Bit tricky at the moment - everything is weird, to be honest. I saw you looking at those handcuffs on Naomi. They were really hard to cut too. Were those police handcuffs?'

'Have you ever thought of joining the police, Uddin?'

'Absolutely not. I'm going to be a lawyer. Why?'

'Although you're quite annoying, you'd probably make a pretty good policeman. You notice things. Yes, they were police handcuffs.'

'So, the cops could be involved in this too?' Uddin asked, his voice a mix of disgust and disbelief. 'Your mates… in bed with these Nazis? I refuse to use the expression neo-Nazi. Makes it sound fashionable and desirable, like a new nightclub.'

'I think so, yes.' The detective was getting short of breath now, as the land began to rise, and the hags and dips of the terrain became more prominent.

'Wow,' the young man deadpanned. 'Nazi cops. Absolute shocker.'

'Is that how you see it?' Smithdown asked.

'Yes, I do. And it appears that I'm entirely right.'

'This is the bit when I tell you about a few bad apples isn't it? About what a great lot we all are - on the whole; just good people doing a tough job as best we can? But under the circumstances, I'm going to say nowt. I don't know what I know anymore. Or who.' Smithdown looked around the darkening landscape. 'I'm a bit lost, to be honest.'

'Maybe if you got out of the bubble of your own world, your own experience. Your own kind. That would help. That's the problem with Oldham. It's completely compartmentalised.'

'No, I mean I'm literally a bit lost,' the detective pointed out. 'I thought we'd be clear of the open moor by now.'

'I see,' Uddin smiled. 'You're not a great one for introspection are you, Mr Smithdown.'

'Not if I can help it mate, no.'

Once Smithdown had satisfied himself they were indeed going the right way, they carried on without speaking. They walked through a walled plantation of trees, criss-crossed another stream and eased their way up and across the final stretch of moorland.

Then they crested the final hill that hid the Mermaid's Pool from view from the moors below. It looked smaller than when the detective had been here to view what they'd thought had been the body of Naomi Wells just a few days earlier. The water level seemed lower too. One end now had so little water in, it had turned to mud. The pool had a haze of blue dragonflies over it, dancing and darting around the reeds as the last of the sunlight disappeared over the ridge behind them.

A pile of bottles and cans had appeared next to the water; the police divers who'd searched the water had placed them neatly at one end, but none of them had apparently decided that it might be a good idea to take them away. So, there they had stayed, like a bizarre memorial cairn to where Councillor Sharmeen Chowdhury's life had been ended, as she reached out to try to end her indescribable suffering.

'Is this where it happened?' Uddin asked, his voice quiet now, all the confidence and humour scrubbed away.

'Yes,' Smithdown confirmed. 'Right here.' The two were silent for a moment. 'She must have begged,' the detective said. 'Over and over again. All the way here. Begged when they had her hand away, begged when they got the petrol out and begged when they made her swallow it. Then they set fire to her anyway.'

Uddin looked at the blackened patch of grass near to the pool. It had grown a little, the burnt areas where the fire had been now formed the top of the blades where the grass had grown through. 'Are we going in there?' Uddin asked, turning away from the burnt grass and looking across the peaty-coloured surface of the pool.

'Yes, I'm afraid that we are,' Smithdown replied. 'If this all works out okay, I'm sure there'll be some compensation fund that will get you some new trainers. Potentially, anyway. Which end do you want?'

'What?' Uddin replied.

'The pool, the detective pointed out. 'We need to search it methodically. Which end do you want to start at? Then we can meet in the middle.'

'The un-muddy end.'

'Thought you might say that. Right. See you in the middle.'

Smithdown stepped into the water up to his knees and his feet immediately dropped a few inches into the silt at the bottom. He remembered what one of the mountain rescue team members had said to him about the water in the Mermaid's Pool: how it was salted because the lake was somehow connected to the sea. He dipped a finger into the water and put it into his mouth. It tasted a little stagnant and mossy, but there was no hint of salt. *Mumbo jumbo bollocks.*

The detective went in another few feet then bent over and began a fingertip search of the bottom of the pool.

Uddin, meanwhile, was still standing by the water's edge, gingerly poking at the bottom of the pool with his crowbar. 'I can smell smoke,' he said. 'Can you smell smoke? Should we be smelling smoke way out here?'

'Nothing to worry about,' Smithdown said, reassuringly. 'You're in the countryside now, lad. All sorts of weird and wonderful smells out here. Stop being mardy - get in the water and start searching.'

CHAPTER FORTY-SIX

6.25 pm Tuesday 5 April 1988

Aleem had just finished on the phone when there was a knock at the door. 'Good evening sir, sorry to trouble you. It's Mr Aleem, isn't it?'

He looked at the two police officers. Both young, both keen-looking and both smiling. Both white.

'Yes, it is. Good evening. Can I ask what it's about?' Aleem asked.

'We just need a moment of your time,' the first PC said. 'It's in connection with the attack and the injuries you sustained.' He nodded at Mr Aleem 's bandaged arm. 'We've got a bit of news. Could we come in for a moment please?'

Aleem hesitated. He glanced inside the house and immediately regretted it. 'Is there anyone else here with you this evening, sir?' the second officer asked.

'No there isn't - just myself,' he replied. Smithdown had insisted that Naomi stay out of sight until they received a call from him to head for Glossop police station. If anyone else were to ask, he was to deny all knowledge of her.

'Officer, as you know - as you can see - I was quite badly injured a few days ago. I'm not feeling anywhere near well enough to speak to you, though I'm keen to hear the news you have. Could you possibly come back tomorrow? I'd be so grateful.'

The two officers looked at each other. The first one smiled and nodded. 'Of course. We'll come back then. Not a problem. Sorry to trouble you.'

'I very much appreciate it,' Aleem said. He pushed the door to close it just as both the PCs kicked the door, sending him crashing against the hallway wall.

Naomi called out from upstairs. The police officers didn't understand the word Naomi had screamed. Aleem did and as the blows came down it broke his heart.

Daddy.

CHAPTER FORTY-SEVEN

6.50 pm Tuesday 5 April 1988

Bent nearly double, with water up to the tops of their legs and their arms totally submerged, Smithdown and Uddin had been in the Mermaid's Pool for nearly 15 minutes when the younger man did a combined shout and scream, fell backwards and sat down. He immediately leapt up, windmilled both arms, stumbled forwards and waded to the water's edge. 'There!' Uddin shouted. 'Where I just was. There's something there. I'm not touching it. That's your job.'

'Technically, it isn't any more,' the detective said quietly, pushing through the water to where Uddin had been searching and reached under the surface. He felt something soft and round and lifted it up. It felt like a ball of uncooked chicken. It was heavier than he was expecting it to be, but the detective felt there would be a logical explanation for that when he lifted it clear of the water. There was.

The small areas of Sharmeen Chowdhury's hand that he could actually see were just as bloated and puffy as the one he'd looked at on the edge of Alexandra Park boating lake just a few days earlier. Probably more so. But that hand was supposed to be found. This one wasn't. It had been crudely Gaffa-taped to a rock to make sure it sank into the waters of the Mermaid's Pool. The flesh had begun to break down in the water. The detective examined the find more closely. The tape - and the fact that the fingers were pressed into the rock – appeared to have protected the integrity of the fingerprints. Smithdown felt elated. *We've got the fuckers.* Then almost immediately there was a jab of guilt. *These are human remains, John lad. A hard-working, decent person who wanted the best for*

Oldham. She was the exact opposite of the racist fucks who did this. It's not the time for celebrating. 'I think our work here is done, Uddin,' he said quietly as he made his way to the shore.

'Is that what I think it is?' the young man asked, hugging his knees as he sat on the grass.

'It's exactly what you think it is,' the detective confirmed.

He looked around for something to wrap the hand in. There was nothing. 'I don't suppose you have an evidence bag on you, Uddin.'

'No,' the young man replied. 'I feel a bit stupid now for not bringing one with me when I left the house this morning.'

Smithdown remembered the care that the mountain rescue team had taken in bringing Sharmeen Chowdhury's body down from the same spot. He felt embarrassed that he couldn't offer the same level of respect with the last of her remains.

He thought for a moment, then took off his jacket, shirt and vest. All three were wet. He carefully - he hoped respectfully - wrapped the hand in his vest and put the hand into his jacket pocket. Then he put his shirt and mac back on. Not ideal, but better than nothing. 'Come on,' the detective said, bone tired but with the end in sight. 'Time to go, mate.' He put his hand onto Uddin's shoulder and gave it an appreciative squeeze. 'Thank you. You've done brilliantly. You didn't have to come, but you did.'

'Well, it was an experience I won't forget, I'll say that,' the young man replied.

'We'll be at the front desk of Glossop Police station in less than an hour. Can't risk going to Oldham. We'll meet up with Mr Aleem and Naomi, tell the local cops what we know, then this will all be over.'

They walked away from the pool and headed downhill. 'I can still smell smoke,' Uddin said. 'And the smell's getting stronger.'

'It'll be the gamekeepers,' Smithdown said. 'They do controlled burning to get rid of the dead vegetation. It's very carefully managed, we're quite safe.'

'How do you know that?' Uddin asked, sounding slightly cynical about Smithdown's confident-sounding display of countryside knowledge.

'A friend of mine told me,' the detective replied. He thought about Jenny Seddon for the first time in a few hours, remembering once again that she hadn't shown up to see DS Pym earlier in the day. 'She knows these hills. I mean really knows them. If Jenny Seddon says it's safe, then that's good enough for me.'

CHAPTER FORTY-EIGHT

7.00 pm Tuesday 5 April 1988

As the sun set behind White Brow, the soft ridge that ran above Kinder Reservoir, Tom Lennon questioned several of the Wolves about the firelighters they'd bought. 'How many did you buy in each shop?' he asked.

'Two packs in each. Like you said,' one replied.

'I actually got three in one shop,' replied another.

'What the fuck did I tell you?' Lennon shouted, his voice carrying across the empty car park they were standing in.

'There was an offer on!' the Wolf replied. 'Buy two, get a third one free. It would have looked weird if I'd turned it down.'

'Fine,' said Lennon. 'Always nice to get a bargain. How many packs in all?'

'I've got twelve,' said one Wolf.

'Thirteen, here,' the second one replied, quietly.

'Twenty-five packs with two dozen firelighter blocks in each,' Bob Donaldson said to King. 'That should send half of Derbyshire up in flames, let alone this moor.'

Adam Griffin, one of his eyes now completely swollen shut, spoke: 'If this moor goes up, we could all go up with it.'

Donaldson stepped forward, grabbed the younger man's face and pushed him backwards. 'If you hadn't decided to keep her hand like a little fucking weirdo, we wouldn't be here in the first place, would be?'

'The wind will be behind us,' Lennon said. 'It'll send the fire in their direction.'

'Sure?' Griffin said. 'I've seen these fires on the telly. They're mad.'

'Fookin hell,' Donaldson said, getting ready to properly hit Griffin this time.

'I know these hills,' Lennon stated, as if trying to show Donaldson he was still in control of Griffin and the other Wolves. 'And I know that if the fire doesn't get them, the panic created by the heat and smoke will send them into a gully. Then the fire and smoke will get them anyway.'

Donaldson pointed at Griffin: 'You. Get the little 'un and let's get cracking.'

Becky Wells was wedged between some rocks close to the path. She seemed to be moaning, crying and laughing quietly to herself all at the same time. Griffin took her arm, stood her up and lifted her onto his shoulder. Lennon addressed the Wolves: 'Right. Listen up. Adam, we'll take the girl up to the plantation. That's where the fire will burn the hardest. Give us 15 minutes head start so we can get clear off towards the side of Kinder Scout, then the rest of you take five packs a piece, spread out in a line at the bottom end of the moor, spark up the firelighters and drop them. Do it all at the same time then fuck off out of it. That'll create a nice strong line of fire. First there'll be a cold burn across the top of the moss. Then when it hits the peat it'll create a hot burn and that's when the fun will start. It could keep burning for weeks - months even.'

Bob Donaldson - there was no question as to who was really in charge now - spoke to the assembled Wolves. There were fifteen of them in all: as well as Lennon and Griffin there were several other members of the Kingdom security team, four members of well-known Manchester crime families and three convicted football hooligans - all the rest were police officers. As Donaldson spoke two more officers arrived - the pair who'd visited Mr Aleem's house.

'Right, I need to get back to Oldham, raise the alarm about Smithdown going crackers and get things in place at that end. This is simple, lads. Dump the little girl. Burn the moor. The evidence disappears. All sorted. Then it's all clear for St George's Day.'

He looked at each of them in turn. Then he asked: 'Who

are we?'

'WOLVES!' they shouted in unison.'

'What are we?'

'WHITE AND RIGHT!'

CHAPTER FORTY-NINE

7.45 pm Tuesday 5 April 1988

Heat. Fuel. Oxygen.

The perfect fire triangle was crackling into life at the bottom end of the moor, just as Smithdown and Uddin left the area at the top end close to the Mermaid's Pool.

With heat from the Wolves' firelighters and fuel in every direction, the fire was spoilt for choice as to where it would head, but the wind took control and pushed it up the moor in the direction of the pool. The fire was low-key to start with, the accompanying smoke was white and hissy, producing a steam engine-like smell. As it grew hotter and dug into the peat, the smoke became yellowy brown, taking on the more sweet and smoky flavours of the moor that surrounded it.

The smoke folded itself into the contours of the land as the fire became more confident and reacted to the ever-changing environment the landscape provided. Large boulders made the flames stop momentarily, reassess, then find a way around; tempting, tufted hags - grassy islands of especially combustible vegetation - made it stay a while, burning hard, flaring in the darkened landscape before moving on. Gullies forced it to stop and spread right and left until it found a new route or built up enough intensity to leap the break in the landscape and carry on regardless.

Smithdown and Uddin were halfway through the walled plantation of trees that separated the upper and lower areas of the moor when the smoke, emboldened by the wind, began to flood uphill towards them. It swirled around their legs, which were still wet from wading into the Mermaid's Pool. Through the trees and behind the smoke they saw the orange and red line of the fire moving in their direction. It stretched left and right as far as they could see and seemed to be moving at a sprinter's pace. 'I thought you said it was a managed fire,' Uddin said. 'That doesn't look managed to me. That looks really, really un-managed.'

'Yes, it does look a little unruly, doesn't it?' Smithdown admitted. The detective had picked up a little knowledge from the other emergency services of the years - one thing had always stuck in his mind: never be in front of a fire with smoke in your face. *And that's exactly where you are John lad.*

'We need to go back up the moor,' the detective said. 'Right now.'

The detective turned around and began to walk uphill when he saw something that made him stop and reluctantly go back towards the flames. 'No, no, no,' Uddin cried, pointing back up the moor. 'It's this way. It's totally this way and not that way, which is where the fire is. Trust me, I might not know much about the countryside, but this is the way we should definitely be going.'

'Not any more it isn't,' Smithdown replied, walking downhill through the smoke until he got to the collapsed figure of Becky Wells. The little girl was leant against the broken gate at the low end of the plantation. She was semi-conscious and dressed in just a t-shirt, jeans and plastic sandals - the same sandals that she'd worn when the detective first saw her at Oldham Police station. Smithdown knelt beside her; he touched her face and checked her pupils. They were huge, turning her brown eyes almost black.

'Oh my God!' Uddin shouted. 'Is that Naomi's daughter - the one who was really, really safe in the care home? My God. Who dumps a little girl out here? Seriously. Who does that?'

'People who want all the evidence destroyed in one go, that's who,' Smithdown pointed out. 'These moors could burn for weeks. No will find us and even if they do, they'll be nowt left worth identifying.'

The smoke was rushing and swirling between the plantation trees now, surrounding the three of them. Becky, lower down than Uddin and the detective, was coughing and spluttering, grey mucus flying from her mouth as her airways tightened. Smithdown knew he had to get her off the ground and up the moor.

He was about to pick her up when he heard shouts from the other side of the smoke. Sprinting towards them, with the leading edge of the fire alarmingly close to her, Naomi Wells was shouting something at them, her voice cracked and hoarse sounding. As she got closer, the detective could see that her face was covered in blood. Her saw her bandaged arm swinging left to right as she ran ahead of the flames. Smithdown also realised what it was she was actually saying: 'Pick her up you dozy twats. Pick her up and fookin' run!'

Seconds after she climbed over the gate, the fire hit the outer wall of the plantation, stopped for a moment, then set about burning the gate down. It wouldn't be long before the fire entered the walled-in space fully; dead, dried out trees, pine needles and vegetation all crammed into one space.

Heat. Fuel. Oxygen.

Smithdown watched as the flames began to take their first steps into the plantation. He was afraid now. Really afraid. They were tired, sluggish with hunger, drained from the cold of the Mermaid's Pool and lacking the skills and knowledge to deal with the situation. The detective might not have been an expert in the outdoors - unlike his colleagues from the Derbyshire Con-stab-u-lary - but he had more than his fair share of common sense. He looked around the plantation. *We're in a stone box filled with stuff that burns really well - it's going to go up like a barrel of fireworks. We need to get out of here right now.*

'Come on you pillocks! Shift yourselves!' Naomi shouted.

The detective slipped his hands under Becky's legs and lifted her out of the smoke; she began to scream and shout, hitting and kicking Smithdown and scratching at his face. He tried to pin her arms down as they moved back through the plantation. Every third step he seemed to stumble over a log or a tree root. Naomi tried her best to calm her daughter - but her quiet, soothing words made no difference. 'She's dosed up,' Smithdown said. 'God knows what they've put inside her. She must be terrified. I'm terrified and I'm not on drugs.'

Uddin, coughing, spitting and shouting almost at the same time, had a question: 'I don't suppose now is a good time to ask WHY SHE IS NOT HIDING AT MR ALEEM'S READY TO ALERT THE POLICE IN GLOSSOP SO THEY CAN ARREST EVERYONE!'

'They dragged me over here and gave me a choice,' she said walking quickly alongside Smithdown so she could stay near to her daughter. 'Die down there with them or die up here with my Becky.' She stroked the little girl's hair. 'No contest.'

'Where's Mr Aleem?' asked Smithdown.

'Back at his house,' Naomi said, quietly.

'How is he?' he continued.

'He's dead.' She looked straight into the detective's eyes. 'They beat him with… what do you call them? Batons. Police batons.'

Smithdown slowed a second. 'Jesus Christ. Not Aleem. He was a bloody good man. And he seemed to care a lot about you and Becky.'

'Yes, Mr Smithdown,' Naomi agreed. 'He really did.'

There was brief silence between the two of them. *Was she going to cry?*

'We need to shift,' Naomi said, firmly.

'Yes, you're right, we need to get out of here quicksticks,' the detective agreed.

Smithdown could feel the heat of the fire now as the last sections of the plantation gate gave way, giving the flames free reign to take hold of the trees and dried out vegetation across the forest floor. To their left and right the fire had started to race ahead of them now, matching them either side as they stumbled through the plantation. The stone walls were protecting them temporarily from the flames, but it wouldn't last. Soon they'd be surrounded. With Becky in his arms, the detective began to run as best he could through the trees. 'We need to get to the other end before the fire does.' The detective was shouting now; the flames had leapt over the walls and were taking a grip of the trees inside the plantation one by one. Rising columns of fire that had wrapped themselves around the trees, were appearing all around them.

The carpet of smoke was turning into a wall. The edges of plantation were now lost in the yellowy haze. Smithdown, his eyes streaming and his throat raw and swollen, was losing all sense of direction. Naomi was holding onto his arm - in reality she was dragging him downwards. Uddin was trying to keep up as best he could but was by now on his knees as often as he was on his feet. Becky, through a combination of fear and the cocktail of drugs she'd been given, screamed and screamed until her voice began to dry up.

They were done. And Smithdown knew it.

'GRAB THIS. GRAB IT. NOW!'

The voice didn't belong to Uddin or Naomi; it was muffled by a decorator's-style white breathing mask and came from a figure in the smoke illuminated by a head torch. A pole was wavering close to the detective's face. At the same time another pair of hands took hold of Becky Wells and lifted the child's limp body onto their shoulders.

Smithdown saw that the pole was a fire beater. He took Naomi's right hand and closed her fingers around the end of the pole. He grabbed the top of her bandaged arm and took a fistful of Uddin's collar with his other hand. It wasn't the most elegant human chain ever, but it seemed to work.

'KEEP TOGETHER AS BEST YOU CAN,' the voice instructed. 'WATCH YOUR FEET AND WATCH OUT FOR EACH OTHER. WE NEED TO GET OUT OF THE SMOKE AND GET CLEAR OF THE FIRE'S PATH.'

Smithdown felt himself pulled along by both the pole and the words of someone who seemed to know what they were doing. But then he noticed that they seemed to be heading back down the plantation towards the fiercest line of the fire. He was about to voice his opinion but realised that he didn't have the breath left in him.

The group then veered off to the left towards a break in the wall where it had been damaged. Fallen stones lay scattered either side of the gap and, by starving it of fuel, had made a small gap in the fire which created a way through.

Their rescuers dragged them through the opening and out of the plantation, extinguishing any remaining snatches of fire with their beaters.

They stepped into a triangle of moor that was a respite from the fire and the worst of the smoke. Behind them the plantation was now fully ablaze. To their right, the main line of fire was still approaching; to their left was the imposing edge of Kinder Scout.

Brian McIntyre dropped the fire beater and pulled off his mask. His face was blackened from the smoke save for an oval of white skin where the mask had been. 'Brian, lad,' Smithdown wheezed. 'You big, beautiful bastard. I could kiss you, I really could.'

'Something for me to look forward to for when we're properly safe,' Brian replied.

'Agreed,' the detective said, hawking up a big glob of phlegm and spitting the blackened mass onto the grass. 'But thank you anyway. I'm glad to see you. What brings you out here on this fine evening?'

'To be fair,' Brian replied, 'You can see this fire from Manchester city centre, but it was your friend Mr Aleem who told us you'd be out here. He called the Glossop cops.'

'It must have been the last thing he did before they got to him,' the detective said. 'I told him to wait. Thank God he didn't.'

'They've already rounded up a gang of nutcases heading out of the village,' Brian explained. 'Fucking neo-Nazis, apparently. In Hayfield! They say some of them were off duty cops from Oldham. Whether they got them all, I don't know.'

Smithdown looked at Naomi. She was too busy being sick to hear the conversation. 'I was worried for Jenny,' the detective said, quietly. 'She never showed up at Oldham nick.'

'You were right to be worried,' Brian replied as Jenny pulled off her mask to show her bruised and heavily swollen face. 'She shouldn't be here, she should be in hospital, but since when did she ever listen to me?'

'I was the nearest,' she said, her voice barely registering from the injuries to her throat. 'It made sense for me to come with you when we got the call. Now shut it and let's get moving. I assume that is Naomi?'

Wiping the sick from her mouth, Naomi nodded. 'Well, we don't want her dying a second time, do we?' Jenny said. She turned to Brian. 'We can't go back the way we came, and the fire has cut us off from the Mermaid's Pool.' She pointed up at the dark groove that stretched up to the edge of Kinder Scout. 'Our best bet is Red Brook.'

CHAPTER FIFTY

7.45 pm Tuesday 5 April 1988

'You can fuck right off,' Smithdown said to Jenny and Brian, looking up at the cluster of giant boulders and scree that formed the base of Red Brook, an intimidating upward gash in the landscape. 'Red Brook? That's not a brook, it's a fucking waterfall.'

'It's a dry waterfall - a smaller version of the Kinder Downfall,' Brian explained, trying to sound reassuring. 'There's hardly been any rain for weeks - by usual standards around here anyway. It's a fire-proof escape route and we are going up it.'

'What about this lot?' Smithdown said, indicating towards Naomi, Becky and Uddin. 'They're half dead as it is.'

'They can stop here and be 100 per cent dead if you'd prefer,' Jenny replied in her dry, whispery voice.' How about that?'

'Upwind and downhill is the safest place to be right now,' Brian added. 'But that's not going to happen. We can't go sideways so we've got to go up. Apart from the fire there's 150 years' worth of industrial pollution in the peat on these moors and the fire is releasing it. This is not a good place to be for a lot of reasons. We need to get out of this smoke and away from the path of the fire.'

Smithdown was about to speak again when Jenny leant in: 'Just for once, you stubborn bastard, just accept that someone else might know a bit more than you do. It's possible, isn't it?'

'Of course, I wasn't saying that...'

'Good. Glad to hear it. Time to go, then.'

'We will get you all off this moor, John,' Brian added. 'I

promise you. You're in good hands.'

'Okay, understood,' Smithdown conceded. 'Thank you both. But little Becky there has been dosed. God knows what drugs she's got rattling around inside her. She's still hallucinating and even more frightened than I am. And I'm fucking terrified.'

'We'll have to tie her up,' Jenny said, looking to where Naomi was trying to comfort her daughter as the little girl feebly kicked out and continued to hoarsely cry. Exhaustion seemed to be overcoming the child as her struggles became weaker and less aggressive.

Jenny went to them: 'I'm sorry about this… it's Naomi, isn't it? And Becky? I'm Jenny.'

The women looked at each other's damaged faces for a moment. 'Alright?' Naomi said. 'You look worse than me.' Naomi waved her bandaged arm in the air. 'In the face department, anyway.'

Jenny allowed herself the smallest of smiles, then regretted it with the pain that it caused. 'I know it sounds harsh, but we need to tie little Becky up. It's the only way to ensure her safety - and ours - on the way up. I'm sorry. I hope you understand.'

Naomi nodded as she stroked her daughter's face. Becky struggled a little as Jenny and Brian tied her hands and then her feet with light cord. Brian put her over his shoulder then Jenny tied a third cord between her hands and feet across Brian's chest. She was becoming more still now; the fight seemed to have all but gone from her.

Brian and the Becky led the climb as the fire edged towards the lower slopes of Red Brook. It had easily jumped the small stream that came from the downfall and was now approaching them from both sides. Smithdown had seen moorland fires on television before, but the local news crews always filmed them from above - aerial shots from a helicopter to give an impression of scale. To be this close to the fierce, orangey heat was a very different experience - it was frightening, choking and overwhelming.

Uddin was next to climb, moving left to right on the giant

rocks at the base of Red Brook - he was silent now, all his chatty bravura gone. Next came Naomi helped by Smithdown with Jenny at the rear, her headtorch providing a little light for them to find their way. They zig-zagged their way slowly up the vertical split in the Kinder landscape. Apart from the occasional instruction as to where best to place a hand or foot, the group were largely silent. The more they climbed, the larger the rocks they scrambled up seemed to become. What started as small steps were now wider, more difficult stretches; soon they became jumps as they cut left and right up the dry waterfall. To Smithdown's eyes the edge of Kinder Scout was no closer now than it had been when they started.

There was something hypnotic about the repetitive moves - Smithdown realised he had lost all sense of time. Had they been climbing for twenty minutes or two hours? He ached from his shoulders to his ankles - but wasn't about to admit it - as he tried to keep his eyes on his hands and feet. It was a difficult task, made worse by the fact that the fire was matching them step for step, catching hold of the moss and heather either side of them. The detective could feel the heat and taste the smoke but despite how close it came as it darted in and out of the rocks alongside Red Brook, the gully protected them. The sheer volume of rocks either side of them deepened, putting more and more distance between the group and the fire. *This might just fucking work.*

Brian - despite having Becky strapped across his shoulders and back - pulled ahead as the others helped Naomi navigate a particularly large set of moss-covered boulders. Jenny scaled them first - making it look easy - then pulled Uddin, Naomi and Smithdown up one after the other.

'I can see the ridge,' Brian shouted from above them. 'Not long now. Then we can take the Pennine Way path down to Kinder Low End and come down around the other side of the fire. We can beat it! You okay down there?'

'Oh yes,' gasped Smithdown. 'We're having an absolute hoot.'

'You're nearly there, John,' Brian cried. 'We'll sign you up as a mountain rescuer when this is done.'

'You fucking well won't,' the detective muttered, taking hold of another slab of rock and pulling himself upwards.

'Can we stop, please?' Uddin asked, sitting on a square, level boulder. 'Just for a minute?'

'You big mard arse,' Naomi said. 'I'm doing this one-handed.'

'One minute,' Jenny responded. 'Literally. I'm going to time it.'

The two detectives, the young man who wanted to be a lawyer and the single mum everyone thought was dead, rested for a moment and looked out across Greater Manchester and beyond. In the distance they could see the centre of Manchester. To the left was Stockport, the runway lights of Manchester Airport and then the Cheshire Plains; to the right, Ashton and the southern edge of Oldham. Below them were huge, curved fire walls that cut the moors into a series of impassable, blazing sections. They could see a mix of fire, plus ambulance and police flashing lights, scoping and illuminating the area behind the fire. More were arriving from all directions, heading for the car park where the White Wolves had gathered earlier in the evening. The four of them looked at the scene and then each other. 'Mad,' Uddin stated in a quiet, flat voice. 'Just... mad.'

'We need to go,' Jenny said, her voice now just a cracked whisper. 'Brian and Becky will already be on the Kinder edge path. Not long now.'

By now, Jenny and Uddin were helping Smithdown as much as they were helping Naomi. The detective was hurting. Hee was more than 30 years older than Uddin - the youngest of the group - and the detective's arms and legs burned with pain. But the ridge was now was almost in sight; the end point of Red Brook was just ten feet above them - two sides of the gully that came together in a V shape, with a tiny trickle of water going over the edge. Crossing it left to right was the Pennine Way path. Sheer black rock was behind the thin walkway.

Naomi went over the edge first, then Uddin. Smithdown was next, then Jenny. The detective was hoping to rest for a while to ease the searing ache the climb had created.

He immediately saw that wasn't going to happen.

On an outcrop of rock 20 feet from the edge of Red Brook, Adam Griffin was holding Becky Wells; his arm was across the little girl's mouth with the point of a machete touching the side of her head. She didn't seem tired and woozy now - her eyes were wide with fear and her body shook.

Next to them was Tom Lennon, standing over Brian McIntyre's body with a machete held above his head. He hacked at Brian's neck and shoulders once, then twice. A third machete blow came down. Lennon's legs shielded them from the worst of what had happened, but the detective could see that Brian's head was now resting on his shoulder at a sickening angle, the light from his headtorch stretched out into the night. Lennon turned, looked directly at Smithdown - then Jenny - and pushed Brian's body off the edge and down into the Red Brook gully.

Uddin's eyes flickered then closed; he swayed, fell against the rocks to the side of him and bounced off them, falling towards the edge in a dead faint.

Smithdown was surrounded by shouts and screams - he didn't know which belonged to Jenny, Lennon, Griffin or Naomi. Some were probably his own. Into the mix of noise came distant sirens, the sound of the fire below and the wind scraping across the rocks of Kinder Scout.

The four of them clung to each other on the ledge. 'If you move,' said Lennon. 'The little 'un goes next,' he said. He traced a finger through the air in an arc and made a descending whistling noise.

The screams and shouts dipped a little, but not by much. Smithdown's head was reeling from what he saw; he tried to focus on a way out, a resolution, a plan of action. *That's what detectives do, isn't it? Sort it out? Make it right?*

He tried to think of something - anything - that could bring a halt to the madness that was around him. For once he had nothing. There is no way out. All the detective could do was plead. 'Tom, please. This is madness, lad. Please. I'm begging you. No more.'

Lennon stood next to Griffin and Becky and pointed his machete at Smithdown and the others. The smoke from the moor fire was creeping over the edge now, snaking around their feet. 'SHUT THE FUCK UP,' Lennon shouted. 'Not fucking interested. You don't get a say any more. Your time is up. Your generation had your chance and you fucked it. This is not the time for talking. It's time for action. St George's Day is when things will really start. Then nothing will get in our way.'

'You bastards killed Brian,' Jenny screamed. 'Deprived my kids of his dad - and for what reason? He's a teacher… a fucking mountain rescue volunteer. What possible reason can you rustle up to justify that?'

Griffin, still holding onto Jenny, screamed back at Jenny: 'We are at WAR you stupid bitch. It's a fucking RACE WAR. Our race - your race - is under threat. This swarm of filth, drowning our people, ruining our way of life, has to end. It's a battle to the death and we are going win it.'

'You're not the same race as me,' Jenny shouted back. 'You bastards aren't even the same fucking species.'

Lennon spoke more quietly now: 'We'll wipe the slate clean in Oldham, then across Greater Manchester and then the whole country. But first we need to clean things up right here.'

He nodded to Griffin who loosened his grip on Becky and pushed her downwards until she lay on the path. He placed his foot onto the small of her back and raised his machete. The little girl seemed to have shaken off the last of her drug-induced lethargy. She turned her head and looked up at Griffin who laughed and let out a wolf-like cry. Becky matched him with a terrible scream.

The crowbar whooshed across the gap and hit Griffin square in the face. No one seemed more surprised than Uddin that the piece of metal he'd doggedly kept hold of since they were in Lennon's house had found its target and then clattered and clanged down Red Brook. Uddin's arm was still outstretched, frozen in time, as the blood spurted from Griffin's already battered nose. He lowered the machete slightly, wavered a little, then two seconds later raised the machete again over his head. Griffin had both hands on it now and was ready once again to bring it down on the little girl.

Naomi saw her chance the moment Uddin let fly with the crowbar. She ran, jumped the small V at the top of Red Brook, hit the path on the other side and kept on running. A moment after the blood had hit Griffin's jacket, she hit him straight on, wrapping her arms and legs around him in a crab-like grip. Griffin held firm, fury in his face but fear in his eyes. Then he staggered. Then fell. The momentum, plus Naomi's weight, took them both straight off the edge and down into the darkness.

'Look after Becky,' Jenny said to Smithdown in her sandpaper voice as she sprinted after Tom Lennon who had turned and run the moment Griffin and Naomi went over the edge.

The path at Kinder Edge was in total darkness now, the only light came from the flames below and Jenny's headtorch. Despite her injuries, she moved at astonishing speed, vaulting over rocks and deftly following the swerve of the path until she was within six feet of Lennon. Sensing she was behind him, he stopped, swung his machete back like a baseball bat, aiming it at Jenny's head as she hurtled towards him. She skidded to a halt and bent her neck back, allowing the blade to whistle past her face. As Lennon's weight followed the machete, she landed a kick to the side of his knee that unbalanced him. His leg buckled and he was brought low. The DC punched him in the throat. Lennon dropped the weapon, put his hands to his neck and wheezed for air as he dropped to his knees.

Smithdown could see them from Red Brook, their shapes highlighted by the glow of the fire below. Jenny grabbed Lennon by his jacket collar and looked as though she was readying herself to push him off the path. She leant him right out over the edge, letting him see the drop. For a moment she caught a flash of colour and light from the rocks below - it was Brian's jacket and torch.

Lennon saw it too.

Jenny swung him back from the edge and smashed his head against the wall of rocks that ran alongside the path. Then she pulled him back and did it again. 'Once more for good luck,' Smithdown whispered quietly, as he held Becky in his arms on the other side of Red Brook. 'Go on, girl.'

There was no way that Jenny could have heard him. But she did it once more anyway.

'Manchester Radio News at eleven, this is Beth Hall. Emergency crews from several counties have descended on a tiny village in north Derbyshire after a huge moorland fire broke out earlier this evening. It's thought the fire may have been started deliberately and several arrests have already been made. Mountain Rescue Teams have also been searching for the bodies of at least two people who are reported to have fallen from the edge of Kinder Scout - the highest point in the Peak District. Robert Crane joins us live from the scene and has the very latest.'

'The village of Hayfield is in chaos tonight as fire crews from several counties try to bring the blaze under control. It's thought to have started on moorland close to Kinder Reservoir and quickly spread up through a small plantation of trees and then on to an area known as Red Brook.

At least ten people have been arrested at the scene - they've now been taken to Glossop Police Station.

Meanwhile, Hayfield Mountain Rescuers - who've been searching for two people thought to have fallen from the edge of Kinder Scout - say they've now recovered a total of three bodies at the scene. At least one of the dead is thought to be that of a local rescue volunteer. Another is believed to be that of Naomi Wells. Bizarrely, the same woman who is thought to have already died at Kinder Scout several days ago.

It's not yet known how many of the fatalities died as a direct result of the fire, but I understand the moor - and Kinder Scout itself - have now both been declared murder scenes. This is Robert Crane, Manchester Radio News, in Hayfield.'

CHAPTER FIFTY-ONE

12.45am Wednesday 6 April 1988

After they'd been treated by an ambulance crew at the base of Kinder Scout - and a call had been made to Jean Smithdown - it was time to go. Smithdown and DC Seddon had both refused the offer to accompany Uddin and Becky to hospital. They didn't want further treatment, thank you. They had other business to attend to; Jenny Seddon had insisted on it. They said their goodbyes then asked to be taken to Glossop Police Station.

They passed a long line of fire engines as they drove away from Kinder Scout. Crews from three counties had answered the call to help put out the fire and the narrow road between Kinder and Hayfield was rammed with emergency workers preparing for one of the biggest fires they'd ever dealt with. Outside broadcast vehicles from Granada TV, the BBC and Manchester Radio were gathered at the far end of the road - police officers were directing the traffic as best they could, but it was a chaotic scene. A cordon had been formed to keep the journalists at bay. Smithdown recognised some of them from the TV. *What a story we have for you.*

Jenny leant her head against the window of the car as they drove away. The flashing lights illuminated her bruised and swollen face. A few dabs of rain touched the window. She waved weakly at one of the police officers who were trying to hold back a particularly pushy reporter with a microphone: 'Derbyshire Con-stab-u-lary,' she whispered and smiled at Smithdown. He took her hand and squeezed it.

As they weaved slowly but steadily through the tide of oncoming traffic towards Hayfield, Smithdown spotted something in the car park close to the mountain rescue centre and asked the driver to stop. Derbyshire Constabulary officers were holding several men ready to be taken away. The detective recognised some of them as Oldham police colleagues, mainly young constables. They were shouting and swearing as they were handcuffed and bundled into the back of a series of police vans. When they spotted Smithdown they directed their anger towards him as they disappeared through the van's rear double doors. One of the arrested men was more still than the others; he stood quietly waiting his turn. It was DC Bob Donaldson.

'One minute, please,' Smithdown said, as he stepped out of the car. 'This won't take long.'

'Fucking Nora,' Jenny Seddon muttered to herself as she watched the detective get out of the car.

Donaldson - handcuffed and being held by two PCs - half-smiled as he saw the detective walk across the car park towards him. It began to rain more steadily as the two men faced each other; a few dots and dashes at first, then it became steadily heavier as grey sheets of rain bounced off the ground around them. Black streaks of soot began to slide down Smithdown's face as the water washed his smoke-darkened skin.

'It's nasty out tonight, Bob,' Smithdown said, lighting up a JPS.

'Yeah,' Bob said, waiting his turn to be loaded into the back of the van. 'And now it's pissing it down too. Grim.'

'The rain's not so bad though,' Smithdown said. 'I don't mind it. It'll put the fire out. I hope so anyway. Wash all the burnt shit away. It looks terrible right now - fucking awful, in fact - but it'll be better by the morning.'

'You reckon?' said Donaldson.

'I reckon,' Smithdown confirmed, 'I spoke to Jean, just now.'

'Did you?'

'I did. She says you paid another call to Kate in the hospital.'

Donaldson was silent for a few beats. 'I suppose I did,' he

confirmed.

'I hope you enjoy being in prison, Bob. Because everyone in there will know you're a cop. I'll make sure of it.' Smithdown took a step closer and looked Donaldson in the eye. The Derbyshire officers holding him weren't quite sure what to do. The situation confused them. As the rain came even more heavily, Smithdown gave them a reassuring look. Then he hawked up a gob of blackened phlegm and spat it right into Bob Donaldson's face.

Donaldson said nothing. Smithdown turned and walked back to the car. 'Let's go,' the detective said. This time, Jenny squeezed *his* hand.

Fifteen minutes later they walked through the front doors of Glossop Police Station and asked for the Duty Sergeant. 'Jesus, Jenny,' the middle-aged officer said as he approached the front desk from a back room and looked at the three blackened and bleeding faces in front of him.

'Sergeant,' she began. 'This is Thomas Lennon of Snipe Street, Oldham.' Jenny pushed Lennon closer to the front desk. His hands were tied with the same cord that had been used to restrain Becky on their climb up Red Brook. His face was a tangle of cuts, gashes and bruises from being slammed against the Kinder rocks. Lennon stared at the ceiling, refusing to engage with what was happening. 'I've arrested him on suspicion of a number of offences both here and within the Greater Manchester force area. It's my belief that, because of the nature of the alleged crimes, it is better for him to be placed in custody here, rather than with the Greater Manchester Police.'

'DC Seddon,' the Duty Sergeant said. 'Are you sure you're in a fit state to do this…'

'Never been surer of anything in my life,' she replied.

'Okay - what have you arrested Mr Lennon in connection with, DC Seddon?' the Duty Sergeant asked.

She paused. 'I've arrested him in connection with the murder of Sharmeen Chowdhury of Oldham, Greater Manchester. She is a local councillor and was recently reported missing-from-home. It's my belief that it was her body that was discovered last week at the Mermaid's Pool near Hayfield and not that of one Naomi Wells. Ms Wells is in fact one of three fatalities that have occurred over at Kinder Scout this evening.

'Right you are,' the Sergeant said, writing the details onto the custody record sheet as fast as he could.

'I've also arrested Lennon in connection with the murder of a Mr Aleem …' she turned to Smithdown. 'Sorry, what was Aleem's first name?'

'Amir,' the detective replied. 'His name was Amir Aleem .'

'… in connection with a Mr Amir Aleem, of Queen's Road, Oldham.'

Just for a beat, Jenny hesitated. She breathed in and out, heavily. Then continued: 'Also, he is under arrest in connection with the murder of Brian McIntyre of number 70, Old Glossop Road…'

The Duty Sergeant looked directly at DC Seddon. For a moment he was silent. 'My God, Jenny,' he finally said. 'Brian? Christ… I mean, I'm so sorry…'

'Brian McIntyre is the second of the three fatalities at Kinder Scout. The third is Adam Griffin, also of Snipe Street, Oldham.'

The Duty Sergeant was struggling to keep up. 'Also,' Jenny continued, 'I'll be speaking to Lennon in connection with offences of attempted murder… unlawful imprisonment… rape… grievous bodily harm and Section 18 wounding. Plus, offences under the Public Order Act of 1986 that are frankly too fucking numerous to go into right now.'

'I've never heard anything like this in all my life, DC Seddon,' the Sergeant said, shaking his head.

'I agree, Sergeant. It really is quite the shopping list, isn't it? There's more. I'll also be seeking to speak to a Mr Richard T. King, a businessman based in Oldham, Greater Manchester and to a Detective Constable Bob Donaldson of Greater Manchester Police, also based in Oldham.'

'And who is this gentleman here?' the Sergeant said,

pointing his pen in Smithdown's direction.

'This is Detective Inspector John Smithdown, also of Oldham Police. His testimony will be vital to the case against Mr Lennon and others. I may wish to put Mr Smithdown into witness protection as I believe his life may be in danger from elements within his own force.'

'You're alright, Jenny. I'll be fine. Soon as we're done here, I'm off home to see my Jean.'

'Whatever you say, Mr Smithdown,' Jenny said before addressing the Sergeant again: 'That's your lot, Sergeant.'

'Jesus wept...' the Sergeant said in an exhaled whisper. 'Do you have any pieces of evidence you wish to book in at this time?'

Smithdown dug deep into his jacket pocket and pulled out Mr Aleem's small tape recorder that contained their discussion with Naomi. He placed it on the counter. Then he felt around in his other pocket and pulled out his vest, still bundled into a tight ball. He carefully unwrapped it and placed Sharmeen Chowdhury's gaffa-taped hand next to the tape recorder. 'Just these two,' he said.

CHAPTER FIFTY-TWO

10am Thursday 7 April 1988

'Come in John,' said DS James Pym. 'Take a seat.'

Pym put out a hand and offered Smithdown a handshake. The detective's hands were criss-crossed with scratches from the rocks of Red Brook. He still smelled of smoke despite takings several baths. He took the DS's hand and the two men shook. Pym normally favoured an overly firm grip - what Smithdown considered to be a golf club bullshit handshake. Not today; it was soft and compliant. Maybe Pym was being cautious of his injured hands? Maybe not.

'John, let me be frank,' Pym sighed.

Here we go.

'We've got a balancing act on our hands here. A delicate one. We need you to see GMP's dilemma - and understand it.'

Smithdown said nothing.

Eyes open, gob shut.

'No one - absolutely no one - doubts that what you did was extraordinary. What you've uncovered in this division, maybe in this force, is going to be felt across the land. You've sent a shockwave thought the policing community. No question. You instinctively felt something wasn't right about the Wells case and you went with it. And you were dead right. Fair play to you.'

'I'm sure you would have done exactly the same thing in my circumstances, Jim,' Smithdown said. He was aiming for a low-key tone of deadpan sarcasm and was slightly concerned that he might have underdone it.

'You saved that kiddie, Becky Wells,' Pym continued. 'You saved that lad Uddin too. Though what he was doing out there on the moors with you in the first place is something I'm looking forward to hearing all about. Or maybe I'm not.' Pym smiled. He didn't get one in return. So, he continued. 'This is going to take a long time to… untangle.'

'Is it?'

'Yes, John. It really is.'

Smithdown went silent again. He was in no rush. 'It's going to be in everyone's interest to get this to trial as soon as possible,' Pym continued. 'But it's still going to take time. They're all saying nowt, so far. Bob, King, Lennon… these so-called Wolves… the lot of them. But maybe that will change. It'll be interesting to see if Bob survives being on remand. A cop, facing the kind of charges he's got coming down the pipe? He'll have more targets on him than a Mod's parka.'

'Let's hope no harm comes to him then,' Smithdown offered. 'That would be a bad thing in all sorts of ways.'

'Yes, it would. Absolutely. So, John. What I'm saying is… you're going to have to bide your time. We need to get the trial done before we can even look at your disciplinary. There's obviously going to have be an inquiry into the whole… *infiltration* of the force thing. What went on etcetera. Root and branch, lessons learnt - all that. It could take a year or so to sort out. But maybe the timing's perfect. Kate's on the mend. Jean needs you at home now more than ever. Get yourself off home. You might even be able to stretch this to your retirement. You're not far off doing 30 years, then that's you done.'

'I'm in no hurry to retire, Jim,' Smithdown said. 'Sooner I can get back to work, the happier I'll be.'

The two men looked at each other. 'So that's it, John,' Pym said. 'Sit tight. Wait for the process to work itself out, then we'll take it from there.'

'That it?' Smithdown asked.

'Yes, it is John. Give my regards to Jean and of course we all wish a speedy recovery to Kate.'

Smithdown got up from his chair. He looked at the

scratches on his hands. 'Just one thing before I go, Jim…'

'Of course. Anything, John.'

'You knew, didn't you?'

EPILOGUE

9am Sunday 1 April 1990

'Radio Manchester News at nine, this is Beth Hall. A policeman, hailed a hero after his part in exposing the neo- Nazi infiltration of Oldham Police, is set to return to work tomorrow after spending nearly two years on suspension. Detective Inspector John Smithdown was told to step down from his duties after allegations he harmed a child in his custody in 1988. But an internal Greater Manchester Police inquiry has found that there was no case to answer. Mr Smithdown is due back at his desk first thing tomorrow morning. The investigation had to be put on hold untilthe end of the so-called 'Nazi Cops' trial. Several Oldham police officers, including Detective Constable Bob Donaldson were finally jailed on Thursday for their part in a string of murders and racist attacks in Oldham. Danny Johnston reports.'

'What started as a murder inquiry into the apparent death of sex worker Naomi Wells in April 1988, turned into one of the biggest police scandals the UK has ever seen. Officers from Oldham Police were found to have been conspiring with neo-Nazi groups to seize power on the local Council by any means possible - that included murder, kidnapping and inciting a riot. Their aim was to provoke a race war to push an extremist, racist agenda. Nine people are now serving life sentences for their part in the scandal - six were serving police officers, including Detective Constable Bob Donaldson.

Donaldson, along with neo-Nazi activist Thomas Lennon, conspired to stage a series of murders and attacks to further their aim of generating a backlash against South Asian communities in Oldham. Their ultimate goal was grabbing political power and making money from land sales brought about by forced repatriation.

Yesterday a memorial was unveiled outside the town hall, dedicated to those who lost their lives during those tragic events of Easter 1988. Those include murdered local Councillor Sharmeen Chowdhury, mountain rescue volunteer Brian McIntyre, local businessman Amir Aleem and teenager Tariq Shamsi. Oldham MP Peter Jeffries says it's their names - not those of the guilty - that we should remember:'

"These evil people used fear to generate hate and divide our

communities. But they failed. This town showed it was better than that and rose above their hate-filled message. The Oldham we had before all this was a good place, full of good people. The Oldham we have today is even better."

'The memorial was paid for by local businessman Richard T King - one of ten people originally set to stand trial. He was cleared of all charges after a search of offices above his Oldham nightclub was deemed to have been unlawful. The incident forced a retrial of the remaining accused.

Detective Inspector John Smithdown is now in line for a police bravery award for his actions in exposing the scandal, alongside DC Jennifer Seddon of the Derbyshire Constabulary. Oldham teenager Mohiuddin Rahman will receive a civilian award. Posthumous awards will go to DC Seddon's late partner Brian McIntyre and to Naomi Wells, the woman whose disappearance sparked the initial inquiry.

Detective Superintendent James Pym of Oldham Police, says that he is looking forward to welcoming DI Smithdown back to work on Monday:'

"DI John Smithdown exemplifies everything this force and this division is about: honesty, integrity, decency and fairness. We are forever in his debt. The policing community in Oldham have been through some tough times in the last two years, but we are a family. And we're looking forward to welcoming back one of the most important members of that family on Monday."

'After the initial arrests of DC Donaldson and several of his colleagues, Greater Manchester Police promised what was described as a 'root and branch' investigation into further links between its officers and neo-Nazi groups. So far, no other officers have been suspended and GMP describe the 'Nazi Cops' case as a one-off incident. Danny Johnston, Manchester Radio News, at GMP Headquarters in Old Trafford.'

CHAPTER FIFTY-THREE

5am Monday 2 April 1990

When the phone rang, Jean Shipdown knew full well the call wouldn't be for her and barely stirred. 'Bloody hell,' Jean muttered. 'First day back and they're ringing already?'

She'd enjoyed the peace that her husband's nearly two-year suspension had given them - no phone calls at strange times of the night or morning, no coming and going when regular people were asleep, no aching worry for the harm that might come her husband's way. That, it appeared, was all over, but then Smithdown had received the news confirming he was to be reinstated on the previous Wednesday. The official letter had arrived by recorded delivery first thing on Friday morning. She was happy for him but had cried later when he wasn't in the room.

John and Jean Smithdown had spent that Saturday in nearby Uppermill. They'd had a pub lunch, done a little shopping and called in to see Becky Wells, settled and happy now that her adoption had been confirmed with Mr Aleem's widow and her extended family.

Then they'd walked a little on the Huddersfield Canal that cut gently though the centre of the town, but Jean had tired quickly and he'd taken her home.

After what seemed like real progress with her treatment, the cancer had started to make inroads back into their lives again. The disease seemed harsher this time; fiercer - more determined. The options open to them looked narrower, the words from her oncologist quieter and more final. Smithdown had told his wife that he wanted to take retirement. She'd said no. 'I'm sick of you knocking around this house,' she'd lied. 'You're driving me mad. You should get back to work. You need to walk back into that police station with your head held high. I'm not going to deny you that.'

Reluctantly, he'd agreed.

'Smithdown,' the detective said into the trimphone receiver.

'It's DC Cave, sir. Sorry to ring so early.'

'It's okay, Jan. Strangeways, is it?'

They'd planned to spend Sunday visiting friends but had stayed in to allow Jean to rest and to follow events at Strangeways Prison. A riot had broken out during a service at the jail's chapel. The Smithdowns watched as rioters took control of the prison, then broken through to the roof, taunting prison officers from their vantage points, knowing the authorities couldn't touch them as the drama played on television. 'If they don't regain control today - they've had it,' Smithdown had told his wife.

Bob's in that jail. The other inmates will be gunning for him. He's had it.

After seeing the rioters on the news, the detective had volunteered to come back to work a day early - but Detective Superintendent James Pym had told him to wait, take the day with Jean and arrive fresh on Monday. Perhaps the DS had changed his mind.

The detective had then phoned Kate, but she wasn't in. Then he'd tried the *Oldham Messenger* where she was working, but he'd been told that she was on her way to the jail - several prisoners spotted on the roof were thought to be from the Oldham area. *You've always got to get a local angle.*

'No, you're not required at Strangeways, sir,' DC Cave continued. 'Bit closer to home. Literally close to your home, in fact. We've got a report of body - possibly a child - out at Black Moss reservoir. That's near you, isn't it?'

'It is, just up the Huddersfield Road,' he confirmed. 'Bang on the Yorkshire border, in fact. Are we sure it belongs to GMP? It might be a case for the Tykes not us if the body's on the other side of the Pennine Way.'

'It was called in from the Manchester side, so I assume so,' DC Cave said. 'Mr Pym told me to pass it straight to you as you know the area. Is that okay?'

'It's fine, Jan. I can be there in ten minutes, though it's another 20 to walk to the reservoir down the Pennine Way.'

'There's two uniforms there already, securing the scene. That's all I know. I'll leave you to it.'

'No problem, Jan.'

'Good to have you back, sir,' she said.

'A dead kiddie by a reservoir out on the moors? Who wouldn't want to come back to work to a treat like that? Tell Pym I'm on it. Thanks Jan.'

Smithdown replaced the receiver and got out of bed. He pulled his trousers over his pyjama bottoms and swapped the top for a shirt. He pulled his mac from the wardrobe. He hadn't worn in for nearly two years.

'Straight back to it then?' Jean said, propping herself up in bed. There was barely anything left of her now. The cancer had whittled her away. But her eyes and smile were enough for Smithdown.

'Yes love,' he replied, putting a tie around his neck and rummaging in a chest of drawers for some socks. 'Straight back to it.'

THE END

DI John Smithdown and his family - along with Danny Johnston from Black Moss - will return in the third of the Manc Noir novels, The Ballad of Hanging Lees.

Postscript

The Mermaid's Pool is a work of fiction but, like my previous novel *Black Moss*, it has its basis very much in fact. Real-life riots took place in Oldham in 2001. At the height of the disturbances 500 youths were involved and 15 police officers were injured. Here is a section of the Minutes of Evidence from the House of Lords Select Committee on Religious Offences in England and Wales 2002-3. Full details at www.parliament.co.uk

A Case Study On Oldham

The classic example of the nature and impact of Far-Right activities against the Muslim community is provided by the northern city of Oldham. The upsurge in the level of activities by Far-Right organisations in this city, including the BNP and the NF, are at least partly the catalyst for the civil unrest witnessed there in the early summer of 2001. Two reports seek to illustrate the socially divisive and disruptive role played in this city by Far-Right organisations.

The first report, produced by the Black Racial Attacks Independent Network, entitled *The Oldham Riots - Shattering the Myths*, states:

'. . . the result of years of . . . institutional attitudes combined with media hysteria has given legitimacy and created a climate for the racists and the BNP (British National Party) to gain a foothold to propagate and stir hatred… It is important to note the BNP's strategy of blaming Muslim communities for the problems in the northern towns. Articles have appeared on BNP websites and literature, with titles such as: '*The Situation in Oldham: Ethnic Cleansing Muslim Style*', calling for a boycott of Muslim businesses, but not Chinese or Hindu. On the BBC's Newsnight programme, in an interview by Jeremy Paxman with Nick Griffin, Griffin stated that: "It's not an Asian or black problem but a Muslim one". The existence of Islamophobia in society endorsed by Government policies on refugees, asylum, terrorism . . . etc., in conjunction with the media's subsequent portrayal [of these people] further adds to Islamophobic attitudes which the BNP turn into political gain by claiming to disillusioned whites that these fundamentalist Muslims live only up the road from them...'

The second report, produced by the Islamic Human Rights Commission, entitled *The Oldham Riots - Discrimination, Deprivation and Communal Tension in the United Kingdom*, offers similar insights:

'Political leaders in the town have admitted that the riots had been stirred up by right-wing white extremists. Both the Police and the Prime Minster concurred . . . Even [a local] Chief Superintendent highlighted the particular role of the National Front (NF) and British National Party (BNP)... Statements by right-wing groups reveal that their efforts were primarily directed against Oldham's Muslim Community. An article on the race riots on the BNP's website commented that "this is how extremists within the Muslim community in Oldham are repaying the hospitality of the people who built the town and allowed them to settle there by the tens of thousands." Another BNP article remarked on how the Party has been able to use the riots to further exacerbate racist and Islamophobic sentiment to thereby recruit members: 'Media coverage and the personal experience of scores of thousands of white people every year are combining to make gangs of Muslim thugs the best recruiting sergeant the British National Party has ever had... it is a perceived distinction... and one which indicates the current state of anti-discriminatory legislation in the UK.'

About the author:

David Nolan is a journalist, television producer and author. He's written 13 books including *Black Moss* and *Tell the Truth and Shame the Devil*, the true story of the largest historic abuse investigation ever mounted by Greater Manchester Police. David's reporting on the case won him a Royal Television Society Award, a New York International Festival award and a Rose d'Or. He lives in south Manchester, within sight of Kinder Scout.

Acknowledgements

If you need help, enlist an expert. So, thank you to Jim Harries of Kinder Mountain Rescue in Hayfield and to Station Manager Dave Swallow, Wildfire Officer from Greater Manchester Fire and Rescue Service based at Staybridge. They kindly gave me their time and expertise, despite me asking such weird questions.

Former Detective Constables Nicola Graham and Phil Selley helped with police procedure; Stockport councillor Tom Dowse did the same with local government matters.

Thanks also to Parmita Paul of BBC Bangladesh and all my friends at the BBC in Islamabad, Pakistan.

Dee Graham and Neil Summers assisted greatly with their personal knowledge in the areas of cancer treatment and the taking of ecstasy. In that order.

For more information about the (real life) Kinder Mountain Rescue Team visit: www.kmrt.org.uk

More books from Fahrenheit Press

Black Moss by David Nolan

In April 1990, as rioters took over Strangeways prison in Manchester, someone killed a little boy at Black Moss.

And no one cared.

No one except Danny Johnston, an inexperienced radio reporter trying to make a name for himself.

More than a quarter of a century later, Danny returns to his home city to revisit the murder that's always haunted him.

If Danny can find out what really happened to the boy, maybe he can cure the emptiness he's felt inside since he too was a child.

But finding out the truth might just be the worst idea Danny Johnston has ever had.

"As one would expect from a writer with the skill and experience of David Nolan, this haunting book deals with very difficult issues in an incredibly sympathetic manner while at the same time throwing a light onto one of the most complicated and shaming areas of our society - the failure to protect those who are the most vulnerable."

Rubicon by Ian Patrick

Rubicon has recently been optioned by the BBC with a view to making a 6 episode series.

Two cops, both on different sides of the law – both with the same gangland boss in their sights.

Sam Batford is an undercover officer with the Metropolitan Police who will stop at nothing to get his hands on fearsome crime-lord Vincenzo Guardino's drug supply.

DCI Klara Winter runs a team on the National Crime Agency, she's also chasing down Guardino, but unlike Sam Batford she's determined to bring the gangster to justice and get his drugs off the streets.

Set in a time of austerity and police cuts where opportunities for corruption are rife, Rubicon is a tense, dark thriller that is definitely not for the faint hearted.

'A sharp, slick, gripping and compelling novel'

Know Me From Smoke by Matt Phillips

Stella Radney, long-time lounge singer, still has a bullet lodged in her hip from the night when a rain of gunshots killed her husband.

That was twenty years ago and it's a surprise when the unsolved murder is reopened after the district attorney discovers new evidence. Royal Atkins is a convicted killer who just got out of prison on a legal technicality. At first, he's thinking he'll play it straight. Doesn't take long before that plan turns to smoke—was it ever really an option?

When Stella and Royal meet one night, they're drawn to each other. But Royal has a secret. How long before Stella discovers that the man she's falling for isn't who he seems? A noir of gripping suspense and violence, Know Me from Smoke is a journey into the shadowy terrain of murder, lost love, and the heart's lust for vengeance.

"A beautifully written, brutal & brilliant slice of hardboiled crime fiction. A Knockout."

Printed in Great Britain
by Amazon

60351293R00154